BLAKE'S

Maths Guide

for Upper primary students

AF585065

Bev Dunbar

Blake's Maths Guide
Upper Primary

Copyright © 2011 Blake Education and Bev Dunbar
Reprinted 2012, 2014 (twice), 2016, 2018

ISBN: 978 1 74215 904 1

Published by Pascal Press
PO Box 250
Glebe NSW 2037
www.pascalpress.com.au
contact@pascalpress.com.au

Author: Bev Dunbar
Publisher: Lynn Dickinson
Edited by Karen Jayne
Design and illustration by Janice Bowles
Typset by Patricia Tsiatsias
Printed by Vivar Printing/Green Giant Press

Reproduction and communication for educational purposes
The Australian *Copyright Act 1968* (the Act) allows a maximum of one chapter or 10% of the pages of this work, whichever is the greater, to be reproduced and/or communicated by any educational institution for its educational purposes provided that the educational institution (or that body that administers it) has given a remuneration notice to the Copyright Agency Limited (CAL) under the Act.

For details of the CAL licence for educational institutions contact:
Copyright Agency Limited
Level 15, 233 Castlereagh Street
Sydney, NSW 2000

Reproduction and communication for other purposes
Except as permitted under the Act (for example a fair dealing for the purpose of study, research, criticism or review) no part of this book may be reproduced, stored in a retrieval system, communicated or transmitted in any form or by any means without prior written permission. All inquiries should be made to the publisher at the address above.

© Australian Curriculum, Assessment and Reporting Authority 2010.

Strands, Sub-strands and Content descriptions – This is an extract from the Australian Curriculum

Elaborations: This is a modified extract from the Australian Curriculum and includes the work of the author. ACARA neither endorses nor verifies the accuracy of the information provided and accepts no responsibility for incomplete or inaccurate information. In particular, ACARA does not endorse or verify that:

- The content descriptions are solely for the relevant year;
- That all the content descriptions for the relevant year have been used; and
- The Author's material aligns with the Australian Curriculum Content Descriptions for the relevant year.

You can find the unaltered and most up to date version of this material at http://www.australiancurriculum.edu.au/Home

This material is reproduced with the permission of ACARA.

CONTENTS

AUSTRALIAN CURRICULUM CORRELATIONS – YEAR 5

NUMBER AND ALGEBRA	ELABORATIONS	ACMNA	PAGE
Number and place value Identify and describe factors and multiples of whole numbers and use them to solve problems	★ Explore factors and multiples, and use simple divisibility tests	98	19–26, 31–38
Use estimation and rounding to check the reasonableness of answers to calculations	★ Recognise the usefulness of estimation and apply mental strategies to estimate results of calculations	99	8–9, 14–15, 28–31
Solve problems involving multiplication of large numbers by one- or two-digit numbers using efficient mental, written strategies and appropriate digital technologies	★ Explore different multiplication techniques such as the area model, the Italian lattice method or partitioning ★ Apply the distributive law and use arrays to model and explain calculations	100	26–29
Solve problems involving division by a one digit number, including those that result in a remainder	★ Interpret and represent remainders in context	101	30–36
Use efficient mental and written strategies and apply appropriate digital technologies to solve problems	★ Use calculators to check the reasonableness of answers	291	14–15
Fractions and decimals Compare and order common unit fractions and locate and represent them on a number line	★ Recognise the connection between a unit fraction and its denominator	102	39–41
Investigate strategies to solve problems involving addition and subtraction of fractions with the same denominator	★ Model fraction problems using number line jumps or shape diagrams	103	39–45
Recognise that the number system can be extended beyond hundredths	★ Use knowledge of place value and division by 10 to extend the number system to thousandths ★ Recognise the equivalence of a thousandth and 0.001	104	49–51
Compare, order and represent decimals	★ Locate decimals on a number line and recognise that the number of digits after the decimal point is not the value of the fraction	105	49
Money and financial mathematics Create simple financial plans	★ Create a simple budget ★ Identify GST component in invoices and receipts	106	61–62 65–67
Patterns and algebra Describe, continue and create patterns with fractions, decimals and whole numbers resulting from addition and subtraction	★ Use the number line or diagrams to create fraction and decimal patterns	107	73
Use equivalent number sentences involving multiplication and division to find unknown quantities	★ Use relevant problems to develop number sentences	121	74–75

© Australian Curriculum, Assessment and Reporting Authority 2010.

MEASUREMENT AND GEOMETRY	ELABORATIONS	ACMMG	PAGE
Units of measurement Choose appropriate units of measurement for length, area, volume, capacity and mass	★ Recognise when it is appropriate to use a specific metric unit	108	77–80, 85–90, 95–99, 101–106
Calculate the perimeter and area of rectangles using familiar metric units	★ Explore efficient ways to calculate perimeter and area	109	81–83, 91–94
Compare 12- and 24-hour time systems and convert between them	★ Use hours, minutes and seconds	110	113–117
Shape Connect three-dimensional objects with their nets and other two-dimensional representations	★ Identify the shape and position of each face of a solid to determine the net, including prisms and pyramids ★ Represent 2D shapes in photographs, sketches and digital images	111	123–127
Location and transformations Use a grid reference system to describe locations. Describe routes using landmarks and directional language	★ Compare aerial views and maps with grid references ★ Create a grid reference system and use it to locate objects and describe routes	113	151–152
Describe translations, reflections and rotations of two-dimensional shapes. Identify line and rotational symmetries	★ Identify the effects of transformations by flipping, sliding and turning 2D shapes ★ Identify and describe line and rotational symmetry of 2D shapes by cutting, folding and turning	114	141–146, 146–149
Apply the enlargement transformation to familiar two dimensional shapes and explore the properties of the resulting image compared with the original	★ Use a grid system to enlarge a favourite image or cartoon	115	149–150
Geometric reasoning Estimate, measure and compare angles using degrees. Construct angles using a protractor	★ Measure and construct angles using both 180° and 360° protractors	112	130–133
STATISTICS AND PROBABILITY	**ELABORATIONS**	**ACMSP**	**PAGE**
Chance List outcomes of chance experiments involving equally likely outcomes and represent probabilities of those outcomes using fractions	★ Comment on the likelihood of winning simple games of chance by considering the number of possible outcomes	116	161–162
Recognise that probabilities range from 0 to 1	★ Investigate the probabilities of all the outcomes for a simple chance experiment and verify that their sum is 1	117	159–162
Data representation and interpretation Pose questions and collect categorical or numerical data by observation or survey	★ Conduct data investigations in the playground	118	163–165
Construct displays, including column graphs, dot plots and tables, appropriate for data type, with and without the use of digital technologies	★ Identify the best methods of presenting data and justify the choices	119	164–171
Describe and interpret different data sets in context	★ Use and compare data representations to help decision making	120	164–171

© Australian Curriculum, Assessment and Reporting Authority 2010.

AUSTRALIAN CURRICULUM CORRELATIONS – YEAR 6

NUMBER AND ALGEBRA	ELABORATIONS	ACMNA	PAGE
Number and place value Identify and describe properties of prime, composite, square and triangular numbers	★ Represent composite numbers as a product of their primes factors and use this fact to cancel common primes ★ Understand that if a number is divisible by a composite number it is also divisible by the prime factors of that number	122	21–22, 36–38
Select and apply efficient mental and written strategies and appropriate digital technologies to solve problems involving all four operations with whole numbers	★ Apply a range of strategies to solve small number problems up to large number problems	123	11–18, 24–29, 31–36
Investigate everyday situations that use positive and negative whole numbers and zero. Locate and represent these numbers on a number line	★ Use number lines to position and order positive and negative numbers ★ Investigate everyday uses of positive and negative numbers such as temperature	124	10
Fractions and decimals Compare fractions with related denominators and locate and represent them on a number line	★ Demonstrate equivalence between fractions using drawings and models	125	39–45
Solve problems involving addition and subtraction of fractions with the same or related denominators	★ Solve problems related to equivalence and fractions as operators ★ Model using number line jumps of shape diagrams	126	43–45 45, 47
Find a simple fraction of a quantity where the result is a whole number, with and without digital technologies		127	47–48
Add and subtract decimals, with and without digital technologies, and use estimation and rounding to check the reasonableness of answers	★ Extend whole number strategies to explore and develop strategies for adding and subtracting decimal numbers to thousandths	128	52–54
Multiply decimals by whole numbers and perform divisions that result in terminating decimals, with and without digital technologies	★ Interpret and represent remainders in context	129	56–57
Multiply and divide decimals by powers of 10	★ Understand and use the fact that equivalent division calculations result if both numbers are multiplied or divided by the same amount	130	54–57
Make connections between equivalent fractions, decimals and percentages	★ Move fluently between representations of fractions, decimals and percentages and choose the appropriate one for the problem being solved	131	58–59
Money and financial mathematics Investigate and calculate percentage discounts of 10%, 25% and 50% on sale items, with and without digital technologies	★ Use authentic information to calculate prices on sale goods	132	63–64
Patterns and algebra Continue and create sequences involving whole numbers, fractions and decimals. Describe the rule used to create the sequence	★ Identify and generalise number patterns as the beginning of algebraic thinking ★ Investigate additive and multiplicative patterns	133	69–71 74–75
Explore the use of brackets and order of operations to write number sentences	★ Appreciate the need for rules to complete multiple operations	134	75–76

© Australian Curriculum, Assessment and Reporting Authority 2010.

AUSTRALIAN CURRICULUM CORRELATIONS – YEAR 6 CONTINUED

MEASUREMENT AND GEOMETRY	ELABORATIONS	ACMMG	PAGE
Units of measurement Connect decimal representations to the metric system	★ Recognise equivalent measures such as 125 cm and 1.25 m	135	77–80, 85–90, 95–99, 101–106
Convert between common metric units of length, mass and capacity	★ Identify and use correct operations when converting units, and recognise the significance of prefixes in units of measurement	136	77–80, 85–90, 95–99, 101–106
Solve problems involving the comparison of lengths and areas using appropriate units	★ Recognise and investigate familiar objects	137	81–83, 90–94
Connect volume and capacity and their units of measurement	★ Recognise that 1 mL of water is equivalent in volume to 1 cm^3 of water	138	105
Interpret and use timetables	★ Plan a trip involving one or more modes of public transport	139	120–121
Shape Construct simple prisms and pyramids	★ Construct prisms and pyramids from nets and skeletal models	140	123–127
Location and transformations Investigate combinations of translations, reflections and rotations, with and without the use of digital technologies	★ Understand that transformations can change a shape's position and orientation but not the geometric features or size	142	142–146
Introduce the Cartesian coordinate system using all four quadrants	★ Understand that the Cartesian plane provides a visual way of describing location	143	155–158
Geometric reasoning Investigate, with and without digital technologies, angles on a straight line, angles at a point and vertically opposite angles. Use results to find unknown angles	★ Estimate, compare and classify angles in degrees, and use a protractor to measure angles to the nearest degree ★ Identify the size of a right angle as 90° and define acute, obtuse, right, straight, reflex, full turn by relating them to right angles	141	130–135 134–135

STATISTICS AND PROBABILITY	ELABORATIONS	ACMSP	PAGE
Chance Describe probabilities using fractions, decimals and percentages	★ Investigate popular games of chance and evaluate benefits to organisers and participants	144	161–162
Conduct chance experiments with both small and large numbers of trials using appropriate digital technologies	★ Identify variations between trials and realise that results are closer to the prediction with larger numbers of trials	145	161
Compare observed frequencies across experiments with expected frequencies	★ Predict likely outcomes from chance events and distinguish these from surprising results	146	159–160
Data representation and interpretation Interpret and compare a range of data displays, including side-by-side column graphs for two categorical variables	★ Understand that one symbol can represent multiple data ★ Explore ways to present data such as many-to-one dot plots	147	164–165
Interpret secondary data presented in digital media and elsewhere	★ Understand sampling and other influences on data in order to critique data-based claims in media ★ Identify potentially misleading data displays	148	170–171

© Australian Curriculum, Assessment and Reporting Authority 2010.

HOW TO USE THIS BOOK

Mathematics is a way of thinking. It helps you understand how the world works. *Blake's Maths Guide for Years 5 and 6* helps you see mathematics all around you. This Guide helps you to talk about, to draw and to record mathematics. You will have the tools that you need to be a successful mathematician.

The definitions are clear, concise and written in friendly language. Real-life photographs show you what mathematics is being discussed and how it is used.

In the TRY THIS sections, you practise, make or imagine mathematical concepts. This helps you put the maths ideas inside your head. Selected answers are at the back of the book.

Blake's Maths Guide for Years 5 and 6 contains an index for locating the specific mathematical concept that you might need more information about. A glossary is also provided for quick reference.

This Guide is a vital reference for anyone wanting to be successful at years 5 and 6 mathematics.

ABOUT THE AUTHOR

Bev Dunbar is a highly respected mathematics educator. Over the last 35 years, Bev has worked extensively with students, student teachers, parents and teachers within both government and non-government education systems. She has also lectured in Mathematics Education at the University of Sydney and the Australian Catholic University.

Bev is the author of many educational resources, including *Times Tables 1 and 2*, 16 books for teachers in *The Exploring Maths* series and 10 books for students in the *Excel Maths Early Skill* series.

Bev is dedicated to helping you understand and enjoy Mathematics. Her personal interests include a passion for painting and recreating medieval artworks and, of course, unravelling challenging sudokus.

PLACE VALUE

WRITING NUMBERS USING ROMAN NUMERALS

Ten fingers, ten toes may be the reason why we invented a **decimal** counting system. Decimal is Latin for ten. The word **digit** is Latin for finger.

Ancient Romans used alphabet letters to record their maths. They did not have our digits 1–9. They did not use a symbol for 0.

Romans used the following symbols to record their numbers.

1	5	10	50	100	500	1000
I	V	X	L	C	D	M

They placed a small bar over the letter to record numbers 1000 × larger.

5000	10000	50000	100000	500000	1000000
$\overline{\text{V}}$	$\overline{\text{X}}$	$\overline{\text{L}}$	$\overline{\text{C}}$	$\overline{\text{D}}$	$\overline{\text{M}}$

Letters are repeated to make larger numbers.
XVII is 10 + 5 + 1 + 1 = 17
CCCXX is 100 + 100 + 100 + 10 + 10 = 320
$\overline{\text{M}}\overline{\text{M}}\overline{\text{D}}\overline{\text{C}}$VI is 1000000 + 1000000 + 500000 + 100000 + 5 + 1 = 2600006.

Roman numerals for 4 and 9

There is a special subtraction rule for 4 and 9. If a letter is written to the left of a larger value letter, the smaller value is subtracted from the larger value. For example: XL is 50 − 10 = 40.

4	9	40	90	400	900
IV	IX	XL	XC	CD	CM

Try this

Write these Roman numerals using the 0–9 digits.

1 VIII

2 XXXXIV

3 MMDCCLXX

4 $\overline{\text{M}}\overline{\text{D}}\overline{\text{C}}$CCLV

PLACE VALUE TO 100 000

The digits 0 – 9 are like magic. You use them to write infinitely large numbers. You use them to write infinitely small numbers. It is their position in a decimal place value system that tells you what number they represent.

Number positions to the left of the 1s column are always10 times larger.

Once you have 10 groups of 10 000 you have 100 000 or one hundred thousand.

Using this column you can now write any number up to 999 999.

10 × 10 000	10 × 1 000	10 × 100	10 × 10	10 × 1	1

This house sold for $486 495.
That's four hundred and eighty-six thousand, four hundred and ninety-five dollars.

Place value chart for 486 495

100 000s	10 000s	1 000s	100s	10s	1s
Hundred Thousands	**Ten Thousands**	**Thousands**	**Hundreds**	**Tens**	**Ones**
HT	**TT**	**Th**	**H**	**T**	**O**
4	**8**	**6**	**4**	**9**	**5**

Hundred thousands look like this on a number line:

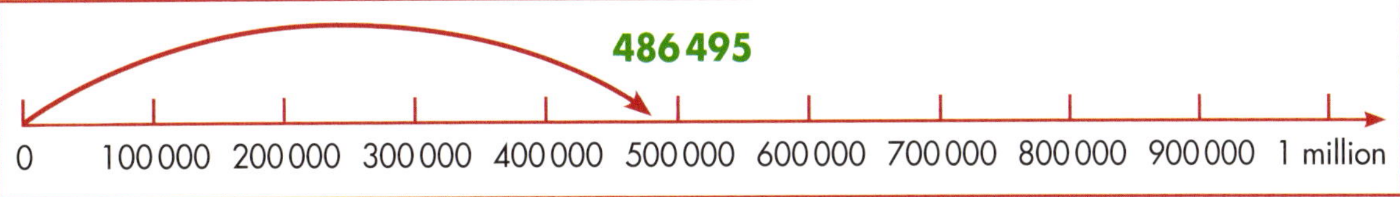

486 495 is:

- smaller than 500 000
- larger than 350 000
- in between 480 000 and 490 000

Zero is a wonderful invention. Zero is used to fill the empty space in a number with no digits in a place value column. If you didn't have 0, this is what 490 003 would look like.

100 000s	10 000s	1 000s	100s	10s	1s
4	9				3

You cannot tell what number you really mean if you only write 493.

490 003 tells you exactly what number you are talking about.

Zeros are written in the place values of 1 000s, 100s and 10s.

PLACE VALUE TO 1 000 000

Once you have 10 groups of 100 000, you now have one million. Using this place value column you can now write any number up to 9 999 999.

My family used 1 503 750 L of water in 3 months.

That's one **million**, five hundred and three thousand, seven hundred and fifty litres.

PLACE VALUE TO 1 000 000 (continued)

Place value chart for 1 503 750

1 000 000s	100 000s	10 000s	1000s	100s	10s	1s
Millions	Hundred Thousands	Ten Thousands	Thousands	Hundreds	Tens	Ones
M	HT	TT	Th	H	T	O
●	●●●●●		●●●	●●●●●●●	●●●●●	
1	5	0	3	7	5	0

The order of digits matters

If your family uses 1 503 750 L of water, this is much less than 5 103 750 L of water.

The **5** in 1 **5**03 750 is ten times smaller than the **5** in **5** 103 750.

Each position to the left is 10 times larger. The digits all have **place value**.

Millions look like this on a number line.

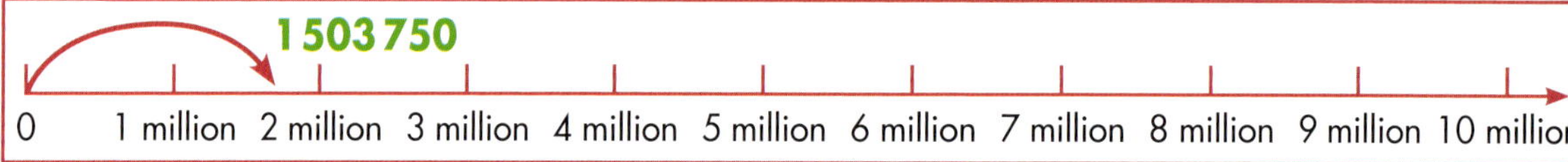

1 503 750 is:

- larger than 1 500 000
- smaller than 1 600 000
- in between 1 500 000 and 1 600 000.

If you rearrange the digits the smallest number you could make is

0	0	1	3	5	5	7

Rearrange the digits in 1 503 750 to make the largest number possible.

Challenge

Rearrange the digits in 1 503 750 to make the second largest number.

PLACE VALUE BEYOND 1 000 000

Large numbers go on forever. Most people today use the American system of place value where after 1 million you use special names for numbers 1000 times larger. One **billion** is 1 000 000 000 or one thousand million.

Most scientists, mathematicians and engineers today do not use any of these number names. Instead they refer to the powers of 10 such as 10 to the ninth power for 1 billion.

Number name	Number	Multiples of 10	Powers of 10
million	1 000 000	10 × 10 × 10 × 10 × 10 × 10	10^6
billion	1 000 000 000 (1000 million)	10 × 10 × 10 × 10 × 10 × 10 × 10 × 10 × 10	10^9
trillion	1 000 000 000 000 (1 million million)	10 × 10 × 10 × 10 × 10 × 10 × 10 × 10 × 10 × 10 × 10 × 10	10^{12}
quadrillion	1 000 000 000 000 000 (1 billion million)	10 × 10 × 10 × 10 × 10 × 10 × 10 × 10 × 10 × 10 × 10 × 10 × 10 × 10 × 10	10^{15}

- In 2009, Zimbabwe printed a 100 trillion banknote. It was worth about $30.
- More than 218 **trillion** emails are sent around the world each day.

GOOGOL

One ridiculously large number is a **googol**.
- It is 10^{100} or 10 to the hundredth power.
- That's 10 multiplied by ten 100 times.
- That's 1 with one hundred 0s after it.

A googol is more than all the grains of sand on earth. It is more than all the stars in our universe. It was named for fun and lies outside the pattern of naming large numbers. The name was created by the 9-year-old nephew of an American mathematician in the 1930s. This is what a googol looks like:

EXPANDING LARGE NUMBERS

The population of Australia at 3.00 pm on 22 May 2011 was 22 615 410. That's twenty-two million, six hundred and fifteen thousand, four hundred and ten.

10 000 000s	1 000 000s	100 000s	10 000s	1 000s	100s	10s	1s
Ten Millions	M	HT	TT	Th	H	T	O
●●	●●	●●●●●●	●	●●●●●	●●●●	●	
2	2	6	1	5	4	1	0

To expand this number, you write each number separately using its place value name. This is called **expanded notation**.

20 000 000 + 2 000 000 + 600 000 + 10 000 + 5 000 + 400 + 10 + 0

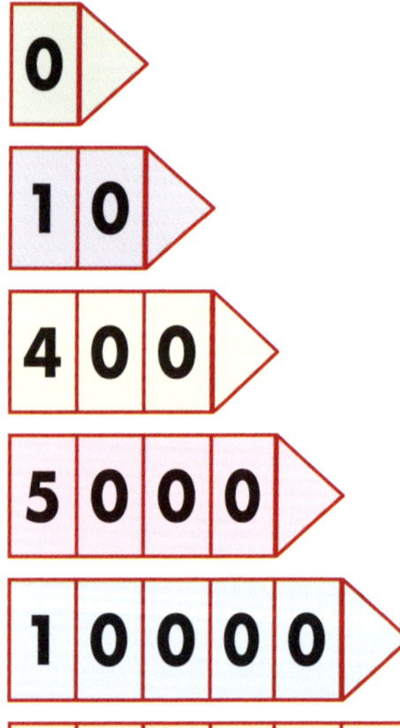

You could also record this number with Montessori arrow cards. Maria Montessori was a famous teacher in Italy over 100 years ago. She developed a range of mathematics resources that we still use today. Each arrow card represents one of the powers of 10. Once you have the matching cards, place all the pointed ends together to reveal the whole number like this:

In the metric system you do not need commas as a thousands marker in large numbers. Just use a space.

ORDERING LARGE NUMBERS

To put a mix of large numbers in order, use a ***count the number of digits strategy***. If the number of digits is different, the number with the most digits is the largest.

$102 675 is more than either $38 965 or $84 995 as it has **6** digits.

If you have the same number of digits, use a ***front end strategy***. Look at the left digit first. The larger number has the larger digit on the left. It doesn't matter what the digits on the right are.

8 is larger than **3**, so $**8**4 995 is more expensive than $38 965.

Don't get tricked

- 900 is smaller than 1000, even though 9 is more than 1, because 1 is in the 1000s place.
- 7000 is larger than 899, even though 7 is smaller than 8, because 7 is in the 1000s place.
- 40 000 is larger than 4692 because the 4 is in the 10 000s place.

ORDERING LARGE NUMBERS (continued)

Try this ...

Place the circumferences of these planets in order from the smallest to the largest.

Mercury	15 329 km
Venus	38 035 km
Earth	40 075 km
Mars	21 343 km
Jupiter	449 113 km

Earth

Challenge

Place the length of these orbits in order from the smallest to the largest.

Uranus	2 870 658 186 km
Earth	149 598 262 km
Saturn	1 426 666 422 km
Jupiter	778 340 821 km
Mars	227 943 824 km

Mars

ROUNDING LARGE NUMBERS

To estimate a number you do not need to be exact.

- Did you know that a sneeze can release 39 874 droplets? To help you remember how many droplets are in a sneeze, you can round 39 874 up to 40 000. It is still disgusting!
- A sneeze can travel up to 10.168 metres. Did you need to be so precise? You can round 10.168 metres down to 10 metres.
- A sneeze can travel at a speed of 158.88 km per hour. Will you remember this? You can round 158.88 km per hour up to 160 km per hour.

Don't get tricked

Numbers like 700 000 are already rounded to the nearest 10, 100, 1000 and 10 000. You don't need to change anything.

How to round to the nearest 10

If the ones digit is **5 or more**, round it **up** to the next multiple of 10 and write 0 ones.

146 65**7** rounds up to 146 6**60**

If the ones digit is **less than 5**, round it **down** to the 10s digit and write 0 ones.

230 19**4** rounds down to 230 1**90**

How to round to the nearest 100

If the 10s digit is **5 or more**, round it **up** to the next multiple of 100 and write 0 in the 10s and 1s place.

146 6**5**7 rounds up to 146 **700**

230 1**9**4 rounds up to 230 **200**

If the 10s digit is **less than 5**, round it **down** to the 100s digit and write 0 tens and 0 ones.

729 3**4**8 rounds down to 729 **300**

How to round to the nearest 1000

If the 100s digit is **5 or more**, round it **up** to the next multiple of 1000 and write 0 in the 100s, 10s and 1s place.

146 **6**57 rounds to 14**7 000**

If the 100s digit is **less than 5**, round it **down** to the 1000s digit and write 0 in the 100s, 10s and ones.

230 **1**94 rounds to 23**0 000**

How to round to the nearest 10 000

If the 1000s digit is **5 or more**, round it **up** to the next multiple of 10 000 and write 0 in the 1000s, 100s, 10s and 1s place.

14**6** 657 rounds up to 1**50 000**

If the 1000s digit is **less than 5**, round it **down** to the 10 000s digit and write 0 in the 1000s, 100s, 10s and ones.

23**0** 194 rounds down to 2**30 000**

POSITIVE AND NEGATIVE NUMBERS

If you think of numbers as starting from 0, imagine them going on forever in a straight line to the right. They look like this on a number line.

But sometimes numbers can go backwards too. They can go backwards forever. This time they start at 0 but go in a straight line to the left. They look like this on a number line.

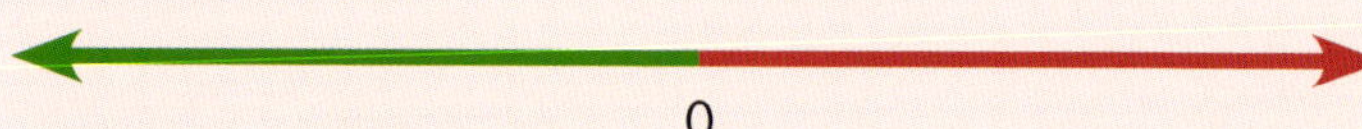

Negative numbers go backwards. Positive numbers go forwards.

Use the – sign for negative numbers.
Use the + sign for positive numbers.

If you have no money saved but you need $10 to buy your lunch, you can borrow $10. You are minus $10.

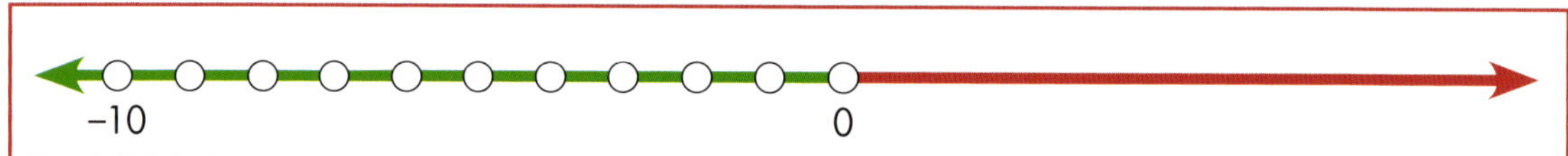

If you later pay back $5, you are still minus $5.

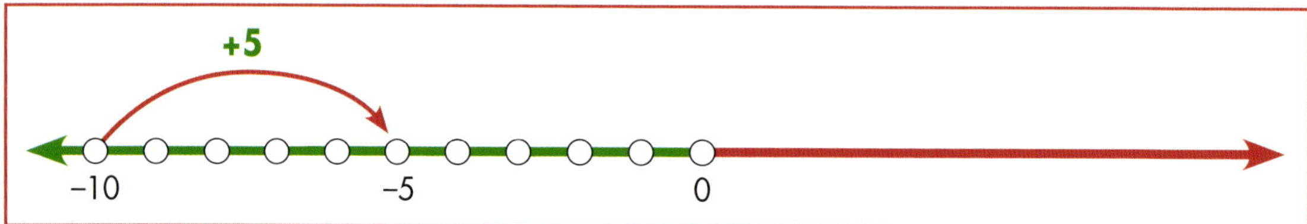

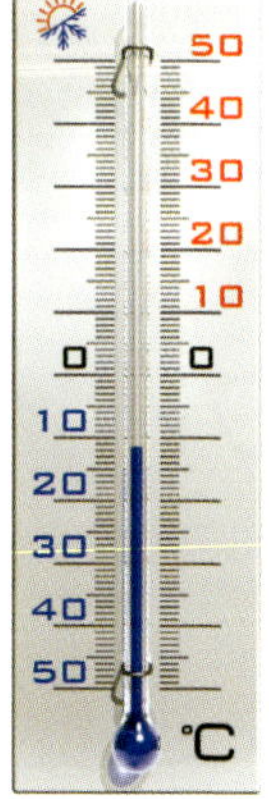

You use positive and negative numbers to measure temperature.

The temperature on this thermometer measures minus 11 degrees Celsius. That's –11 °C.

Architects use negative numbers to describe rooms or floors below ground level. The basement floor might be 4 m below the ground level. You can record this as –4 m.

ADDITION & SUBTRACTION

ADD AND SUBTRACT FACTS TO 20

When you add numbers, it does not matter in what order you add the numbers. The sum of 8 + 9 is the same sum as 9 + 8.

So when it comes to remembering your basic facts, you only need to memorise half of them. All the blank spaces in the table below are reversals.

You need to know the basic facts with 100% accuracy.

+/–	0	1	2	3	4	5	6	7	8	9	10
0	0										
1	1	2									
2	2	3	4								
3	3	4	5	6							
4	4	5	6	7	8						
5	5	6	7	8	9	10					
6	6	7	8	9	10	11	12				
7	7	8	9	10	11	12	13	14			
8	8	9	10	11	12	13	14	15	16		
9	9	10	11	12	13	14	15	16	17	18	
10	10	11	12	13	14	15	16	17	18	19	20

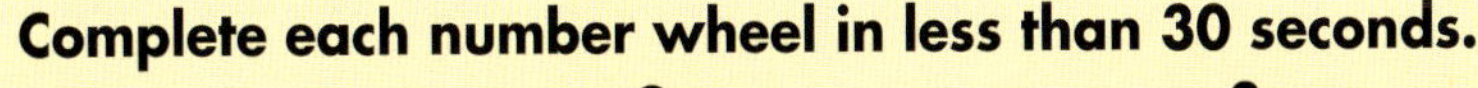

Complete each number wheel in less than 30 seconds.

1

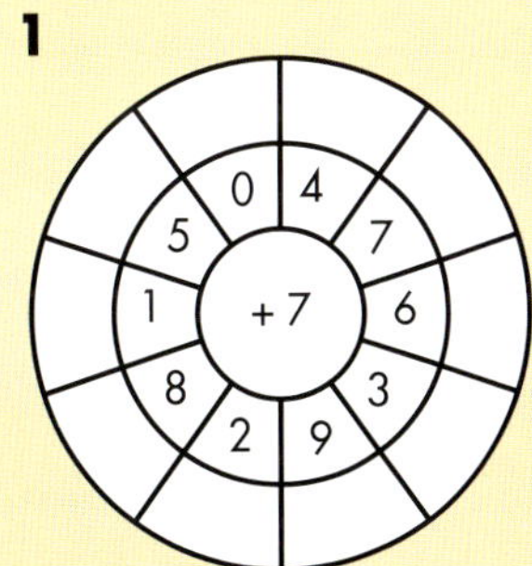

2

3

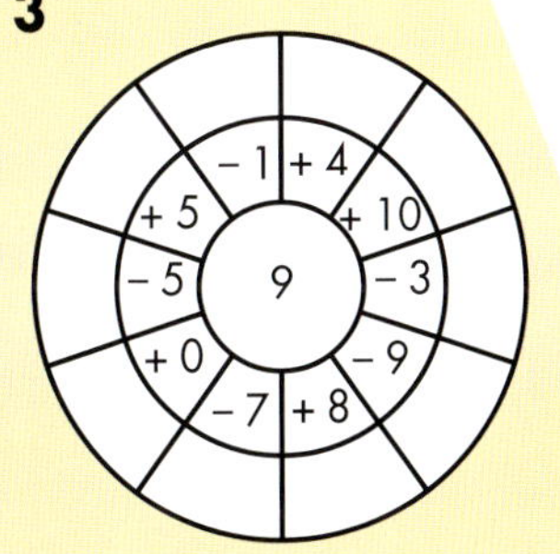

MAGIC SQUARES

Magic squares are special addition puzzles to help you practise your basic facts. Every row, column and diagonal has the same sum. Puzzles like this were used in ancient China. They were used 500 years ago in Europe as a charm to protect you from bad luck.

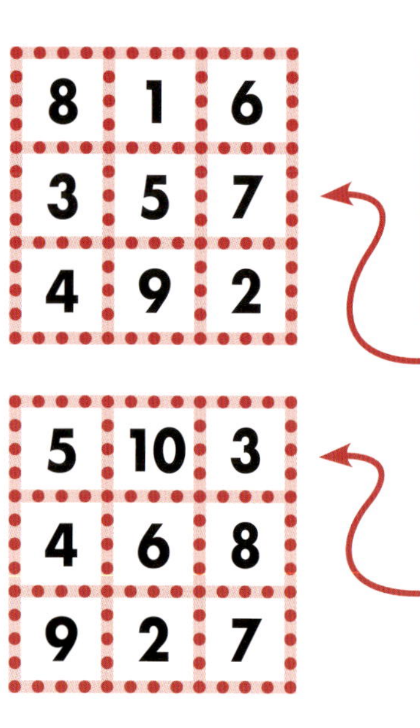

In this magic square, every row, column and diagonal adds to **15**, using the digits 1–9 only.

In this magic square, every row, column and diagonal adds to **18**.

In this magic square, every row, column and diagonal adds to **45**.

Finish these Magic Squares. Every row, column and diagonal adds to 15 using the digits 1–9 only.

Challenge

Complete this 'adds to 30' Magic Square.

Complete this 'adds to 45' Magic Square.

'COUNTING UP TO' STRATEGY

To add or subtract large numbers, your first strategy is to try to work out the answer in your head. Try ***counting up to*** the higher number from the lower number.

What is the difference in length between these two rivers?

Nile River 6693 km long

Amazon River 6436 km long

It might look like this on a number line:

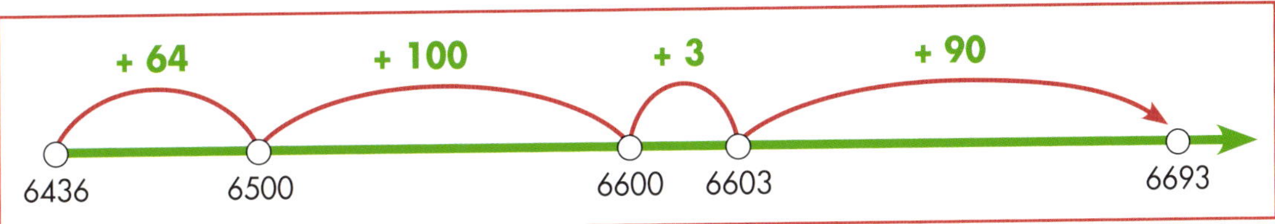

6436 is the lower number.
What do you add to 436 to get 500?
Adding **64** more takes you to 500.
Adding another **100** takes you to 6600.
That's an extra 164 so far.
Now add the **93**.
164 and 3 more is 167.
90 more is **257**.
So the difference is 257 km.

Think of another way to use this strategy.
Practise adding to the next 100 then next 1000.

Adding to the next 1000

342 → 1000
You add 58 to 342 to make 400.
You add 600 more to make 1000.
So that's 658 more to make 1000.

734  1000
You add 66 to 734 to make 800.
You add 200 more to make 1000.
So that's 266 more to make 1000.

'COUNTING UP TO' STRATEGY (continued)

Try this

Use a 'counting up to' strategy to work out the difference for these number sentences. Demonstrate one strategy on a number line.

1 256 + ____ = 1000 **2** 481 + ____ = 1000

3 805 + ____ = 1000

USING A CALCULATOR

Suan-pan abacus

There are many types of calculator. An **abacus** has columns and rows of beads like a place value table.

The Chinese suan-pan has helped Chinese people calculate quickly for over 2000 years. The Japanese use a soroban abacus to help students calculate mentally. They imagine the place value positions in their head.

The most popular calculators today are digital devices. You find them on computers and mobile phones too. Before using a **digital calculator** to add or subtract, **estimate** the sum or difference mentally, just in case you press the wrong buttons. Try rounding up or down to the nearest 5, 10, 50, 100, 500, 1000 or 5000. It all depends on the size of the numbers you are working with.

What is the difference in length between these Chinese rivers, Chang Jiang River and Huang He River?

Chang Jiang River 6370 km

Huang He River 5464 km

Estimate first → You might round to the nearest 500.
Round 6370 to 6500 and 5464 to 5500.
Now subtract mentally to get your estimate.
6500 – 5500 is 1000.
So you expect a difference of about 1000 km.

To work it out on a calculator, press:

The answer is 906 — 906 km, close enough to what you expected.

USING A WRITTEN ALGORISM

Our word **algorism** or algorithm comes from the name of a famous Persian mathematician Al Khorezme. His maths books introduced us to the Hindu-Arabic digits 0–9 and methods for operating with large numbers. An algorism is a procedure for working out an answer to a real-life problem that you cannot work out in your head.

The examples below are based on the following information:

Lake Michigan-Huron

Lake Victoria

Lake Baikal

	Name of lake	Place	Area (m²)	Length (m)	Depth (m)
a	Michigan-Huron	Canada/USA	117 502	710	282
b	Victoria	Africa	69 485	322	84
c	Baikal	Russia	31 700	636	1637

Addition algorism

To find the total of the areas of the three lakes, line up all the digits in place value columns.
You do not need to write an addition sign.

- Add the 1s first. If you get 10 or more, trade into 10s. Write any traded number at the top of the 10s column.
- Add the 10s next. If you get 10 or more, trade into 100s. Write any traded number at the top of the 100s column.
- Add the 100s. If you get 10 or more, trade into 1000s. Write any traded number at the top of the 10 000s column.
- Add the 10 000s.

HT	TT	Th	H	T	O
1	1	1			
1	1	7	5	0	2
	6	9	4	8	5
	3	1	7	0	0
2	1	8	6	8	7

The total area covered by water in the three lakes is 218 687 square metres.

Use the table of the lakes to write and solve three more addition algorisms of your own.

Subtraction algorism using trading

Use the ***trading* method** if you cannot solve a problem mentally or on a number line.

1. Write the larger number in place value columns.
2. Write the smaller number under it.
3. Write the subtraction sign on the left.
4. Subtract the 1s first. If you don't have enough 1s, trade a 10 and write the new number on top of the 1s.
5. Subtract the 10s next. If you don't have enough 10s, trade a 100 and write the new number on top of the 10s.
6. Subtract the 100s next. If you don't have enough 100s, trade a 1000 and write the new number on top of the 100s.
7. Subtract the 1000s last.

What is the difference in the depth of water between Lake Victoria and Lake Baikal?

1637 – 84 Estimate first → Try 1600 – 100 = 1500

	Th	H	T	O
	1	6	3	7
–			8	4
				3

	Th	H	T	O
		5	13	
	1	~~6~~	~~3~~	7
–			8	4
			5	3

	Th	H	T	O
		5	13	
	1	~~6~~	~~3~~	7
–			8	4
	1	5	5	3

The difference in depths between Lake Baikal and Lake Victoria is 1553 metres.

What is the water area difference between Lake Michigan-Huron and Lake Baikal?

117 502 – 31 700 Estimate first → Try 120 000 – 30 000 = 90 000

	HT	TT	Th	H	T	O
			6	15		
	1	1	~~7~~	~~5~~	0	2
–		3	1	7	0	0
				8	0	2

	HT	TT	Th	H	T	O
			6	15		
	1	1	~~7~~	~~5~~	0	2
–		3	1	7	0	0
			5	8	0	2

	HT	TT	Th	H	T	O
	0	11	6	15		
	~~1~~	~~1~~	~~7~~	~~5~~	0	2
–		3	1	7	0	0
		8	5	8	0	2

The difference in water area between Lake Michigan-Huron and Lake Baikal is 85 802 square metres.
Use a calculator to check.

Use the information about the three lakes to write and solve three more subtraction algorisms of your own.

OTHER SUBTRACTION ALGORISMS

Trading can be tricky to use when there are lots of 0s. Try the ***'subtract 1' trading* method** when you have lots of 0s.

Your family has saved
$7000 for a holiday.
Plane tickets cost $2125.
How much is left for other expenses?

Remember 7000 is the same number as 700 × 10. Trade one of the seven hundred 10s for ten 1s. That leaves 699 tens and ten 1s.

	Th	H	T	O
	6	9	9	10
	~~7~~	~~0~~	~~0~~	~~0~~
–	2	1	2	5
	4	8	7	5

You have $4875 left for other holiday expenses.

If it was $70 000, that is the same as 7000 tens.
If it was $700 000, that is the same as 70 000 tens.
If it was $7 000 000, that is the same as 700 000 tens.

Another method is to subtract 1 from both numbers to turn your problem into an easy algorism to solve.

7000 – 1 = 6999
2125 – 1 = 2124

	Th	H	T	O
	6	9	9	9
–	2	1	2	4
	4	8	7	5

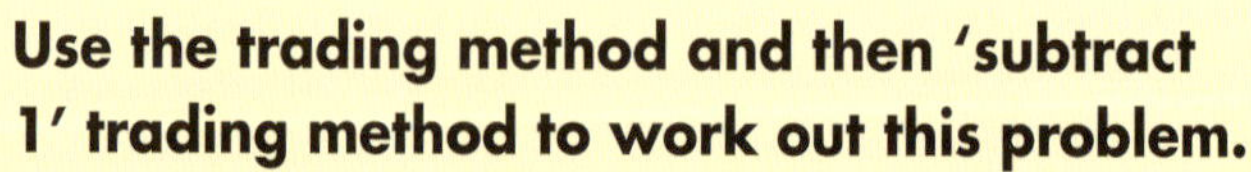

Use the trading method and then 'subtract 1' trading method to work out this problem.
Which method is easier for you to use? Why?
Remember there are 14 000 tens in 140 000.

There are 140 000 strands of blonde hair on Sally's head.
Jack has 87 457 strands of red hair.
How many more strands does Sally have?

MULTIPLICATION & DIVISION

WHAT IS MULTIPLICATION?

Multiplication is **repeated addition**. It helps you count equal rows of objects in an array.

This carton has 6 rows of 5 eggs. Turn the array a quarter turn and there are now 5 rows of 6 eggs. Both 6 × 5 and 5 × 6 make 30 eggs altogether.

6 rows of 5 eggs = 30 eggs

Multiplication helps you calculate units of area in a rectangle. It doesn't matter which side you measure first. It saves you having to add up all the units in each row.

7 × 8 = 8 × 7 = 56 square units

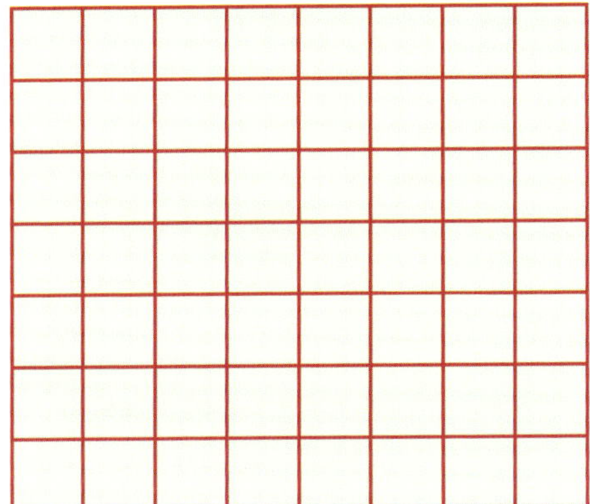

7 units

5 rows of 6 eggs = 30 eggs

Multiplication helps you work out combinations. If you have 3 pairs of shorts and 4 shirts, each pair of shorts can have 4 different shirts. There are 12 different outfits.

FACTORS AND MULTIPLES

Multiplication uses repeated addition of factors.
Division uses repeated subtraction of factors.

A **factor** is a number that can be added over and over again to create new numbers. Two or more factors can be multiplied together to make a product.

A large red kangaroo can leap 9 metres seven times and travel 63 m in total.
9 + 9 + 9 + 9 + 9 + 9 + 9 = 63

A small kangaroo can leap 7 metres nine times and travel 63 m in total.
7 + 7 + 7 + 7 + 7 + 7 + 7 + 7 + 7 = 63
9 and **7** are both **factors** of **63**

A number can have more than two factors.
1 + 1+ 1+ 1+ 1+ 1+ 1+ 1+ 1+ 1+ 1+ 1= 12 × 1 = 12
2 + 2 + 2 + 2 + 2 + 2 = 6 × 2 =12
3 + 3 + 3 + 3 = 4 × 3 =12
4 + 4 + 4 = 3 × 4 =12
6 + 6 = 2 × 6 =12
12 = 1 × 12 = 12
1, **2**, **3**, **4**, **6** and **12** are all factors of 12.

A **multiple** is the repeated addition of one number. It is also the product of two or more factors.
multiples of **7**: 7, 14, 21, 28, 35, 42, 49, 54, 63, 70, 77, 84, 91, 98 …
multiples of **9**: 9, 18, 27, 36, 45, 54, 63, 72, 81, 90, 99, 108, 117 …

A **product** is the result you get when two or more numbers are multiplied together.

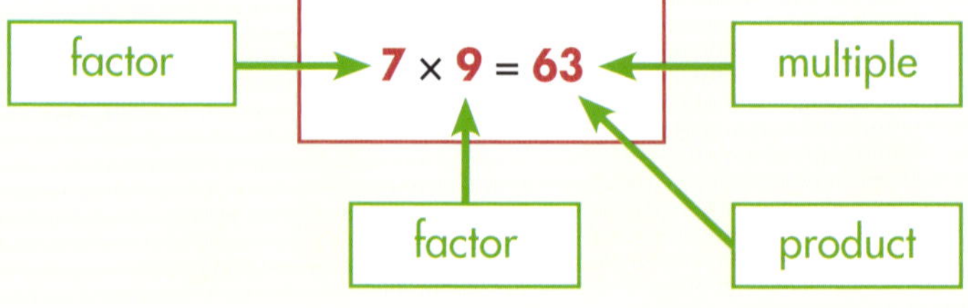

1 What are four different factors of 24?
2 What are ten different multiples of 8?

PRIME AND COMPOSITE NUMBERS

A **prime number** is larger than 1. A prime number has only two factors as it is divisible only by 1 and itself. The number 1 is not a prime number as it only has one factor.

If you use counters to model a prime number as a rectangle, you can only make one row.

11 is a prime number. It can only make one row, 1 × 11.

What are the first ten prime numbers?

2 3 5 7 11 13 17 19 23 29

There are 25 prime numbers up to 100. Prime numbers are the building blocks of our number system.

Mathematicians have tried to discover a pattern in prime numbers. They have even programmed computers to search for a pattern. No-one has found a pattern yet.

Every even number can be made by adding two prime numbers.
8 = 5 + 3
or
20 = 13 + 7

A composite number is divisible by three or more factors. If you use counters to model a composite number as a rectangle, you can make two or more equal rows.

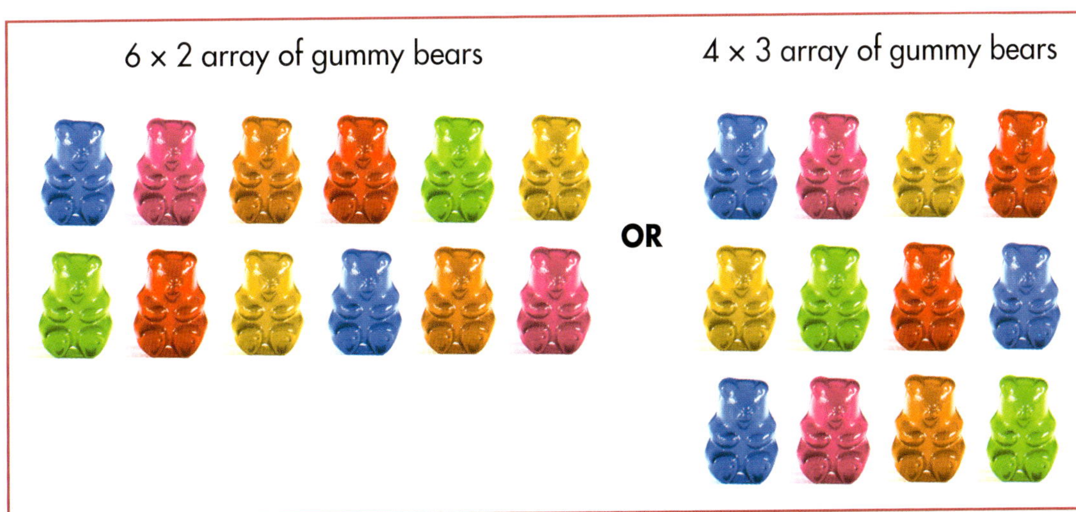

PRIME AND COMPOSITE NUMBERS (continued)

12 is a composite number
It can make:

- 1 row of 12
- 12 rows of 1
- 2 rows of 6
- 6 rows of 2
- 3 rows of 4
- 4 rows of 3

The factors of 12 are 1, 2, 3, 4, 6 and 12.
There are 74 composite numbers up to and including 100.

Try this

What are the first ten composite numbers?

SIEVE OF ERATOSTHENES

The Greek mathematician Eratosthenes discovered this sieve method to identify prime numbers on a 0–99 chart.

1. Shade 0 and 1 pink, as they are not prime. A prime number is always larger than 1.
2. Next circle 2, then shade all its multiples green.
3. Repeat for 3 and its multiples. Shade them blue.
4. Repeat for 5 and its multiples. Shade them lilac.
5. Repeat for 7 and its multiples. Shade them orange.
6. The remaining prime numbers will now be revealed by the sieve. Draw a circle around them.

0	1	2	3	4	5	6	7	8	9
10	11	12	13	14	15	16	17	18	19
20	21	22	23	24	25	26	27	28	29
30	31	32	33	34	35	36	37	38	39
40	41	42	43	44	45	46	47	48	49
50	51	52	53	54	55	56	57	58	59
60	61	62	63	64	65	66	67	68	69
70	71	72	73	74	75	76	77	78	79
80	81	82	83	84	85	86	87	88	89
90	91	92	93	94	95	96	97	98	99

ESSENTIAL TABLES FACTS TO 10 × 10

There are 121 multiplication and division facts up to 10 × 10 and 100 ÷ 10. You need to remember all of these with 100% accuracy. Phew! That's quite a task. These are usually written as a large grid or table that looks quite daunting.

×	0	1	2	3	4	5	6	7	8	9	10
0	0	0	0	0	0	0	0	0	0	0	0
1	0	1	2	3	4	5	6	7	8	9	10
2	0	2	4	6	8	10	12	14	16	18	20
3	0	3	6	9	12	15	18	21	24	27	30
4	0	4	8	12	16	20	24	28	32	36	40
5	0	5	10	15	20	25	30	35	40	45	50
6	0	6	12	18	24	30	36	42	48	54	60
7	0	7	14	21	28	35	42	49	56	63	70
8	0	8	16	24	32	40	48	56	64	72	80
9	0	9	18	27	36	45	54	63	72	81	90
10	0	10	20	30	40	50	60	70	80	90	100

But if you already know your facts for × 0, × 1 and × 10, that's 57 facts you already know. These are marked green.

And because you know 9 × 6 is exactly the same answer as 6 × 9, or 54 ÷ 6 = 9 and 54 ÷ 9 = 6 you can remove 28 reverse facts too. These reverse facts are marked orange.

The amazing thing is you now just need to memorise the 36 white facts. This seems much more achievable!

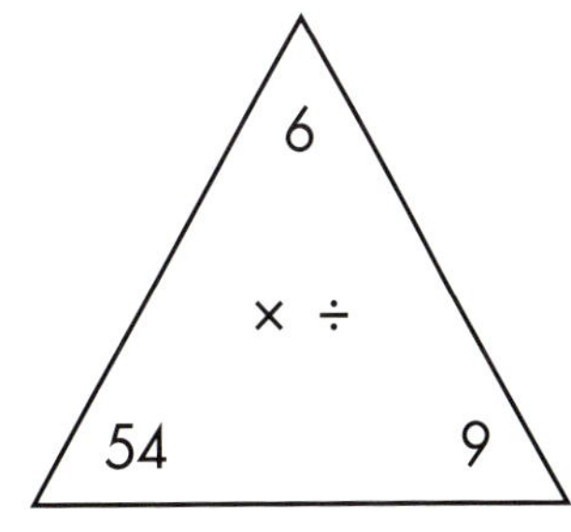

Caroline Herschel was too old to learn her × and ÷ tables when she became a famous astronomer late in life. She kept a copy of all her tables facts on a piece of paper in her pocket. Was this an efficient method?

ESSENTIAL TABLES FACTS TO 10 × 10 (continued)

Complete each number wheel in less than 30 seconds.

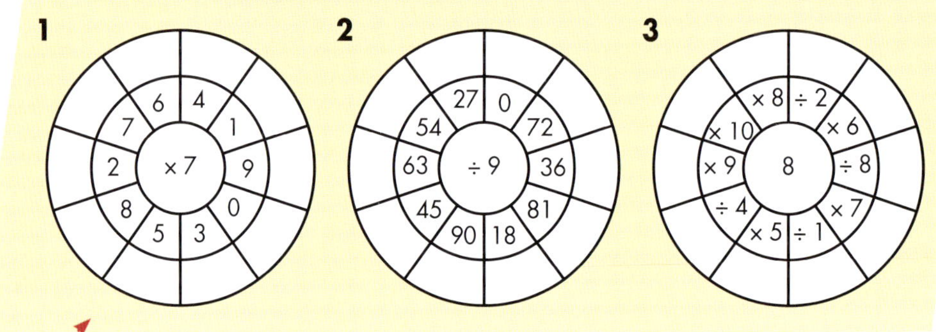

MULTIPLY AND DIVIDE BY 11 AND 12

Your grandparents learnt how to multiply and divide by 11 and 12 when they were at school. They used measurements that were based on 12. Today knowing your 11s and 12s tables is no longer as important. It is a bonus skill.

×	0	1	2	3	4	5	6	7	8	9	10
11	0	11	22	33	44	55	66	77	88	99	110
12	0	12	24	36	48	60	72	84	96	108	120

MULTIPLY BY MULTIPLES OF 10

When you multiply a number by 10, the digits slide **one** place to the left and you write **0** in the empty 1s place. Each digit is now 10 times larger.

1 000s	100s	10s	1s
	7	5	2

1 000s	100s	10s	1s
7	5	2	**0**

752 × 10 = 7520
10**0** is 10 groups of 10
30**0** is 10 groups of 30
70**0** is 10 groups of 70
Can you see the pattern?

39 × 10 = 39**0**
450 × 10 = 450**0**
7269 × 10 = 72 69**0**

To multiply by a multiple of 10 try to mentally calculate with the 10s digit, then write **0** in the 1s place.

56 × 70 → 56 × 7 = (50 + 6) × 7 = (50 × 7) + (6 × 7) = 350 + 42 = 392
→ 392**0**

MULTIPLY BY MULTIPLES OF 100

When you multiply a number by 100, the digits slide **two** places to the left and you write **0** in the empty 10s and 1s place. Each digit is now 100 times larger.

1 000s	100s	10s	1s
	4	1	9

10 000s	1 000s	100s	10s	1s
4	1	9	**0**	**0**

419 × 100 = 41 900
10**00** is 100 groups of 10
90**00** is 100 groups of 90
70**00** is 100 groups of 70
Can you see the pattern?

83 × 100 = 83**00**
790 × 100 = 79 0**00**
4025 × 100 = 402 5**00**

To multiply by a multiple of 100 try to mentally calculate with the 100s digit, then write **0** in the 10s and 1s place.

48 × 600 → 48 × 6 = (40 + 8) × 6 = (40 × 6) + (8 × 6) = 240 + 48 = 288
→ 28 8**00**

MULTIPLY MENTALLY WITH EASY MULTIPLES

Look for easy multiples. Try to make products of 10, 100 or 1000.

Here are some useful easy multiples:

20 × 5 = 100	200 × 5 = 1000	75 × 2 = 150	75 × 4 = 300
25 × 4 = 100	250 × 4 = 1000	750 × 2 = 1500	750 × 4 = 3000
50 × 2 = 100	500 × 2 = 1000		

325 × 4 is the same product as 4 × 325 or
(300 × 4) + (25 × 4)

That's 1200 plus 100 or 1300 altogether.
Four 325 kg zebras have a total mass of 1300 kg.

975 × 4 is the same product as 4 × 975 or
(75 × 4) + (900 × 4)

That's 300 plus 3600 or 3900 altogether.
Four 975 kg crocodiles have a total mass of 3900 kg.

MULTIPLYING USING AN AREA MODEL

The area model breaks factors into place value sections that can be multiplied mentally.

Imagine a helicopter view of a farm divided into different paddocks, measured in metres.

In this 457 × 7 m area, there are three paddocks:

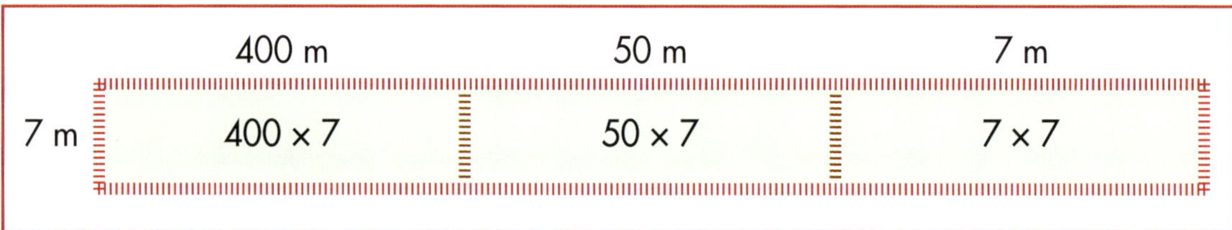

The total area is 400 × 7 plus 50 × 7 plus 7 × 7.
That's 2800 m^2 + 350 m^2 + 49 m^2 = 3199 m^2.

In this 312 × 24 m area, there are six smaller sections:

	300 m	10 m	2 m
20 m	300 × 20	10 × 20	2 × 20
4 m	300 × 4	10 × 4	2 × 4

The total area is
300 × 20 plus 300 × 4 plus 10 × 20 plus 10 × 4 plus 2 × 20 plus 2 × 4

6000 + 1200 + 200 + 40 + 40 + 8 = 7488 m^2

If you cannot do this in your head, write each product in place value columns and add.

6 0 0 0	What is 300 × 20?
1 2 0 0	What is 300 × 4?
2 0 0	What is 10 × 20?
4 0	What is 10 × 4?
4 0	What is 2 × 20?
8	What is 2 × 4?
7 4 8 8	Add all the products to find the total.

MULTIPLY USING THE ITALIAN LATTICE METHOD

This method was popular in ancient India and also in Italy 500 years ago. Another name is the Gelosia method. Think of place value diagonally and not vertically.

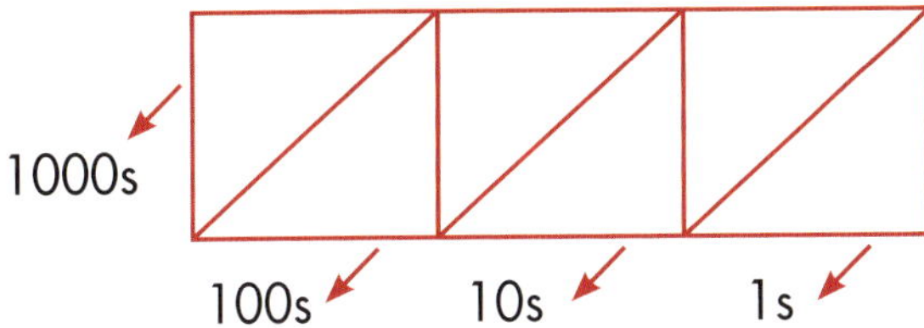

What is the mass of seven 215 kg gorillas?

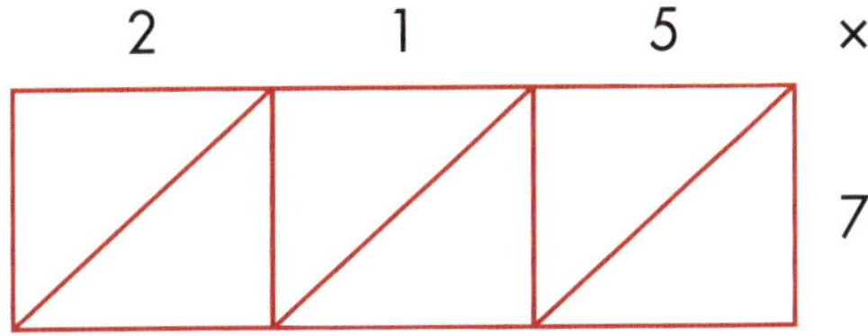

Place the larger number to be multiplied on top of the grid and the smaller number at the side.

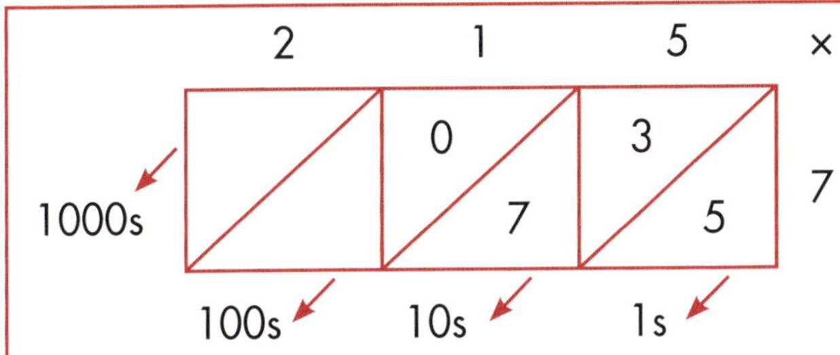

7 × 5 = 35
7 × 1 = 07
(place the 0 in the 100s diagonal)

Multiply each digit pair and write the product.

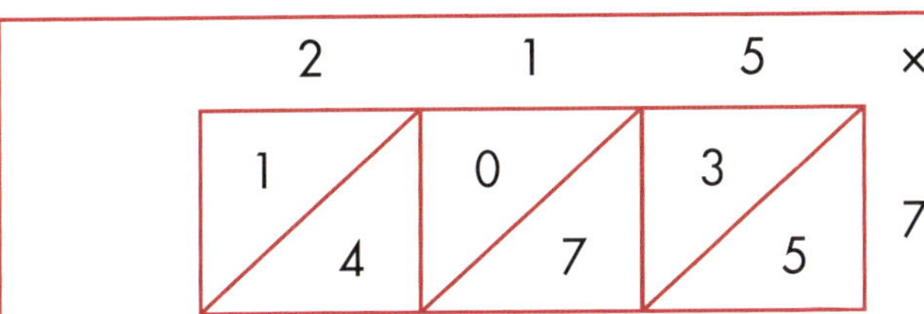

7 × 2 = 14

Add all the numbers in each diagonal to get your product. Trade where necessary.

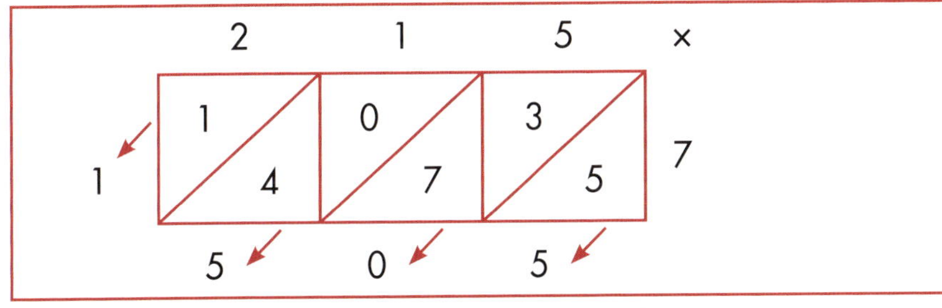

The mass of seven 215 kg gorillas is 1505 kg.

MULTIPLY USING LONG MULTIPLICATION

Long multiplication is when you calculate all the separate products, like in the area model. Write each number in place value columns with all numbers lined up correctly. Estimate your answer before starting to calculate.

A fly beats its wings 198 times each second. How many times does it beat its wings in one minute?

Estimate first → 200 × 60 = 12 000

In expanded notation:
198 is the same as 100 + 90 + 8
So 198 × 60 is the same product as 100 × 60 plus 90 × 60 plus 8 × 60

Record these smaller products in order.

	1 9 8	
×	6 0	
	4 8 0	What is 8 × 60?
	5 4 0 0	What is 90 × 60?
	6 0 0 0	What is 100 × 60?
	1 1 8 8 0	Add all the products to find the total.

A fly's wings beat 11 880 times in 1 minute.

MULTIPLY USING A SHORT ALGORISM

Once you are successful at using long multiplication, try more of the calculations in your head, recording each answer as you go.

Start by multiplying the 1s. If you need to trade, write it in the matching column and add it after you have multiplied. Keep multiplying like this to get your product.

2-digit × 1-digit

A hippo eats 42 kg of grass in one day.

How much grass does it eat in one week?

Estimate first ⟶ 40 × 7 = 280

and another 2 × 7 =14.

You can actually work out the exact answer in your head.
280 + 14 = 294

If you need to do it on paper it looks like this:

	~~1~~	
	4 2	7 × 2 = 14 (ones), write 4 and trade one 10.
×	7	4 × 7 = 28 (tens) and 1 more 10 is 29
	2 9 4	Cross out the 1 to show you used it

A hippo eats 294 kg of grass each week.

2-digit × 2-digit

For a dance performance,
19 people earn $67 each.
How much will the group earn altogether?

Estimate first ⟶ 70 × 20 = 1400

If you cannot work this out in your head use an algorism.
Calculate 67 × 9 and record your answer.
Then work out 67 × 10 and record this underneath.
Add the two answers to get your product.

	~~6~~	
	6 7	
×	1 9	9 × 7 = 63 (ones), write 3 and trade six 10s
	6 0 3	9 × 6 = 54 (tens) plus the extra 6 (tens) is 60
	6 7 0	Cross out the 6 to show you used it
	1 2 7 3	10 × 67 = 670

The dance group will earn $1273 altogether.

WHAT IS DIVISION?

Division is:

- repeated subtraction
- about sharing or grouping
- to take away the same amount each time until nothing is left
- the opposite of multiplication
- undoing multiplication
- to start with the product and find the factors.

If 7 people share 30 pancakes, each person will get 4 pancakes because 7 × 4 = 28 but there will be 2 left over.

Remainders can be a whole number, a fraction or a decimal.

Here are three ways to record remainders:

whole number	**30 ÷ 7 = 4 r 2**
fraction	$\mathbf{30 \div 7 = 4\frac{2}{7}}$
decimal	**30 ÷ 7 = 4.29**

A calculator gives you a decimal remainder.

The problem will determine the kind of remainder you calculate.
Two pancakes might go to the hungriest person. Or they can each get cut into 7 parts and shared equally. But you would not slice up the two extra pancakes into 0.29 pieces, even though this is mathematically correct.

Four words help you talk about division like a mathematician:

dividend → **30 ÷ 7 = 4 r 2**

divisor (7), quotient (4), remainder (2)

A **dividend** is the division start number, the product of the other two numbers.
A **divisor** is the division sharing or grouping number.
The **quotient** is the division answer.
The **remainder** is any leftovers after sharing or grouping.

DIVISION ESTIMATES

To estimate in division problems you need to look for the nearest easy multiple that you can divide mentally. This is not always the nearest 10, 100 or 1000.

A cheetah can travel 6 m in one stride. How many strides can the cheetah travel in 1000 m?

Estimate first ⟶ 1020 divided into 6 equal groups is 170

A quick calculator check shows 166.66 so about 167 strides is the answer.

Here are more examples of finding an easy multiple:
437 ÷ 6 think 420 ÷ 6 = 70
502 ÷ 7 think 490 ÷ 7 = 70
785 ÷ 4 think 800 ÷ 4 = 200
368 ÷ 3 think 360 ÷ 3 = 120

Once you have your estimate, calculate your answer using a mental strategy or a written algorism. Use a calculator to check.

Try this

Write your easy multiple and estimate beside each division.

1 213 ÷ 4, think .... ÷ 4 =
2 534 ÷ 6, think .... ÷ 6 =

DIVISION USING A MENTAL STRATEGY

Only $\frac{1}{9}$ of an iceberg is visible above water.

If an iceberg is 181 m high, about how much of it is visible above water?

There are at least three different ways to record this division using symbols:

$181 \div 9$ $\quad 9\overline{)181}$ $\quad \frac{181}{9}$

DIVISION USING A MENTAL STRATEGY
(continued)

Use your known division facts to work out an answer.

One easy mental strategy is to **think multiplication**.

9 × ____ = 181 ⟶ 9 × 10 = 90

so 9 × 20 = 2 × 90 = 180

About 20 m of the iceberg is above sea level.

DIVIDE MENTALLY BY 10 AND 100

A grasshopper can jump 10 times its body length.

If it jumps 85 cm, how long is its body?

Think multiplication to solve 85 ÷ 10

10 × ____ = 85 ⟶ 10 × 8 = 80 and there is an extra 5 cm.

So the grasshopper must be 8 and $\frac{5}{10}$ cm long.

That's $8\frac{1}{2}$ or 8.5 cm long.

Notice the digits slide one place to the right.

To mentally divide a number by 10 slide the digits one place to the right.

The decimal point never moves.

1 000s	100s	10s	1s	•	$\frac{1}{10}$
4	8	3	9	•	

1 000s	100s	10s	1s	•	$\frac{1}{10}$
	4	8	3	•	9

4839 ÷ 10 = 483.9

Here are some more example of division by 10:

56 ÷ 10 = 5.6 234 ÷ 10 = 23.4 4839 ÷ 10 = 483.9

98 ÷ 10 = 9.8 405 ÷ 10 = 40.5 8700 ÷ 10 = 870.0

To mentally divide a number by 100 slide the digits two places to the right.

1000s	100s	10s	1s	•	$\frac{1}{10}$	$\frac{1}{100}$
2	0	2	5	•		

1000s	100s	10s	1s	•	$\frac{1}{10}$	$\frac{1}{100}$
		2	0	•	2	5

2025 ÷ 100 = 20.25

37 ÷ 100 = 0.37   551 ÷ 100 = 5.51   2025 ÷ 100 = 20.25

46 ÷ 100 = 0.46   829 ÷ 100 = 8.29   9876 ÷ 100 = 98.76

Mentally divide each of these numbers and record your answer.

1 23 ÷10 =
2 79 ÷100 =
3 398 ÷ 10 =
4 502 ÷ 100 =
5 1440 ÷ 10 =
6 8569 ÷ 10

DIVISION USING CHUNKING

Use **chunking** only when you cannot divide mentally. Use your × and ÷ facts to look for the **largest multiple** you can subtract easily. Start from the largest place value column.

1. Find a chunk, multiply, subtract.
2. Trade if necessary.
3. Continue finding the next easy multiple until you have none left or a remainder.
4. Add up all the quotients to get your answer.

DIVISION USING CHUNKING (continued)

The total money collected for a charity in one week was $5035.

What is the daily average?

Write the **divisor** and **dividend** like this:

```
7)5035
 -4900   700
   135
 -  70    10
    65
 -  63     9
     2
```

1 What is the largest easy multiple of 7 close to 5000?
$7 \times 1000 = 7000$ is too large
$7 \times$ **700** $= 4900$ is a large chunk that you can take away.
Write this first **quotient** on the far right.
Write the total under the dividend and subtract
$5035 - 4900 = 135$, so you still have 135 left

2 What is the largest multiple of 7 close to 135?
$7 \times 20 = 140$ is too large.
Try $7 \times$ **10** $= 70$
Record the quotient on the right, multiply then subtract.
$135 - 70 = 65$, so you still have 65 left

3 What is the largest multiple of 7 close to 65?
$7 \times$ **9** $= 63$ and you have **2 left**.

$700 + 10 + 9 = 719$ with 2 left over, or $\frac{2}{7}$ or 0.29.

So the daily average collected for charity must be $719.29.

Try this ...

The telescope costs $4765. It costs 6 times more than the binoculars. How much are the binoculars?

DIVISION USING LONG DIVISION

Use **long division** only when you cannot divide mentally or if you do not want to use a calculator. You must have 100% accuracy for all your × and ÷ facts before you attempt it.

Start to divide from the largest place value column first. Use multiplication and subtraction to help you work it all out.

Six hummingbirds have a total of 5628 feathers. How many feathers on one bird?

Imagine the place value columns as feathers packed into boxes.

1 000s	100s	10s	1s
5	6	2	8

There are 5 boxes with 1000 feathers inside. There are 6 boxes with 100 feathers inside. There are 2 boxes with 10 feathers inside and there are 8 extra feathers.

Write the **divisor** and **dividend** like this:

$6 \overline{)\,5\,6\,2\,8}$

Are there enough boxes of 1000 for each bird to get one?
No, there are only 5 so trade them for 100s.

You now have 56 boxes with 100 feathers in each.
6 × **9** = **54** so each bird can get 9 boxes of 100.
Trade the extra 2 boxes for 10s.

You now have 22 boxes with 10 feathers in each.
6 × **3** = **18** so each bird can get 3 boxes of 10.
Trade the extra 4 boxes for 1s.

You now have 48 single feathers.
6 × **8** = **48** so each bird can get 8 feathers.
Altogether each bird gets 9 × 100 plus 3 × 10 plus 8 feathers.
So each bird must have 938 feathers.

DIVISION USING LONG DIVISION (continued)

Your final recording looks like this:

```
     9 3 8
6) 5 6 2 8
  -5 4        What is 6 × 9?
     2 2
   - 1 8      What is 6 × 3?
       4 8
     - 4 8    What is 6 × 8?
         0
```

Challenge

Don Maclurean walked from Perth to Sydney in 67 days.
He walked 3283 km.
What was his daily average?

DIVISIBILITY TESTS

Use the following strategies to see if you can divide a number with a whole number as your answer. You don't want to have any fractions left over.

Divisible by 2

A number is divisible by 2 if it is an even number. Even numbers always end in 0, 2, 4, 6 or 8.

461 is not divisible by 2 because 1 is odd.
358 is divisible by 2 because 8 is even.

Divisible by 3

A number is divisible by 3 if the sum of the digits adds to 3, 6 or 9. If the digit sum is still too large, add the digits again and try to get 3, 6 or 9.

457 → 4 + 5 + 7 = 16 → 1 + 6 = 7
457 is not divisible by 3 as the sum of the digits is not a multiple of 3.

507 → 5 + 0 + 7 = 12 → 1 + 2 = 3
507 is divisible by 3 as the digit sum is a multiple of 3.

Divisible by 4

A number is divisible by 4 if the last 2 digits (the 10s and 1s digits) are divisible by 4.

5031 → 31 is not divisible by 4, so 5031 is not divisible by 4.

1972 → 72 is divisible by 4, so 1972 is divisible by 4.

Divisible by 5

A number is divisible by 5 if the 1s digit is a 0 or 5.

70 052 → does not end in 0 or 5 so is not divisible by 5.

884 615 → does end in 5 so is divisible by 5.

Divisible by 6

A number is divisible by 6 if it is divisible by 2 and it is divisible by 3. So the 1s digit must be even and when you add the digits they must add to 3, 6 or 9.

7133 → $7 + 1 + 3 + 3 = 14$

The sum of the digits is not a multiple of 3 so it is not divisible by 6.

8414 → $8 + 4 + 1 + 4 = 17$

The 1s digit is even but the sum of the digits is not a multiple of 3.

So this number is not divisible by 6.

1830 → $1 + 8 + 3 + 0 = 12$ and $1 + 2 = 3$

The 1s digit is even and the sum of the digits is a multiple of 3. So1830 is divisible by 6.

Divisible by 7

There is no easy way to check if a number is divisible by 7. One way is double the 1s digit and subtract it from the remaining number. If this difference is divisible by 7, then so is the whole number.

586 ⟶ 2 × 6 = 12, 58 – 12 = 46, which is not divisible by 7 so 586 is not divisible by 7.

3668 ⟶ 2 × 8 = 16, 366 – 16 = 350, which is divisible by 7 so 3668 is divisible by 7.

Divisible by 8

A number is divisible by 8 if the last 3 digits (the 100s, 10s and 1s) are divisible by 8.

1428 ⟶ 428 is not divisible by 8 so 1428 is not divisible by 8.

32 968 ⟶ 968 is divisible by 8 so 32 968 is divisible by 8.

Divisible by 9

A number is divisible by 9 if the sum of all the digits is a multiple of 9. If you are not sure, keep adding the digits until you get a single digit. If it is 9, then the whole number is a multiple of 9.

47 563 ⟶ 4 + 7 + 5 + 6 + 3 = 25, which is not a multiple of 9 so 47 563 is not a multiple of 9.

56 880 ⟶ 5 + 6 + 8 + 8 + 0 = 27, which is a multiple of 9 so 56 890 is divisible by 9.

FRACTIONS

COMPARING HALVES, QUARTERS AND EIGHTHS

Halves, quarters and eighths are made by dividing objects into two equal parts and then dividing these parts into halves again and again.

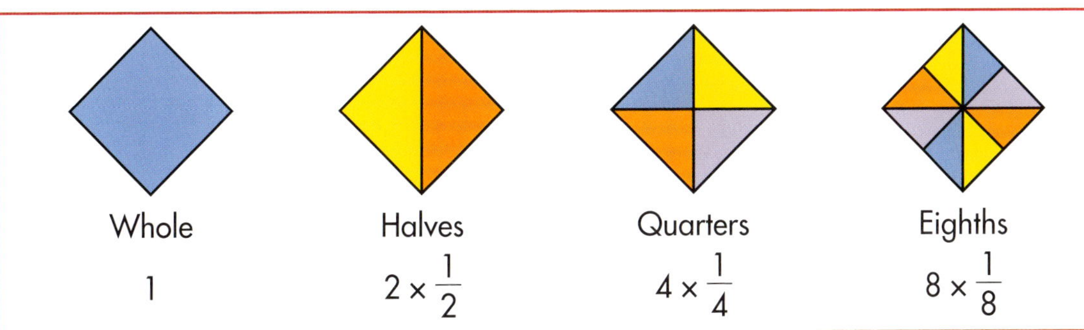

If you keep dividing each piece in half, you get $\frac{1}{16s}$, $\frac{1}{32s}$ and $\frac{1}{64s}$.

You can mark halves, quarters and eighths on a number line to help you compare sizes.

The larger the denominator, the smaller the size of the pieces

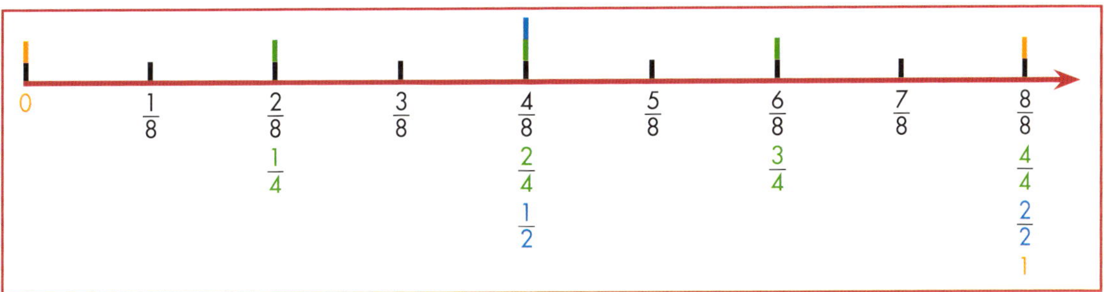

A **unit fraction** has just one piece: $\frac{1}{2}$, $\frac{1}{4}$ and $\frac{1}{8}$.

Compare unit fractions by looking at the denominator.

$\frac{1}{8}$ is smaller than $\frac{1}{4}$

$\frac{1}{4}$ is smaller than $\frac{1}{2}$

Non-unit fractions have more than 1 piece. Compare non-unit fractions by looking at the **numerator** too, not just the **denominator**.

$\frac{1}{8}$ is smaller than $\frac{1}{4}$ $\quad \frac{1}{8} < \frac{1}{4}$

$\frac{2}{8}$ is the same size as $\frac{1}{4}$ $\quad \frac{2}{8} = \frac{1}{4}$

$\frac{3}{8}$ is larger than $\frac{1}{4}$ $\quad \frac{3}{8} > \frac{1}{4}$

COMPARING HALVES, QUARTERS AND EIGHTHS (continued)

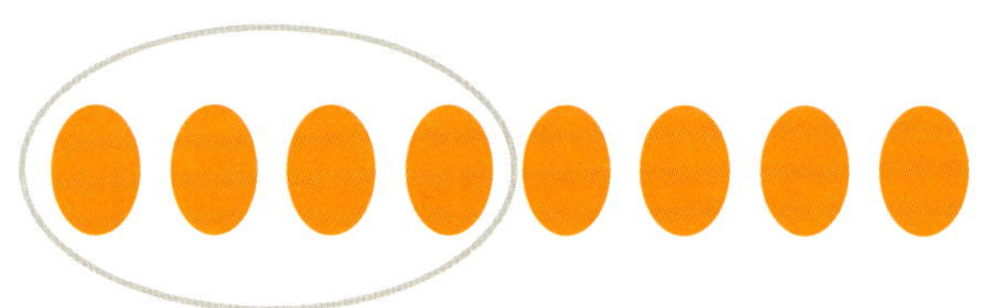

$\frac{1}{2} \times 8 = 4$

$\frac{2}{4} \times 8 = 4$

$\frac{4}{8} \times 8 = 4$

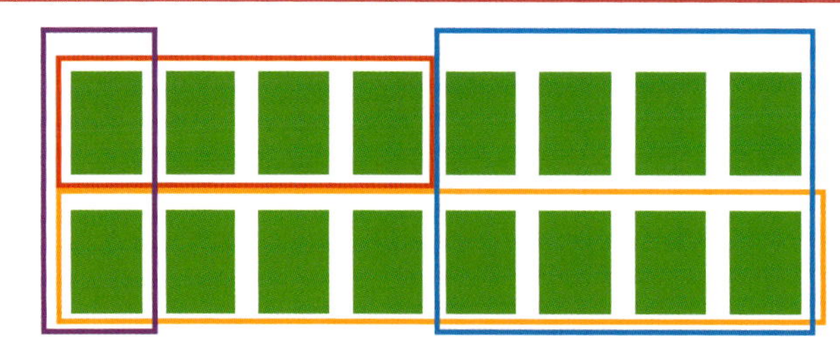

$\frac{1}{8} \times 16 = 2$ $\quad \frac{1}{2} \times 16 = 8$

$\frac{1}{4} \times 16 = 4$ $\quad \frac{4}{8} \times 16 = 8$

Look at the $\frac{1}{2s}$, $\frac{1}{4s}$ and $\frac{1}{8s}$ number line.
Write three more comparison statements.

COMPARING THIRDS, SIXTHS AND TWELFTHS

Thirds, sixths and twelfths are made by dividing objects into three equal parts and then dividing these parts again and again.

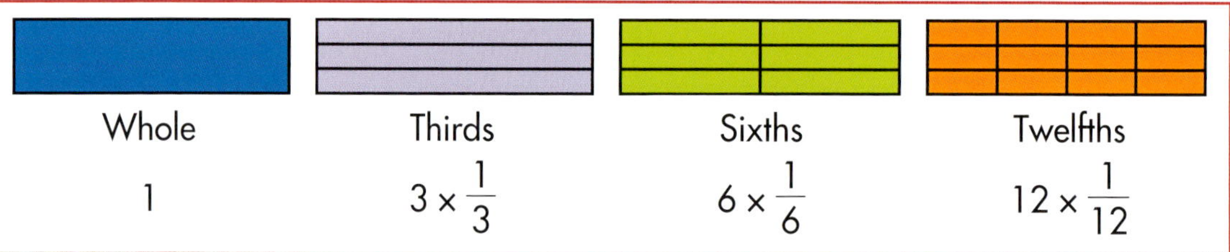

Whole	Thirds	Sixths	Twelfths
1	$3 \times \frac{1}{3}$	$6 \times \frac{1}{6}$	$12 \times \frac{1}{12}$

The smaller the denominator, the larger the size of the pieces.

If you keep dividing each piece into thirds, you get $\frac{1}{24s}$, $\frac{1}{36s}$ and $\frac{1}{72s}$. Thirds are larger pieces than sixths. They are twice the size of sixths. Sixths are larger pieces than twelfths. They are twice the size of twelfths.

A unit fraction has just one piece such as $\frac{1}{3}$, $\frac{1}{6}$ and $\frac{1}{12}$.

Compare the size of unit fractions by looking at the denominator:

$\frac{1}{3}$ is larger than $\frac{1}{6}$ $\quad$ $\frac{1}{6}$ is smaller than $\frac{1}{3}$

$\frac{1}{6}$ is larger than $\frac{1}{12}$ $\quad$ $\frac{1}{12}$ is smaller than $\frac{1}{6}$

When you compare the size of non-unit fractions, look at how many parts are in the numerator, not just the size of the denominator.

$\frac{4}{12}$ is smaller than $\frac{2}{3}$ $\qquad \frac{4}{12} < \frac{2}{3}$

$\frac{3}{6}$ is the same size as $\frac{6}{12}$ $\qquad \frac{3}{6} = \frac{6}{12}$

$\frac{2}{3}$ is larger than $\frac{5}{12}$ $\qquad \frac{2}{3} > \frac{5}{12}$

You can mark halves, thirds, quarters, sixths, eighths and twelfths on a number line to help you compare sizes.

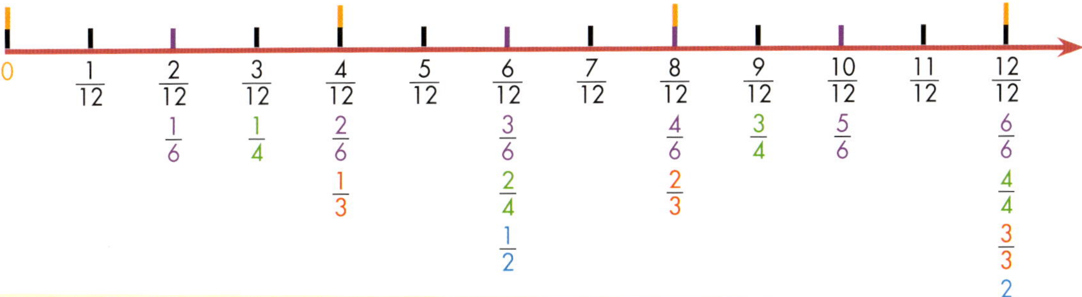

$\frac{1}{3}$ is smaller than $\frac{1}{2}$.
You need $\frac{2}{6}$ to make $\frac{1}{3}$.
You need $\frac{3}{6}$ to make $\frac{1}{2}$.

Write three more comparison statements about $\frac{1}{3}$s, $\frac{1}{6}$s and $\frac{1}{12}$s.

ORDERING FRACTIONS WITH THE SAME DENOMINATOR

To put fractions with the same denominator in **ascending** order place the fraction with the smallest numerator first.

Which fraction has the smallest numerator?

$\frac{9}{12} \quad \frac{3}{12} \quad \frac{6}{12} \quad \frac{1}{12} \quad \frac{11}{12} \rightarrow \frac{1}{12} \quad \frac{3}{12} \quad \frac{6}{12} \quad \frac{9}{12} \quad \frac{11}{12}$

To put fractions with the same denominator in **descending** order place the fraction with the largest numerator first.

Which fraction has the largest numerator? $\rightarrow \frac{11}{12} \quad \frac{9}{12} \quad \frac{6}{12} \quad \frac{3}{12} \quad \frac{1}{12}$

ORDERING FRACTIONS WITH SAME DENOMINATOR (continued)

Try this

Put these fractions in order from the largest to the smallest.

$\frac{4}{6}$ $\frac{1}{6}$ $\frac{5}{6}$ $\frac{3}{6}$ $\frac{6}{6}$ $\frac{2}{6}$

EQUIVALENT FRACTIONS

Look back at the $\frac{1}{2}$s, $\frac{1}{4}$s and $\frac{1}{8}$s or the $\frac{1}{3}$s, $\frac{1}{6}$s and $\frac{1}{12}$s number lines.

Fractions are equivalent if they are exactly the same size as each other, even if they are made from different pieces.

One whole cake is still one cake even if it is cut up into 3, 6 or 12 equal parts.

$\frac{6}{8}$ of a pizza is the same size as $\frac{3}{4}$ of a pizza. You eat the same amount even though one pizza is cut into smaller parts.

Equivalent fractions are marked at the same length on a number line.

If a hot-rod car's petrol tank holds 64 L of petrol and you use $\frac{2}{4}$ or $\frac{4}{8}$, then you used 32 L.

This is the same as half of the petrol tank

$\frac{1}{2} = \frac{2}{4} = \frac{4}{8}$ so $\frac{1}{2} \times 64 = 32$

Two and a half lemons is the same amount as:

- five halves, $\frac{5}{2}$
- ten quarters, $\frac{10}{4}$
- twenty eighths, $\frac{20}{8}$

1 What are five different fraction names for $\frac{1}{2}$?

2 What are five different fraction names for 1?

Challenge

Mark these fractions on this number line:

$\frac{2}{3}$ $\frac{3}{4}$ $\frac{2}{2}$ $\frac{8}{12}$ $\frac{5}{6}$ $\frac{1}{2}$

0

ORDERING FRACTIONS WITH MIXED DENOMINATORS

To place different denominator fractions in order you need to be confident with equivalent fractions.

Look at each fraction and imagine the size. Ask yourself comparison questions. Is it larger than $\frac{1}{2}$? Is it smaller than $\frac{1}{4}$? Is it larger than $\frac{3}{4}$? Is it larger than 1 whole?

If you are not sure, try to write each fraction with the same denominator.

If both robots use the same batteries, which robot will last longer?

Robot 1

$\frac{3}{8}$ battery left

Robot 2

$\frac{5}{12}$ battery left

ORDERING FRACTIONS WITH MIXED DENOMINATORS (continued)

If you have $\frac{3}{8}$ of a wooden shape and $\frac{5}{12}$ of the same shape, you can place them on top of each other to see which one is larger. But if you are just looking at numbers, you need a different method.

Both $\frac{3}{8}$ and $\frac{5}{12}$ are more than $\frac{1}{4}$ but less than a $\frac{1}{2}$.

To change them so that they both have the same denominator, find a denominator that works for both 8 and 12.

Find the **lowest common multiple**.

Double 8 is 16, but this is not a multiple of 12. Double 12 is 24 and it is a multiple of 8. The lowest common multiple is 24.

Divide each $\frac{1}{8}$ into three smaller parts to make 24 equal pieces.

Divide each $\frac{1}{12}$ into two smaller parts to make 24 equal pieces.

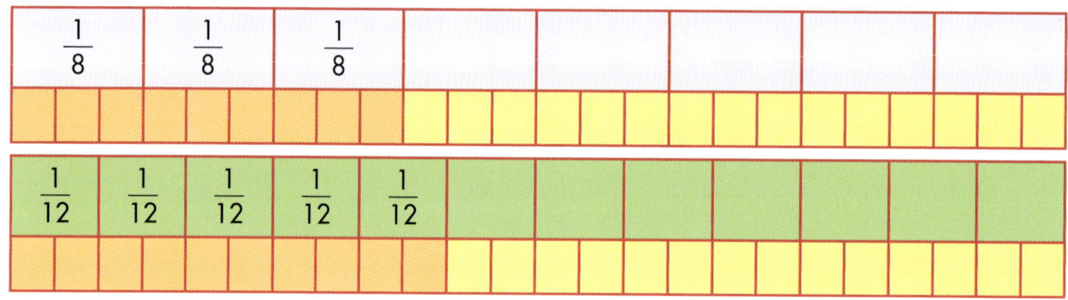

Now you can compare the numerators because the denominators are the same.

Each length is divided into $\frac{1}{24}$ s.

$\frac{3}{8} = 3 \times 3$ twenty-fourths $= \frac{9}{24}$ $\qquad$ $\frac{5}{12} = 2 \times 5$ twenty-fourths $= \frac{10}{24}$

$\frac{5}{12}$ is just a little bit larger than $\frac{3}{8}$ so Robot 2 will last longer.

IMPROPER FRACTIONS

An **improper fraction** is a collection of fractional parts that together are more than 1 whole object. Improper fractions have a numerator larger than the denominator.

Each piece is $\frac{1}{8}$ of a pizza. There are 16 pieces.

$16 \times \frac{1}{8} = \frac{16}{8}$ → $\frac{16}{8}$ is an improper fraction

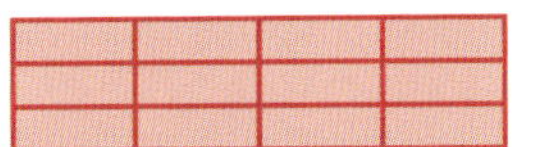

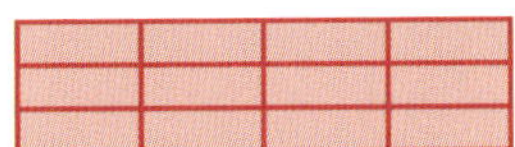

The numerator in an improper fraction can be any whole number, as long as it is larger than the denominator. For example, if you have 37 fifths of a square, that's $\frac{37}{5}$.

Most people like to change improper fractions by collecting parts that make 1 whole.

$\frac{16}{8}$ can be collected together to make 2 whole objects.

MIXED FRACTIONS

Mixed fractions have whole numbers and fractions. To change an improper fraction into a mixed fraction, see how many whole objects you can make.

These sweets come in bags of 6.

$\frac{16}{6}$ is the same as $2\frac{4}{6}$ or $2\frac{2}{3}$ bags

$2\frac{2}{3}$ is a mixed fraction.

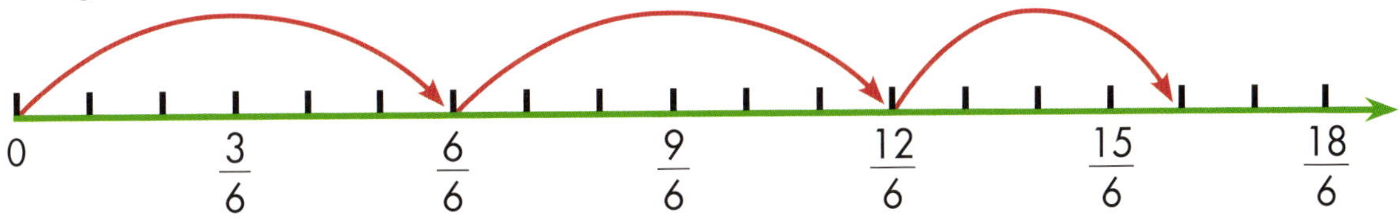

ADDING OR SUBTRACTING FRACTIONS

To add fractions with the same denominator, add the numerators.

$\frac{3}{4} + \frac{3}{4} = 3 + 3$ quarters $= 6$ quarters $= \frac{6}{4}$

That's the same as 1 whole kiwi fruit and 2 more quarters

That's $1\frac{1}{2}$ altogether.

ADDING AND SUBTRACTING FRACTIONS (continued)

Don't be tricked. You do not add the denominators. This is a mistake that many students make. You only add the numerators.

$\frac{1}{2} + \frac{1}{2} = \frac{2}{2}$ $\frac{2}{3} + \frac{3}{3} = \frac{5}{3}$ $\frac{2}{5} + \frac{2}{5} = \frac{4}{5}$

$\frac{5}{8} + \frac{7}{8} = \frac{12}{8}$ $\frac{3}{10} + \frac{5}{10} = \frac{8}{10}$ $\frac{10}{12} + \frac{4}{12} = \frac{14}{12}$

To add fractions with different denominators, make the denominators the same by using equivalent fractions. Then add the numerators.

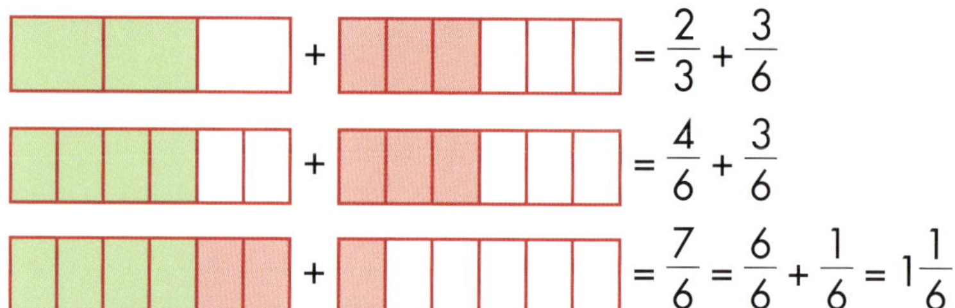

$= \frac{2}{3} + \frac{3}{6}$

$= \frac{4}{6} + \frac{3}{6}$

$= \frac{7}{6} = \frac{6}{6} + \frac{1}{6} = 1\frac{1}{6}$

To subtract fractions with the same denominator, subtract the numerators.

$$\frac{16}{8} - \frac{5}{8} = \frac{16-5}{8} = \frac{11}{8} = 1\frac{3}{8}$$

To subtract fractions with different denominators, make the denominators the same by using equivalent fractions. Then subtract the numerators.

Try to see the numbers as real objects or on a number line in your head.

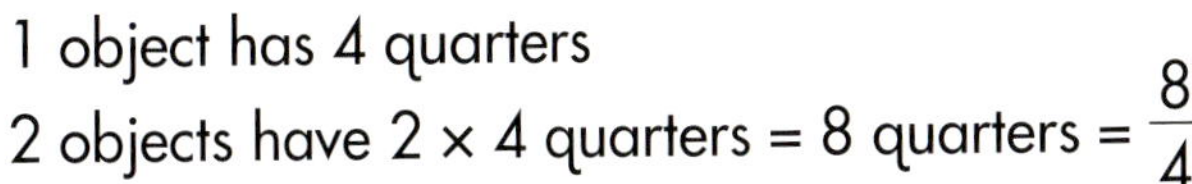

1 object has 4 quarters

2 objects have 2×4 quarters = 8 quarters = $\frac{8}{4}$

$$2 - \frac{5}{4} = \frac{8}{4} - \frac{5}{4} = \frac{3}{4}$$

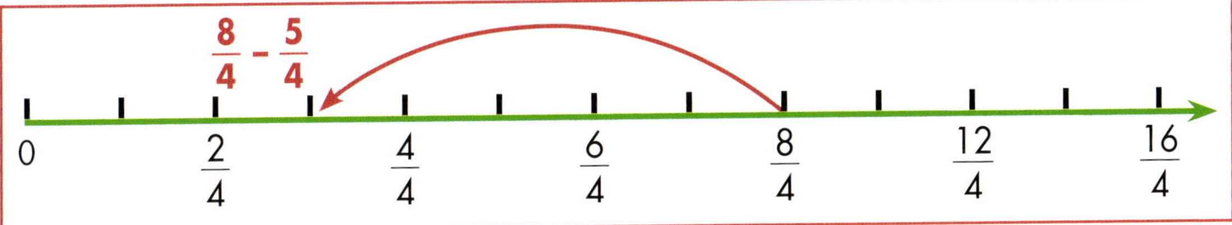

Don't be tricked. You do not subtract the denominators. This is a mistake that many students make. You only subtract the numerators once the denominators are the same size.

MULTIPLYING WITH FRACTIONS

Multiplication is repeated addition.

$6 \times \frac{3}{4}$ is a fast way to write $\frac{3}{4} + \frac{3}{4} + \frac{3}{4} + \frac{3}{4} + \frac{3}{4} + \frac{3}{4}$

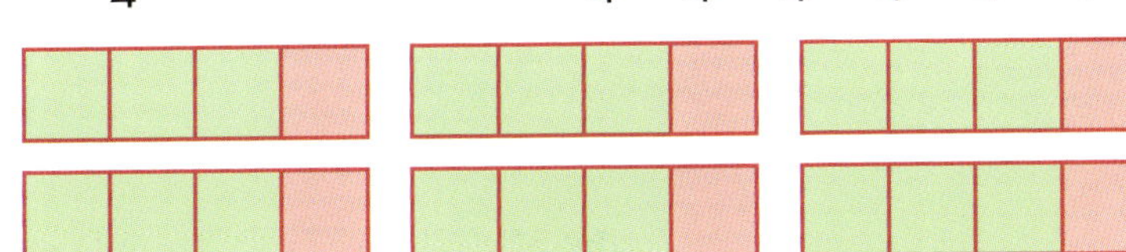

Remember when you add fractions with the same denominator, you add the numerators. So this is the same as

3 + **3** + **3** + **3** + **3** + **3** quarters or 6×3 quarters.

You can write this as $\frac{6 \times 3}{4} = \frac{18}{4}$ or $18 \div 4$

You know there are 4 wholes in 16 quarters, which leaves $\frac{2}{4}$ left over so you have $4\frac{2}{4}$ altogether.

MULTIPLYING WITH FRACTIONS (continued)

$\frac{3}{5}$ of 20 is another way to multiply with fractions.

This asks you to put 20 things into 5 equal groups. Then find how many things in 3 of those groups.

4 triangles in 1 group

3 × 4 triangles in 3 groups

so 12 triangles in $\frac{3}{5}$ of 20

DIVIDING WITH FRACTIONS

Division is repeated subtraction.

$3 \div \frac{3}{4}$ is a fast way to write "How many $\frac{3}{4}$ are there in 3 whole objects?"

The long way is to subtract $\frac{3}{4}$ until you have no more $\frac{3}{4}$ to subtract.

$3 - \frac{3}{4} = 2\frac{1}{4}$ $\quad 2\frac{1}{4} - \frac{3}{4} = 1\frac{1}{2}$ $\quad 1\frac{1}{2} - \frac{3}{4} = \frac{3}{4}$

So that's $4 \times \frac{3}{4} = 3$

Another way is to write it as  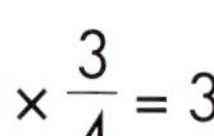 $\times \frac{3}{4} = 3$

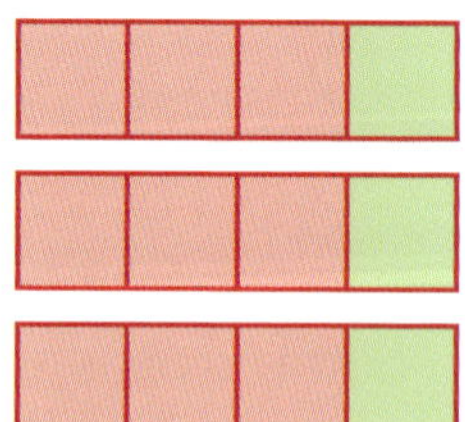

Then find how many $\frac{3}{4}$ you have altogether.

There are $3 \times \frac{3}{4}$ in 3 whole objects

But there are still another $3 \times \frac{1}{4}$ left so that's another $\frac{3}{4}$

So there are 4 three-quarters in 3.

DECIMALS & PERCENTAGES

TENTHS, HUNDREDTHS AND THOUSANDTHS

Decimals are another name for $\frac{1}{10s}$, $\frac{1}{100s}$ and $\frac{1}{1000s}$.

One whole number or object can be divided into 10, 100 or 1000 equal parts. If you kept dividing into 10 equal parts, you would get $\frac{1}{10\,000s}$, $\frac{1}{100\,000s}$ or even $\frac{1}{1\,000\,000s}$

1 millisecond is $\frac{1}{1000}$ of a second

Numbers to the right of the decimal point on a place value chart are decimal fractions. Each place value to the right is 10 times smaller. They are small amounts. They are not the same as the whole numbers on the left of the decimal point.

ones	and	tenths	hundredths	thousandths
1s	•	$\frac{1}{10s}$	$\frac{1}{100s}$	$\frac{1}{1000s}$
1	•	3	4	6

A male peacock eye feather can be 1.346 m long

1.346 is "1 and 346 thousandths"

3 tenths is the same as $\frac{30}{100}$ or $\frac{300}{1000}$

You write it as 0.3 but say "three tenths."

4 hundredths is the same as $\frac{40}{1000}$

You write it as 0.04 but say "four hundredths."
You write 0.006 but say "six thousandths."

1.346 is a three-place decimal

1.346 = 1.0 + 0.3 + 0.04 + 0.006 in expanded notation

1.346 is between 1.3 and 1.4 on a number line

TENTHS, HUNDREDTHS AND THOUSANDTHS
(continued)

1 whole = 1.0 = $\frac{10}{10}$, $\frac{100}{100}$ or $\frac{1000}{1000}$

You use decimals when you measure:

1 000 mL = 1 L

There are 1000 mL in 1 L

1 mL = $\frac{1}{1000}$ L

10 mL = $\frac{1}{100}$ mL

100 mL = $\frac{1}{10}$ L or 0.1 L

There are 1000 m in 1 km

1 m = $\frac{1}{1000}$ km

50 m = $\frac{50}{1000}$ km or $\frac{5}{100}$ km or 0.05 km

1 000 g = 1 kg

There are 1000 g in 1 kg

1 g = $\frac{1}{1000}$ kg

500 g = $\frac{500}{1000}$ kg

or $\frac{50}{100}$ kg or $\frac{5}{10}$ kg or 0.5 kg

There are 10 000 m² in 1 hectare

1 m^2 = $\frac{1}{10\,000}$ hectare

100 m^2 = $\frac{100}{10\,000}$ or $\frac{1}{100}$ hectare

ORDERING DECIMALS

To order a variety of decimal numbers, **first look at the whole numbers on the left of the decimal point**. The largest whole number is the largest number.

16.5 **is larger than** 15.999 because 16 is larger than 15.

42.999 **is smaller than** 43.6 because 42 is smaller than 43.

A long decimal number is not always a large fraction.

0.99999999999999999999 is smaller than 1.0 even though it looks bigger.

If the numbers have the same whole number or no whole number, look at the tenths place. Which number has the larger tenths value?

3.09 **is smaller than** 3.1 because it has no value in the $\frac{1}{10s}$ place

0.89 **is larger than** 0.455 because it has 8 in the $\frac{1}{10s}$ place

0.102 **is smaller than** 0.7 because it only has 1 in the $\frac{1}{10s}$ place

An effective strategy is to make all decimals the same length. Use **0** to fill any empty spaces.

This makes it easier to compare matching place values.

ones	and	tenths	hundredths	thousandths
1s	•	$\frac{1}{10s}$	$\frac{1}{100s}$	$\frac{1}{1000s}$
0	•	1	0	2
0	•	7	**0**	**0**

If the numbers have the same tenths value, look at the hundredths place. Which number has the larger hundredths value?

2.949 **is smaller than** 2.98 because $\frac{4}{100}$ is smaller than $\frac{8}{100}$

0.71 **is larger than** 0.709 because $\frac{1}{100}$ is larger than 0

If the numbers have the same tenths and hundredths value, look at the thousandths place. Which number has the larger thousandths value?

4.572 **is larger than** 4.570 because $\frac{2}{1000}$ is larger than 0

0.333 **is smaller than** 0.337 because $\frac{3}{1000}$ is smaller than $\frac{7}{1000}$

Don't get tricked. 6.0 is exactly the same number as 6.00 or 6.000. It is the same number as 6.00000000000000000000000000000000000000.

Place these numbers in order from largest to smallest.
3.92 0.1 12.0 17.999 1.3 20.855

Try this

ROUNDING DECIMALS

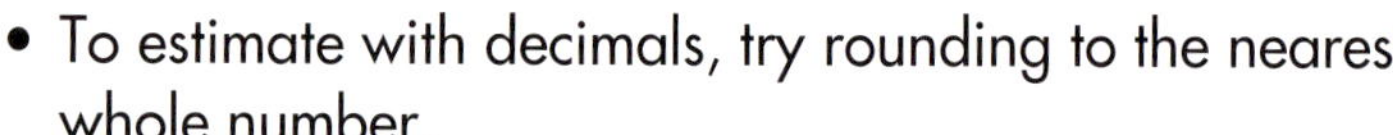

You can round decimals to the nearest whole number, tenth, hundredth or thousandth. It depends on how exact you need to be.

- To estimate with decimals, try rounding to the nearest whole number.
- If the decimal number is 0.5 or more, round up to the next whole number.
- If the decimal number is less than 0.5, round down to the previous whole number or 0 if there is no whole number.

A Tyrannosaurus Rex had a mass of 6.3 tonnes
→ rounds down to 6 tonnes

An adult giraffe has a mass of 0.953 tonnes
→ rounds up to 1 tonne

Round these decimals to the nearest whole number.

1 66.55	**2** 14.2	**3** 0.999
4 1.7	**5** 0.5	**6** 16.09

ADDING DECIMALS

To add decimals, first make sure they all have the same number of decimal places. If the decimals do not have the same number of decimal places, place in **zeros** until they have the same number of decimal places.

Adding 0.6 + 0.38 is not like adding 6 + 38 because 6 is in the $\frac{1}{10\text{s}}$ column and 8 is in the $\frac{1}{100\text{s}}$ column.

You cannot add and subtract decimals the same way as whole numbers. You must look at the place value position of each digit.

0.6 + 0.38 → 0.6**0** + 0.38 = 0.98
They are now both two-place decimals.

54.08 + 1.7 + 0.235 → 54.08**0** + 1.700 + 0.235
They are all now three-place decimals.

Estimate first → 54 + 2 + 0 = 57

If you can't work the exact sum out in your head, use an algorism.

Line up all the digits in their matching place value positions.

Add **0**s if necessary to make the same number of decimal places. If necessary, trade $\frac{10}{1000}$ for $\frac{1}{100}$, trade $\frac{10}{100}$ for $\frac{1}{10}$ or trade $\frac{10}{10}$ for 1 whole number.

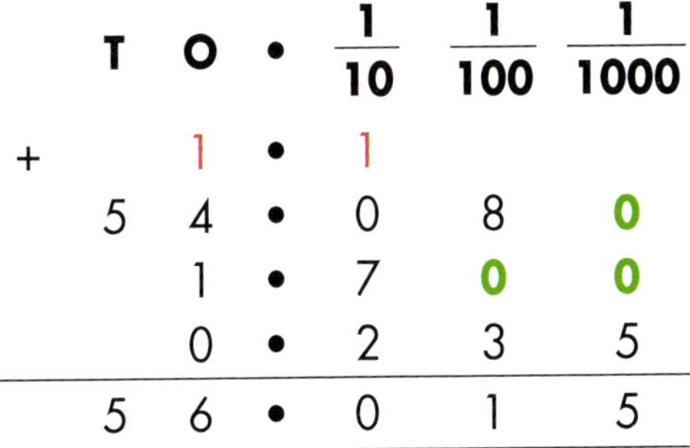

	T	O	•	$\frac{1}{10}$	$\frac{1}{100}$	$\frac{1}{1000}$
+		1	•	1		
	5	4	•	0	8	**0**
		1	•	7	**0**	**0**
		0	•	2	3	5
	5	6	•	0	1	5

This is close to your estimate, so it's probably correct. You can check on a calculator if you want to be sure.

SUBTRACTING DECIMALS

To subtract decimals, first make sure they have the same number of decimal places. If the decimals do not have the same number of decimal places, place in **zeros** until they have the same number of decimal places.

Next try to calculate the answer in your head. If you need to work it out on paper, remember to start with the largest number. If you need to trade, remember 10 tenths is the same as 1.

8.075 – 2.6 **Estimate first → 8 – 3 = 5**

To calculate mentally try a *counting up to* strategy. 2.6 + 0.4 is 3 and another 5 is 8. That's 5.4 so far. Now add the 0.075 to give you 5.475.

SUBTRACTING DECIMALS (continued)

This is what 8.075 – 2.6 looks like as an algorism.

If necessary, trade 1 for $\frac{10}{10}$, $\frac{1}{10}$ for $\frac{10}{100}$, or $\frac{1}{100}$, for $\frac{10}{1000}$.

	T	O	•	$\frac{1}{10}$	$\frac{1}{100}$	$\frac{1}{1000}$
		7	•	10		
		~~8~~	•	~~0~~	7	5
–		2	•	6	**0**	**0**
		5	•	4	7	5

1 What's the difference in mass between a 0.32 tonne zebra and a 0.953 tonne giraffe?
2 What's the difference in mass between a 0.953 tonne giraffe and a 6.8 tonne T-rex?

Try to calculate in your head first. If you can't, then estimate and do the algorism.

MULTIPLYING DECIMALS BY WHOLE NUMBERS

To multiply decimals by a whole number imagine the problem in your head. There are many different mental strategies.

Here are a few examples:

A 1.5 L container of orange juice holds one and a half litres or 1.50 L or 1.500 L.

2 containers hold 2 × 1.5 L.
That's 3 L because I know that double 1 is 2 and $\frac{1}{2} + \frac{1}{2} = 1$.

6 containers hold 6 × 1 L and 6 × 0.5 L.
That's 9 L because I know 6 halves are 3.

A 0.625 L bottle of water has $\frac{625}{1000}$ L.

4 bottles have 4 × 0.625 L of water.
4 × 0.6 is 2.4 L and 4 × 0.025 is 0.1 L so that's 2.5 L.

Another way is to double 0.625, then double that again. Double 0.625 is 1.250 L. Double 1.25 is 2.5 L.

MULTIPLYING DECIMALS BY 10, 100 OR 1000

To mentally **multiply decimals by 10**, slide the digits one place to the left. Write **0** in the empty space. Remember the decimal point does not move.

The mass of 1 small frog is 0.076 kg.

1s	•	$\frac{1}{10s}$	$\frac{1}{100s}$	$\frac{1}{1000s}$
0	•	0	7	6

What is the mass of 10 small frogs?
10 × 0.076 = 0.76 so 10 small frogs have a mass of 0.76 kg.

1s	•	$\frac{1}{10s}$	$\frac{1}{100s}$	$\frac{1}{1000s}$
0	•	7	6	**0**

To mentally multiply decimals by 100, slide the digits two places to the left. It is optional to write 0 in the empty spaces.

The mass of a green tree frog is 0.205 kg.

10s	1s	•	$\frac{1}{10s}$	$\frac{1}{100s}$	$\frac{1}{1000s}$
	0	•	2	0	5

What is the mass of 100 frogs?
100 × 0.205 = 20.5 so 100 green tree frogs have a mass of 20.5 kg.

10s	1s	•	$\frac{1}{10s}$	$\frac{1}{100s}$	$\frac{1}{1000s}$
2	0	•	5	**0**	**0**

MULTIPLYING DECIMALS BY 10, 100 OR 1000 (continued)

To mentally multiply decimals by 1000, slide the digits three places to the left. It is optional to write 0 in the empty spaces.

The mass of a giant cane toad is 2.475 kg.

1000s	100s	10s	1s	•	$\frac{1}{10s}$	$\frac{1}{100s}$	$\frac{1}{1000s}$
			2	•	4	7	5

What is the mass of 1000 cane toads?
1000 × 2.475 = 2475 so 1000 cane toads have a mass of 2475 kg.

1000s	100s	10s	1s	•	$\frac{1}{10s}$	$\frac{1}{100s}$	$\frac{1}{1000s}$
2	4	7	5	•	0	0	0

Multiply each decimal number by 10, 100 and 1000.

		× 10	× 100	× 1000
1	0.08			
2	17.105			
3	91.372			

DIVIDING DECIMALS BY 10, 100 OR 1000

To mentally **divide decimals by 10**, slide the digits one place to the right. Remember the decimal point does not move.

Ten people share 5.3 L of water on a bushwalk. How much for each person?

1s	•	$\frac{1}{10s}$	$\frac{1}{100s}$	$\frac{1}{1000s}$
5	•	3		

1s	•	$\frac{1}{10s}$	$\frac{1}{100s}$	$\frac{1}{1000s}$
0	•	5	3	

5.3 ÷ 10 = 0.53, so each person gets 0.53 L. That's 530 mL. This is the same answer as 53 ÷ 100 and 530 ÷ 1000.

To mentally divide decimals by 100, slide the digits two places to the right.

If you have 137.5 m of rope to cut into 100 equal sections for a playground, how long is each section?

100s	10s	1s	•	$\frac{1}{10s}$	$\frac{1}{100s}$	$\frac{1}{1000s}$
1	3	7	•	5		

100s	10s	1s	•	$\frac{1}{10s}$	$\frac{1}{100s}$	$\frac{1}{1000s}$
		1	•	3	7	5

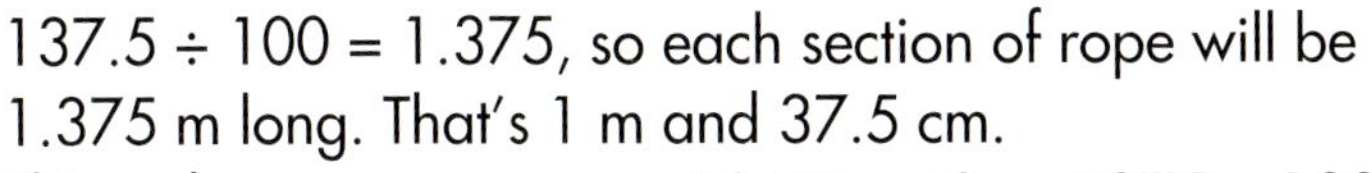

137.5 ÷ 100 = 1.375, so each section of rope will be 1.375 m long. That's 1 m and 37.5 cm.
This is the same answer as 13.75 ÷ 10 or 1375 ÷ 1000.

To mentally divide decimals by 1000, slide the digits three places to the right.

1000 people win $675, how much is that each?

100s	10s	1s	•	$\frac{1}{10s}$	$\frac{1}{100s}$	$\frac{1}{1000s}$
6	7	5	•			

100s	10s	1s	•	$\frac{1}{10s}$	$\frac{1}{100s}$	$\frac{1}{1000s}$
		0	•	6	7	5

675 ÷ 1000 = 0.675, so each person receives $0.675.
That's 67.5 cents.
This is the same answer as 67.5 ÷ 100 or 6.75 ÷ 10.

Divide each decimal number by 10, 100 and 1000.

		÷ 10	÷ 100	÷ 1000
1	2.0			
2	31.4			
3	103.5			

PERCENTAGES

About 60% of our body is water.

Percentages are another way to talk about hundredths. People have calculated with percentages for thousands of years. In Latin, "**per cent**" means "for every 100" or "out of 100". You talk about percentages when analysing statistics and in shopping sales and discounts.

You can draw percentages as parts of a circle. This is useful when analysing data.

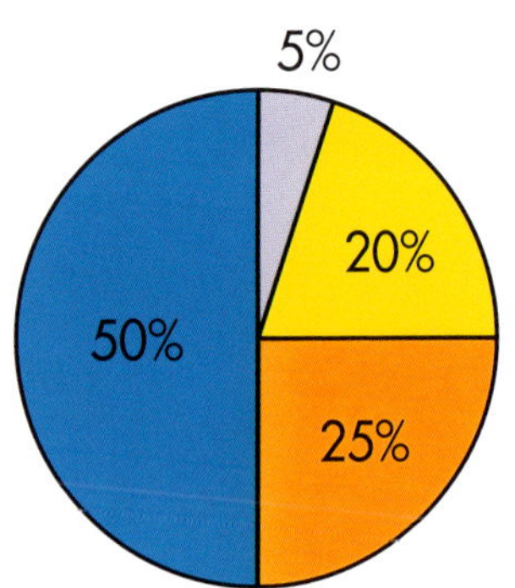

1% is the same as $\frac{1}{100}$ or 0.01.

56% is the same as $\frac{56}{100}$ or 0.56.

100% is the same amount as $\frac{100}{100}$ or 1.0.

This table shows multiples of 10% with their equivalent fraction or decimal.

Percentages	Fractions	Decimals
100%	$\frac{100}{100}$	1.0
90%	$\frac{90}{100}$ $\frac{9}{10}$	0.9
80%	$\frac{80}{100}$ $\frac{8}{10}$ $\frac{4}{5}$	0.8
70%	$\frac{70}{100}$ $\frac{7}{10}$	0.7
60%	$\frac{60}{100}$ $\frac{6}{10}$ $\frac{3}{5}$	0.6
50%	$\frac{50}{100}$ $\frac{5}{10}$ $\frac{2}{4}$ $\frac{1}{2}$	0.5
40%	$\frac{40}{100}$ $\frac{4}{10}$ $\frac{2}{5}$	0.4
30%	$\frac{30}{100}$ $\frac{3}{10}$	0.3
20%	$\frac{20}{100}$ $\frac{2}{10}$ $\frac{1}{5}$	0.2
10%	$\frac{10}{100}$ $\frac{1}{10}$	0.1

Other common percentages:

Percentages	Fractions	Decimals
100%	$\frac{100}{100}$	1.0
75%	$\frac{75}{100}$ $\frac{3}{4}$	0.75
25%	$\frac{25}{100}$ $\frac{1}{4}$	0.25

To change a percentage to a fraction, write it as hundredths.

$$\mathbf{75\% = \frac{75}{100} \text{ or } \frac{3}{4}}$$

A chimp has 32 teeth. If 75% are healthy, how many is that?

$\frac{75}{100} \times 32 = \frac{3}{4} \times 32$

$\frac{1}{4}$ of 32 is 8, so $\frac{3}{4}$ must be $3 \times 8 = 24$

The chimp has 24 teeth that are healthy.

To change a percentage to a decimal, divide it by 100.

$$\mathbf{30\% = \frac{30}{100} = 30 \div 100 = 0.3}$$

To change a number to a percentage, first write it as a fraction then multiply by 100 if you don't know it already.

A donkey has 36 teeth. If 9 are bad, what percentage is that?

9 out of 36 is $\frac{9}{36}$ or $\frac{1}{4}$

$\frac{1}{4} \times 100 = 100 \div 4 = 25$

So 25% of the donkey's teeth are bad.

CALCULATING WITH PERCENTAGES

There are many different strategies. You need to find a way that works for you.

60% of students in our grade have black hair. There are 40 students. How many students have black hair?

Try changing to fractions.

$$60\% \times 40 = \frac{60}{100} \times 40$$
$$= \frac{3}{5} \times 40$$
$$= \frac{3 \times 40}{5}$$
$$= \frac{120}{5} \text{ or } 120 \div 5$$
$$= 24$$

Or find 10% and then multiply by 6.

10% of 40 is $\frac{1}{10} \times 40$.

I know it is 4 because $10 \times 4 = 40$.
$6 \times 4 = 24$

So 24 students have black hair.

Sale 70% off.
How much now for a $200 pair of shoes?

First find 70% of $200

$\frac{70}{100} \times 200$ or $\frac{7}{10} \times 200$

$\frac{7 \times 200}{10} = 1400 \div 10$
$= 140$

Or find 70% of $100 and double it.
$2 \times 70 = 140$

Now subtract this from $200.
$200 - 140 = 60$
The shoes will cost $60.

Or because you get 70% off, that's the same as paying 30%.

$30\% \times 200 = \frac{3}{10} \times 200$

$\frac{1}{10} \times 200 = 20$

$3 \times 20 = 60$

Try this

1 A tiger has 30 teeth. If 20% are decayed, how many is that?

2 A truck delivers 880 yellow and brown bricks. If 75% are yellow, how many are brown?

Challenge

1 A great white shark has 230 teeth, but now 30% are broken. How many teeth are broken?

2 Would you rather have a discount of 60% on an $80 pair of shoes or 70% on a $100 pair? Why?

MONEY & FINANCIAL MATHS

Each country has its own money system so that people can save money or buy and sell products and services. You cannot pay for things in France with Australian dollars. You cannot pay for things in Australia with Japanese yen.

SAVINGS PLAN

You want to buy a bike which costs $249. You get $10 pocket money each week.

You need to work out a **savings plan**. This tells you how much to save each week, each month or each year.

How might you do it? How much time do you have? How much can you save each week? Do you ever get money as a gift? What small jobs can you do to earn extra money?

10 months until Christmas holidays
249 ÷ 10 = 24.90, so I need to save about $25 a month
25 ÷ 4 is about $6 each week
Check:
6 × 4 × 10 = 240
I need to save $6 each week

Try this

A new computer game costs $150.
You save $7 each week from your pocket money.
How long will it take you to save enough money to buy the game?

PLANNING A BUDGET

An average Australian family spends $150 each week on food, as part of their weekly budget. In a **budget** you look at the total amount of money you can spend and what you need to buy. A tight budget means you don't have extra money for luxury items.

You can make a list of essential food spending:

Groceries	$50
Fruit and Vegetables	$50
Butcher	$50
TOTAL on Food	$150

If you stick to your budget, you cannot spend any more than this.

What you spend must total what you have allocated.

So even if you love mangoes, if they are $4 each, you may not be able to afford to buy them. They may be too much for your budget.

Keep a list of how much your family spends on food in one week. Do you spend more on fruit and vegetables than groceries?

DISCOUNTS

When there is a sale in a shop you get a discount.

A discount is a percentage of the total cost that you subtract to find your sale cost.

Your fruit and vegetable shop has a 25% off sale this week.

If your original bill is $60, you subtract 25% from this total.

$\frac{25}{100} \times 60$ is the same as $\frac{1}{4} \times 60$ or $60 \div 4$. That's 15.

$60 - 15 = 45$

So the sale cost for your fruit and vegetables is $45 this week.

Hair Glow salon is offering 30% discount on all haircuts between 4.00 pm and 6.00 pm. How much for 3 children and 2 adults if they go at 4.30 pm?

Hair Glow Salon

Children's Haircut	$20
Adults Haircut	$35
Blow Dry	$15

Weekly Special
30% off all cuts
between 4.00 pm and 6.00 pm

COMPARING DISCOUNTS

Shops advertise discounts in many different ways.

2 for the price of 1

COMPARING DISCOUNTS (continued)

If you want to buy two new chess sets with a friend, you can work out which is the better deal using a table.

Shop	Original Price	Discount	Sale Price for 1 item	Sale Price for 2 items	TOTAL for 2 items
A	$76	75% off your 2nd item	$76	$76 + $(\frac{1}{4} \times \$76)$	$95
B	$95	Half price	$47.50	$47.50 + $47.50	$95
C	$89	2 for 1	$89	$89	$89

Shop C offers the better deal for 2 chess sets. You pay $89 for 2 sets.

Challenge

Which would you prefer?

40% off $70 **OR** 50% off $80

Why?

USING A CREDIT CARD

Notes and coins are **cash**. Notes and coins are real money. If you use a credit card to pay for purchases, you go into **debt**.

A credit card is not real money. It is not the same as cash. It is money you think you will have in the future. This can be dangerous for your budget because you can buy more than you can afford.

Money from a credit card is a loan from a bank to help you pay for an item you cannot afford to pay cash for now. You must pay this money back to the bank within one month. If you do not pay in one month, the bank will charge you interest.

BILLS AND INVOICES

When you buy goods in a supermarket, you receive a **bill** from the cashier. The cash register calculates the total cost for all the individual items you purchased. You pay in cash or with a credit card.

When your family buys lunch in a café, you are given a bill.

This bill lists all the items purchased and the total amount you owe. You pay in cash or with a credit card.

Sometimes you are sent a bill every three months for services you use all the time. Electricity, gas, water and local council rates are sent to your family as a bill. You usually have one month to pay the full amount.

If the vet comes to check your horse, you do not usually pay cash directly. Instead they email you an **invoice**, which is another type of bill. It shows how many hours the vet worked, the cost for each hour of service and the total amount you owe. You usually have one month to pay the money you owe. You can sometimes pay by electronic transfer from your bank to their bank.

Animal Friends Vet
Invoice

Invoice No: **0945**
Invoice: **12.3.12**
Date:

Customer name and address:
Sam and Jill Taylor, 72 Arbour Rd GLEBE NSW 2037
Phone: 02 9843 7676

Date of service	Type of service	Animal	Time	Cost per hour	Unit Price	Total
25.02.2012	Yearly check-up for Blackie	Horse	3.5 hours	$75	3.5 x $75	$262.50
25.02.2012	Medicine				$82.25	$82.25
					Subtotal	$344.75
					10% GST	$34.48
					Balance Due	$379.25

Look at your family's most recent electricity and water bills.

1 Is one bill more than another? Why?

2 Is one bill easier to read? Why?

3 Is one bill easier to pay electronically? Why?

GST

The Australian Government charges a Goods and Services Tax on most products and services sold in Australia. This is called the **GST**. The GST is currently 10%. This 10% is added to the original cost of goods or services.

You find the GST on the bottom of supermarket bills, shopping dockets and invoices, just before the total. So the total usually includes the extra GST amount.

To calculate how much GST you need to pay multiply the cost by 10%. This means the actual amount you pay is 110% of the original cost.

This 10% is given back to the Government by the goods or service supplier. They do not keep this extra 10%. The money is used to pay for roads, hospitals and schools across Australia.

An easy way to work out GST is to multiply the total by 1.1 on your calculator. This is the same amount as 110%.

Original cost of three air tickets $3300

10% GST

$10\% \times \$3300 = \frac{1}{10} \times 3300 = \$330$

Another strategy is to use a calculator. Press

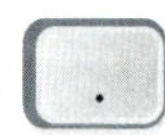

$$\begin{aligned}\text{Total cost} &= \text{original price} + \text{GST} \\ &= \$3330 + \$330 \\ &= \$3630\end{aligned}$$

The full cost of three tickets is $3630.

Collect two different bills and calculate 10% GST.
Does your number match the GST amount on each bill? Why?

RECEIPTS

A **receipt** is a written summary of what money you paid for goods or services and the date you paid it. It is a legal document which shows the purchase is now complete.

You do not owe anything more. If you need to return faulty goods to a shop, you need a receipt to prove you actually purchased the item. If you make a complaint about a service, you need a receipt to show you paid.

If you are organising a party and you have many costs, it is a good idea to keep all the receipts in one folder so that you know exactly how much you have spent. Keep a total of how much you spend to help you keep within your budget.

Holiday Centre
Level 7,115 Bright Parade, Coolangatta 4225 Phone 05 9015 4220

Receipt

To:	The Jackson Family 32 Fitzroy Gardens Brisbane Qld 4000	Invoice Number:	00601
		Date:	25 June 2012
Phone: Fax: Contact:	0585 412 310 Ahmed Jackson	From:	Lucy Humphrey Tour Co-ordinator ABN 73 65 19 23

Holiday details

Quantity	**Description**	**Unit Price**	**Total**
3	Airline Tickets to Tahiti	$1100	$3300
		Subtotal	$3300
		GST	$330
		Total	**$3630**
		Paid in full	$3630
		Balance due	$0

CONVERTING MONEY OVERSEAS

When you travel overseas, you need to swap your Australian money for the local currency.

Sometimes your Australian money is worth more than the local currency, sometimes less. You can find the daily exchange rate in the newspaper or on the internet.

An exchange rate looks like this:

Australian dollar	European euro	Japanese yen	Chilean peso	Indonesian rupiah
$1	0.7	83	480	8886

It tells you how much local money you get for $1. You go to a money exchanger, a bank or an ATM to convert your money. You give them Australian cash to change into the local currency.

An ATM takes the money directly out of your bank electronically.

AUD and euros

If 1AUD = 0.7 euros, how much is 10, 100 or 1000 Australian dollars worth in euros?
AUD is Australian dollars
Euros is the currency for the European zone

$10 = 10 × 0.7 euros = 7 euros
$100 = 100 × 0.7 euros = 70 euros
$1000 = 1000 × 0.7 euros = 700 euros

If an item costs 2000 euros, divide by the local currency rate to see how much that is in Australian dollars.
Use a calculator to divide by 0.7 if you cannot do this in your head.

2000 ÷ 0.7 = $2857
2000 euros is about $2857.

Chilean pesos

If 480 Chilean pesos = 1AUD, what are 240 pesos worth in Australian dollars?

240 pesos = $\frac{1}{2} \times 480$

$\frac{1}{2}$ × 1AUD = 0.50AUD = 50 cents

So 240 pesos = 50 cents Australian

If an item costs 10 080 pesos in Chile, how much is that in Australian dollars?

Divide the amount by the local currency rate.

10 080 pesos ÷ 480 = 21, so it is worth 21AUD

Try this ...

In Vietnam 1AUD = 21 125 Vietnamese dong.

1. What will 10AUD be worth?
2. How many Australian dollars do you get for 2 112 500 dong?

PATTERNS & ALGEBRA

Mathematics is a search for
- patterns and relationships
- tidiness and precision
- what is true and not just a random occurrence.

Mathematicians love to discover, talk about and continue patterns. They love to search for rules.

NUMBER PATTERNS BASED ON SHAPES

This is a hexagon pattern made from sticks.

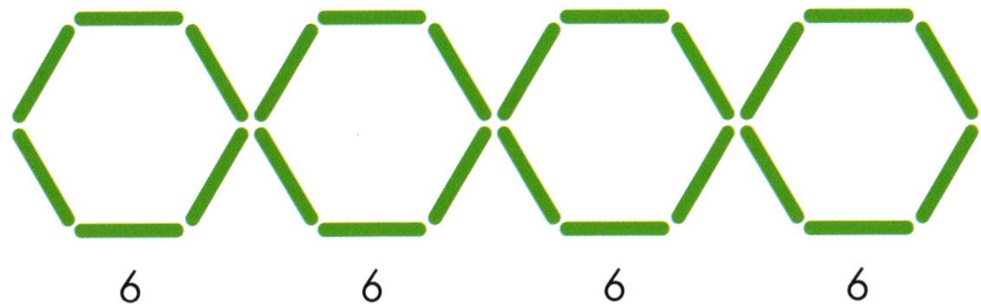

6 6 6 6

To continue this pattern, build more hexagons and write 6 each time. The **running total** is how many sticks you use. Each pair has a difference of 6.

Total number of sticks:

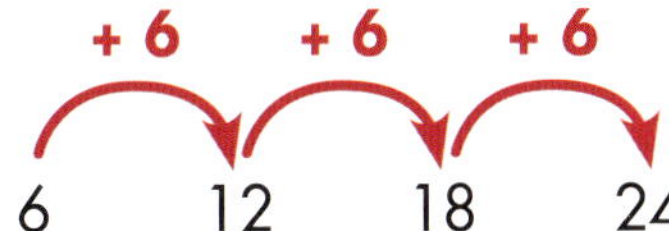

6 12 18 24

Each number is a multiple of 6. To continue this **number pattern**, write the next multiple of 6.

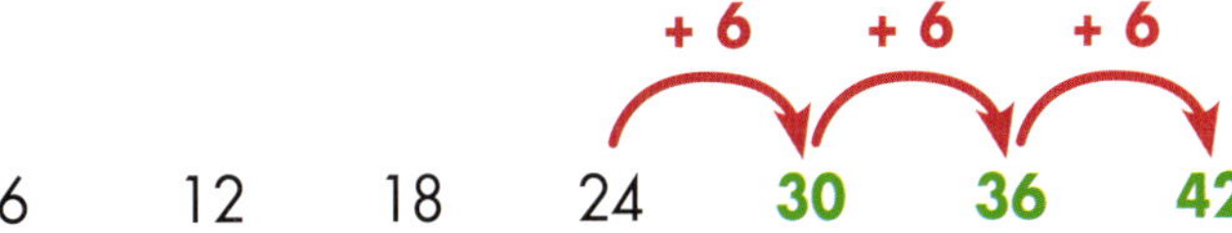

6 12 18 24 **30** **36** **42**

A **table of values** shows you more information about a pattern. It helps you discover other ways to describe a rule. You now see number pairs.

What is the same about each number pair?

What do you do to the top number to get the bottom number each time?

NUMBER PATTERNS BASED ON SHAPES
(continued)

No. of Hexagons	1	2	3	4	5
No. sticks	6 × 6	12 × 6	18 × 6	24 × 6	30 × 6

Rule: To find the total number of sticks, multiply the number of hexagons by 6.

Use this rule to continue the pattern. You do not need sticks now.

5 × 6 = 30, 6 × 6 = 36, 7 × 6 = 42 …

This rule can be used to predict how many sticks you use when making 20 hexagons.
20 × **6** = 120
That's 120 sticks to build 20 hexagons.

Try this

How many matchsticks do you need to build 100 hexagons?
How do you know?

FIND MISSING TERMS IN A TABLE OF VALUES

A small car travels 15 km for every litre, L, of petrol.

A large car travels 8 km for every litre, L, of petrol.

To work out how many kilometres the small car can travel, multiply L × **15**. If it uses 20 L that means it can travel 20 × **15** = 300 km.

To work out how many kilometres the large car can travel, multiply L × **8**. If it uses 60 L that means it travels 60 × **8** = 480 km.

Try this

Use the information about the cars from the previous page.

The two cars start with the same number of litres of petrol.

1 How far can the small car travel if the large car travels 40 km? How much petrol will it use?

Complete this table of values to work it out.

L (number of litres)	1	2	3	4	5
Small car km	15			60	
Large car km	8	16	24		

2 If the large car travels 320 km, how far does the small car travel? How much petrol will it use?

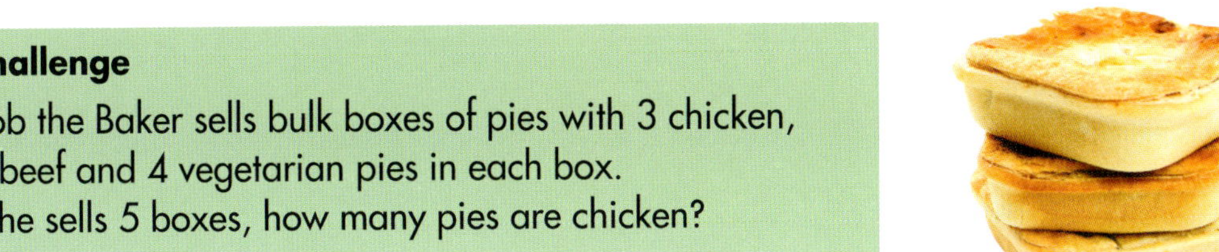

Challenge

Bob the Baker sells bulk boxes of pies with 3 chicken, 5 beef and 4 vegetarian pies in each box.
If he sells 5 boxes, how many pies are chicken?

Draw up your own table of values and find a way to calculate your answer.

No. Boxes					
Chicken					
Beef					
Vegetarian					
TOTAL					

NUMBER PATTERNS WITH WHOLE NUMBERS

A number pattern has a starting number and then a rule to link all the **terms**. Think of the rule as a secret code you are trying to crack.

What is the link between each number? Do you add? Subtract? Multiply? Divide? Sometimes you need to guess and check several times before you discover the rule.

NUMBER PATTERNS WITH WHOLE NUMBERS (continued)

+ 8

74, 82, 90, 98, 106 ... (add 8)

If you have \$74 saved up and you save \$8 each week, this pattern shows how much you will have if you keep saving.

You can show this pattern on a number line.

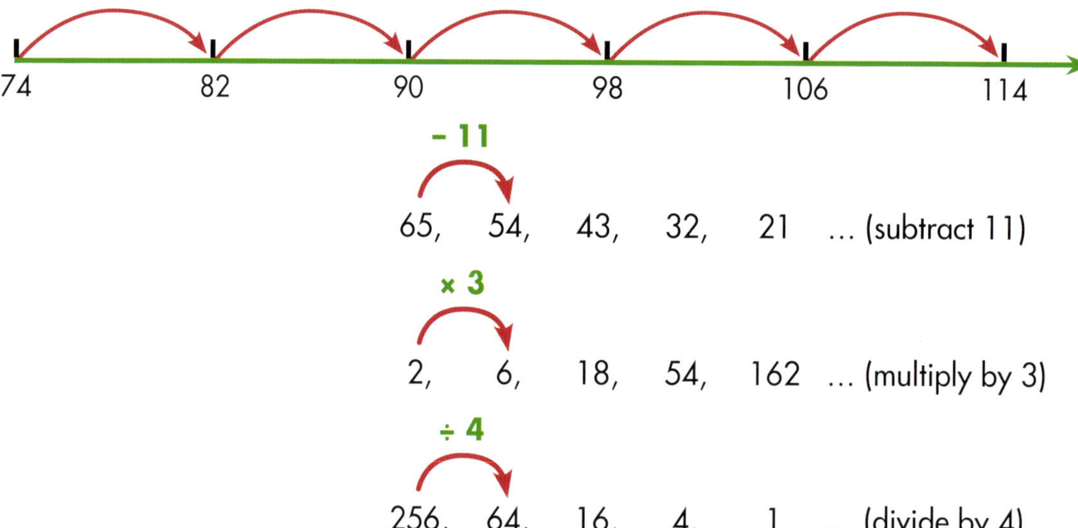

− 11

65, 54, 43, 32, 21 ... (subtract 11)

× 3

2, 6, 18, 54, 162 ... (multiply by 3)

÷ 4

256, 64, 16, 4, 1 ... (divide by 4)

To continue the pattern, keep applying the rule.

+ 8 + 8

74, 82, 90, 98, 106, **114**, **122**

If a number in a pattern is missing, look at the numbers either side. See if they help you work it out.
Try +, then −, then ×, then ÷.

Try this

Crack the code, fill in the missing numbers then write the next two numbers in the pattern. You can use a calculator to help you.

Pattern **A**: 2, 4, ◆, 16, 32, ■

Pattern **B**: 15, 28, 41, ▲, ●, 80

Pattern **C**: 3500, ⬢, 35, ▱, 0.35, 0.035

Pattern **D**: ⬢, 57, 50, 43, ◆, 29

NUMBER PATTERNS WITH FRACTIONS AND DECIMALS

Create rules for money, fraction and decimal patterns too. To continue each pattern, keep applying the rule.

- Multiply the denominator by 2
  $\frac{1}{2}, \frac{1}{4}, \frac{1}{8}, \frac{1}{16}, \frac{1}{32}, \frac{1}{64} \dots$
- Add 85 g (e.g. we can measure spice into 85 g packs)
  0.085 kg, 0.170 kg, 0.255 kg, 0.340 kg …
- Subtract 0.9 m (e.g. we can cut ribbon into 0.9 m lengths)
  5.6 m, 4.7 m, 3.8 m, 2.9 m, 2.0 m, 1.1 m …

Crack the code, fill in the missing numbers and write the next number in the pattern.

Pattern **A**: $2\frac{3}{12}$, $1\frac{10}{12}$, , 1, $\frac{7}{12}$, $\frac{2}{12}$

Pattern **B**: 3.07, , 3.17, 3.22, 3.27,

Challenge

Crack the code, fill in the missing numbers and write the next number in the pattern.

Pattern: 3.25, 9.75, , 87.75, 263.25, 

CONSTRUCT YOUR OWN NUMBER SENTENCES

When you read a word problem you need to work out what mathematics will solve it. Use numbers and symbols to match each part of the problem.

Abassi thinks of a number, triples it and subtracts 4. Her new number is 26. What was her 1st number?

Create a symbol for the missing 1st number e.g.

Write the first part of the problem:  × 3

The 2nd part of the problem says she subtracts 4 and now has 26.

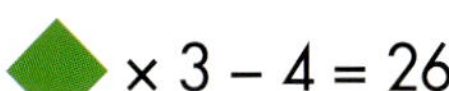 × 3 – 4 = 26

Try working backwards 26 + 4 = 30

 × 3 = 30 so must be 10.

NUMBER SENTENCES

A **number sentence** is a way to write a problem using numbers and symbols. The equals sign means "is the same number as" or "balances with" or "is equal to."

18 + 36 = 54 or 54 = 18 + 36

There are many different names for numbers.
100 – 46 is another name for 54 so 100 – 46 also equals 18 + 36.
It is true that 100 – 46 = 18 + 36.

Turn this type of number sentence into a puzzle by hiding some of the numbers or symbols.

50 – ✹ = 10 + 14

You know 10 + 14 = 24.
Rewrite this problem as 50 – ✹ = 24

What do you add to 24 to get 50?

You add 26. So ✹ = 26.

Check each side to make sure they balance.

50 – **26** = 10 + 14.

24 24

Try this

Find the missing numbers.

1 6 + ▲ = 29 – 18

2 ■ × 9 = 4.5

3 27 ÷ 3 = ● + 4

Try to see a relationship in each side of the number sentence.

Jaya had $45 and spent $7. Sam has $40, bought his lunch and now has the same amount as Jaya.

How much did Sam spend on lunch?

45 – 7 = 40 – ◆ Both sides must balance.

38 = 40 – ◆

◆ = 2

Sam spent $2 on lunch.

Try one using multiplication.

33 × 10 = 11 × 

You know both sides must balance.

33 = 11 × 3

Rewrite 33 × 10 as 11 × 3 × 10

So 11 × (3 × 10) = 11 × 

So   = 3 × 10 = 30

ORDER OF OPERATIONS

Look at these two stories and the matching number sentences.

Gabi has 6 dogs. Each dog has 8 brown spots and 4 black spots. How many spots altogether?

6 × (8 + 4) = 72

Gabi has 6 dogs. Each dog has 8 spots. She buys a new dog with only 4 spots. How many spots altogether?

(6 × 8) + 4 = 52

The stories are not the same. The answers are not the same. Brackets, ( ), show you which numbers belong together to match your story.

Always calculate what is in the brackets first. Without the brackets you do not know which operation to do first.

ORDER OF OPERATIONS (continued)

If you are looking at a complicated number sentence and you do not know the matching story, use the four **order of operations** rules:

1. Calculate anything inside brackets e.g. (6 – 3)
2. Work out any square or cube numbers e.g. 5^2
3. If there are no brackets, calculate × or ÷ from left to right e.g. 4 × 5
4. If there are no brackets, work out + or – from left to right e.g. 27 – 8

Mathematicians agreed to these rules to help you calculate without misunderstanding anything.

$7 \times 3 + 9 \div 3 = (7 \times 3) + (9 \div 3) = 21 + 3 = 24$

If you calculate them in the wrong order, your answer will not be right.

Some people refer to these rules as BODMAS

Brackets first
Orders (square numbers)
Divide or
Multiply
Add or
Subtract

1. Which number sentence matches this story?
2. What is your answer to the problem?

Matt spends $6 a day on bus fares. He earns $65 a day. How much does he have at the end of a 5-day working week?

A: (6 + 65) × 5
B: 5 × (65 – 6)
C: (6 × 65) + 5
D: (5 × 6) + 65

LENGTH

Length is measured in units called millimetres, centimetres, metres or kilometres. The unit you use depends on the length of what you want to measure.

KILOMETRES

A **kilometre** is 1000 metres. Use it to measure distances between towns and cities. Plane travel is also measured in kilometres.

The symbol for a kilometre is km.
"kilo" means one thousand
1000 m = 1 km

The Nile River in Egypt is the longest river in the world. It is about 6650 km long. How many metres is that?

To convert **kilometres** to **metres** multiply by 1000 ⟶ km > m so ×

1000 × 6650 = 6 650 000 so the Nile River is 6 650 000 m long.

The earth's circumference is about 40 000 000 m. How many kilometres is that?

To convert **metres** to **kilometres** divide by 1000 ⟶ m < km so ÷

40 000 000 ÷ 1000 = 40 000 so the earth's circumference is 40 000 km.

The world's longest traffic jam was in Beijing in 2010. It stretched for 96.5 km to Inner Mongolia. How long was the traffic jam in metres?

KILOMETRES (continued)

To show kilometres on a sketch or a map use a scale. The scale on this map is 1 cm = 4 km.

It is 13 km from Clareville to Wanda. How many other length comparisons can you discover?

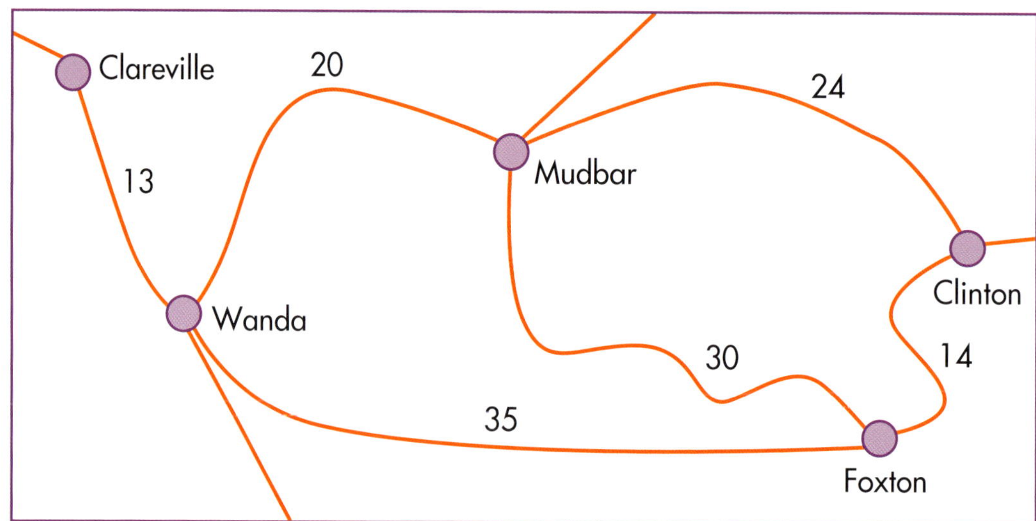

Scale 1 cm = 4 km

Which is the shorter route?
Clareville, Wanda, Mudbar, Clinton
Clareville, Wanda, Foxton, Clinton
Why?

METRES, CENTIMETRES AND MILLIMETRES

The **metre** is the official unit of length. It was created in France over 200 years ago as $\frac{1}{10\,000\,000}$ of the distance from the equator to the North Pole. Since 1983 mathematicians and scientists define a metre as the length of the path travelled by light in a vacuum in $\frac{1}{299\,792\,458}$ of a second.

A metre is 1 thousandth of a kilometre.
The symbol is m.

$$1\ \text{m} = \frac{1}{1000}\ \text{km}$$

$$1\ \text{m} = 0.001\ \text{km}$$

So you need 1000 m before you get the same length as 1 km.

A centimetre is 1 hundredth of a metre.
The symbol is cm.

$$1\ \text{cm} = \frac{1}{100}\ \text{m}$$

$$1\ \text{cm} = 0.01\ \text{m}$$

So you need 100 cm before you get the same length as 1 m.
100 cm = 1 m
1000 cm = 10 m
10 000 cm = 100 m
100 000 cm = 1000 m or 1 km

A millimetre is 1 tenth of a centimetre.
The symbol is mm.

$$1\ \text{mm} = \frac{1}{10}\ \text{cm}$$

$$1\ \text{mm} = 0.1\ \text{cm}$$

So you need 10 mm before you get the same length as 1 cm.
10 mm = 1 cm
100 mm = 10 cm
1000 mm = 100 cm or 1 m

A red kangaroo can jump 2.95 metres off the ground. How many centimetres is this?

To convert **metres** to **centimetres** multiply by 100 → m > cm so ×

2.95 × 100 = 295

so a red kangaroo can jump 295 cm

METRES, CENTIMETRES AND MILLIMETRES
(continued)

A violin is 35.56 cm long. How many metres is this?

To convert **centimetres** to **metres** divide by 100 → cm < m so ÷

35.56 ÷ 100 = 0.356 so a violin is 0.356 m long

The longest jump by a guinea pig is 20.5 cm. How many millimetres is this?

To convert **centimetres** to **millimetres** multiply by 10 → cm > mm so ×

20.5 × 10 = 205 so the guinea pig jumped 205 mm.

A Hercules beetle is 168 mm long. How many centimetres is this?

To convert **millimetres** to **centimetres** divide by 10 → mm < cm so ÷

168 ÷ 10 = 16.8 so the beetle is 16.8 cm long

Try this

Circle the larger length in each pair.

1 2.5 km or 2395 m

2 4.01 m or 497 cm

3 0.99 mm or 6.7 cm

CALCULATING PERIMETERS OF RECTANGLES

The **perimeter** is the total distance around all the sides of a 2D shape. It is a measure of length.

If the shape does not have straight sides, estimate the perimeter using appropriate length units.

To estimate, imagine each unit. You can make small marks to match. Add these up to reveal your estimated perimeter.

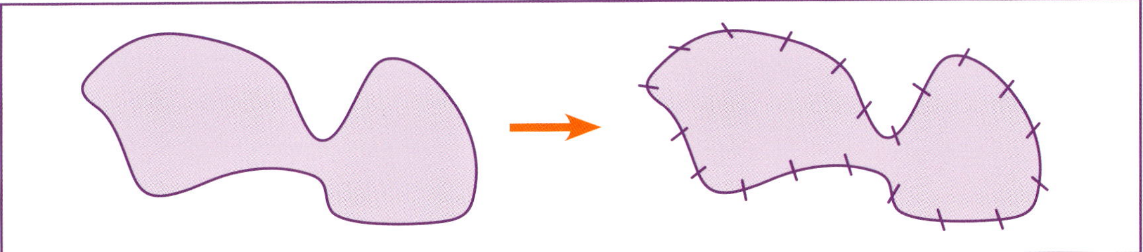

My estimated perimeter is about 20 cm.

Remember you are counting the lengths in between the marks, not how many marks you made.

If the shape does have straight sides, you can measure using **mm**, **cm**, **m** or **km**.

To find the perimeter of a rectangle, measure the length of all four sides using a ruler or tape measure.

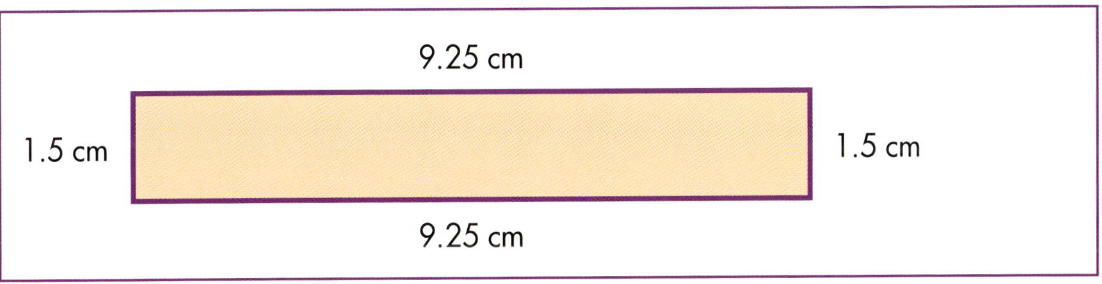

Notice that the two pairs of opposite sides are equal lengths.

The fast way to find the perimeter of a rectangle is to measure only one of each pair and then multiply by 2.

$$\begin{aligned} 1.5 + 9.25 + 1.5 + 9.25 &= (2 \times 1.5) + (2 \times 9.25) \\ &= 3 + 18.5 \\ &= 21.5 \text{ cm} \end{aligned}$$

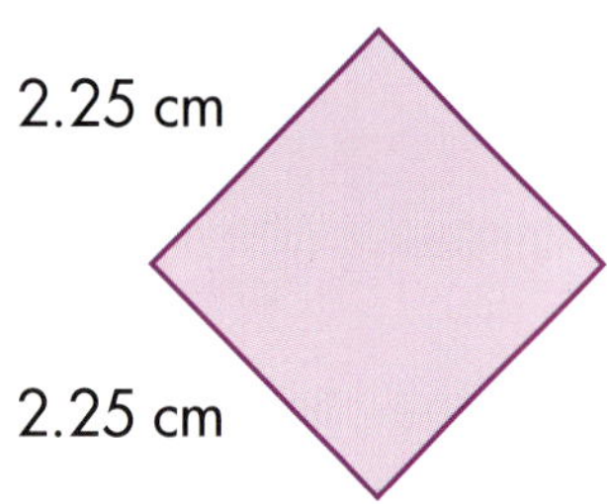

CALCULATING PERIMETERS OF RECTANGLES (continued)

The fast way to find the perimeter of a square is to measure one side and then multiply by 4.

$$2.25 + 2.25 + 2.25 + 2.25 = 4 \times 2.25 = 9 \text{ cm}$$

Use a ruler to find the perimeter of each 2D shape.

1

2

3

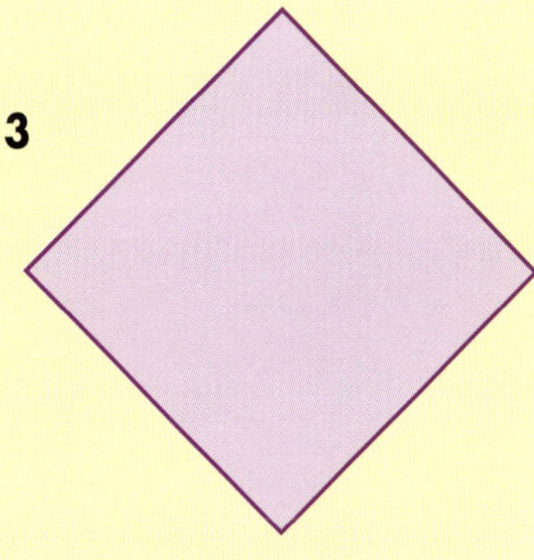

4

CALCULATING PERIMETERS OF OTHER POLYGONS

A **regular polygon** has sides of equal length. To find the perimeter of a regular polygon measure the length of one side and then multiply by the number of sides.

5 × 1.5 = 7.25 cm

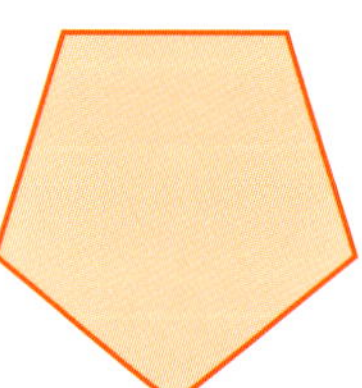

8 × 1.25 = 10 cm

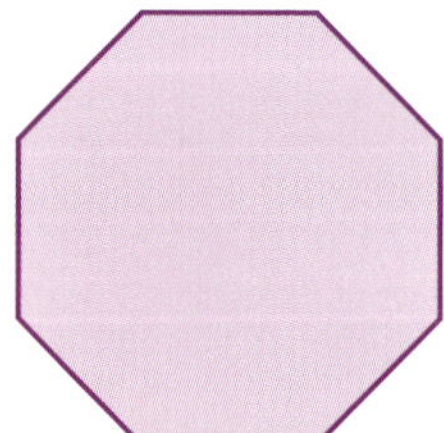

Use a ruler to find the perimeter of each 2D shape.

1

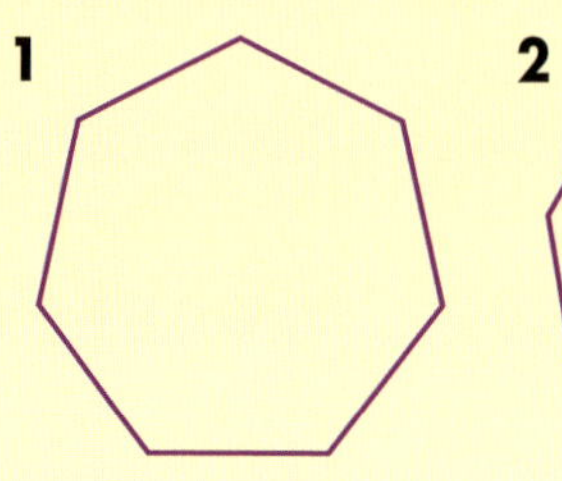

2

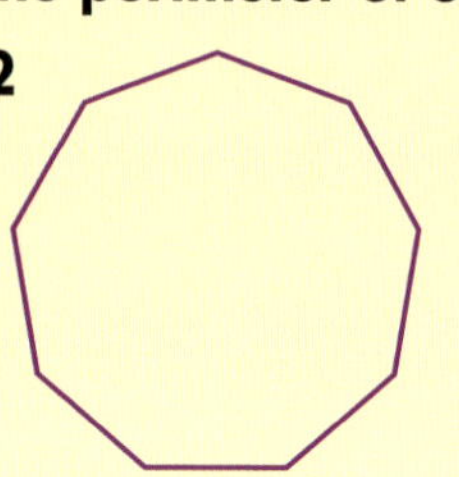

3

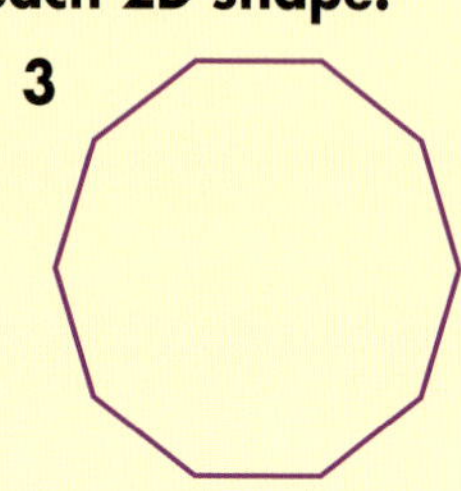

A non-regular polygon has many unequal sides. You may need to measure them all and then add to find the total perimeter. Look for shortcuts. Look for sides that you know must be the same length.

Don't be tricked. If you see a shape where some of the side measurements are shown, check to see if any measurements are missing. You may need to do more measuring before you add to get the total perimeter.

This is a scale map of a play area that needs a new fence.

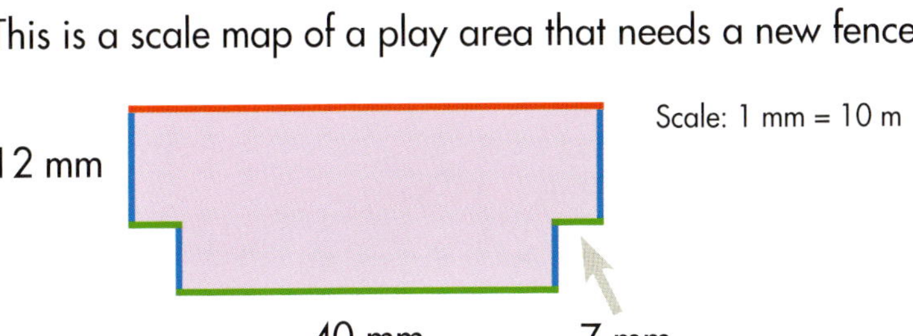

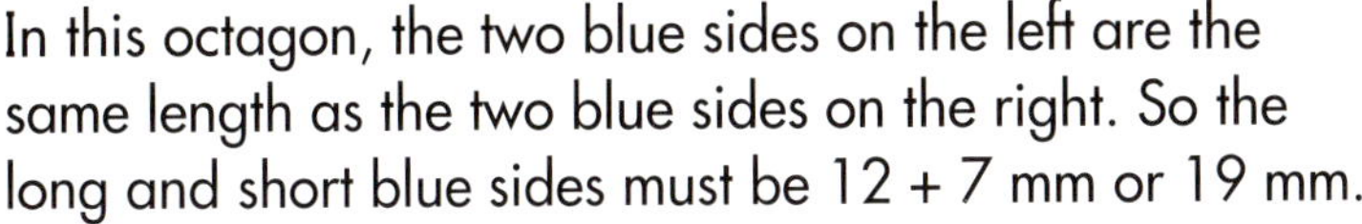

In this octagon, the two blue sides on the left are the same length as the two blue sides on the right. So the long and short blue sides must be 12 + 7 mm or 19 mm.

The three green sides are the same length as the red side. You only need to measure the two small green sides + 40 mm or just measure the length of the red side.

The total perimeter of this octagon is
19 + 50 + 19 + 50 = 138 mm

The scale is 1 mm = 10 m, so the total perimeter of the play area fence is 10 × 138 = 1380 m.

Check the measurements of the scale play area with your ruler.

Find the perimeter of this octagon.

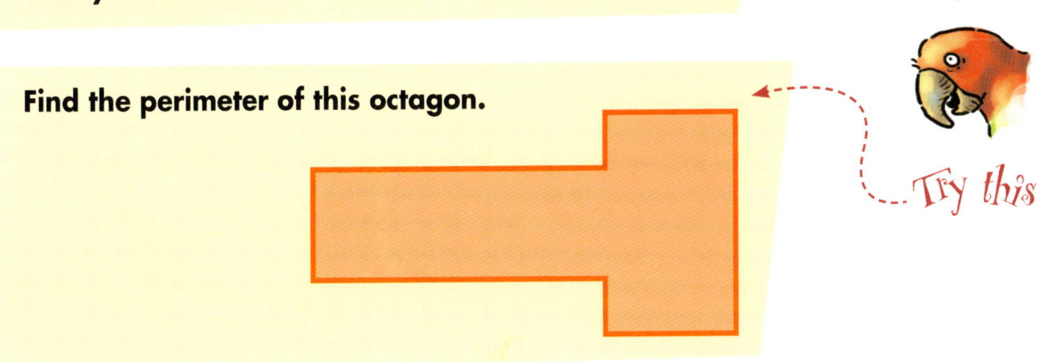

Try this

INTERPRETING SPEED

Speed is a measure of both time and distance.
How far can you travel in 1 minute, 1 hour or 1 day?

The Australian Government has speed rules for safe road use. These are called **speed limits**. Wherever you drive, signs tell you the maximum speed allowed. Most people try to drive at this speed or just under.

If you see a 40 km sign you must slow your car's speed to 40 km per hour or less. The speedometer on the dashboard shows how fast your car is travelling. Written in symbols this is 40 **km/h**.

A red kangaroo can bound at 70 km/h over short distances and 40 km/h over long distances.

To see how far you travel if the speed is 50 km/h, you can create a table of values.

Time in hours	1	2	3	4	5
Distance travelled at 50 km/h	50	100	150	200	250

(1 → × 50 → 50; 2 → × 50 → 100)

To calculate how far you travel:
Time in hours × distance travelled in 1 hour
In 8 hours you will travel 8 × 50 = 400 km.

If you drive at 80 km/h you create a different table of values.

Time in hours	1	2	3	4	5
Distance travelled at 80 km/h	80	160	240	320	400

(1 → × 80 → 80)

So in 5 hours travelling at 80 km/h you travel 400 km.

How far does your family travel if you go 2 hours at 80 km/h, stop for a break, then travel 3 hours at 100 km/h?

AREA

Area is a measure of how much space a flat 2D shape takes up. It is a measure of the space inside a two-dimensional boundary. The unit you use depends on the size of the area you want to measure. Area is measured in **cm²**, **m²**, **hectares** and **square kilometres**.

HECTARES

A hectare is 10 000 m². It is used to measure large land areas like parks and farms.

The symbol for a hectare is ha.
10 000 m² = 1 ha

The term 'hecto' means one hundred and an 'are' is the original metric land measure for 100 square metres. We don't use the are unit anymore, but 100 ares is a hectare or 100 × 100 m².

A hectare can be any shape.
It does not have to be a 100 × 100 square.
1 m × 10 000 m = 1 ha
10 m × 1000 m = 1 ha
500 m × 200 m = 1 ha

The world's largest shopping mall is in Dubai. It covers a total area of 112.4 hectares. How many square metres is that?

To convert **hectares** to **square metres** multiply by 10 000 → ha > m² so ×

10 000 × 112.4 = 1 124 000 so the shopping mall covers 1 124 000 square metres.

HECTARES (continued)

The New South China Mall in Beijing, China, has an area of 65.96 hectares. How many square metres is that?

A football field has an area of (68 × 100) m^2 or 6800 m^2. How many hectares is that?

To convert **square metres** to **hectares** divide by 10 000 ⟶ $m^2 <$ ha so ÷

6800 ÷ 10 000 = 0.68 so the football field covers 0.68 hectares. That's more than half a hectare.

That's about $\frac{7}{10}$ of a hectare.

The Hill family is selling 67 500 m^2 of farmland. How many hectares is that?

SQUARE KILOMETRES

The Sahara is the largest desert in the world. It covers 9 064 958 km^2.

A square kilometre is an area of 1000 × 1000 metres. It is used to measure huge areas such as the areas covered by a local council, a state, a country or an ocean. You see square kilometres when you look out the window of a plane.

The symbol for a square kilometre is km^2.
1 000 000 m^2 = 1 km^2
100 hectares = 1 km^2

Try this

Place these countries in order from the largest area to the smallest area.

Name of Country	Surface Area in km²
Australia	7 692 024
China	9 596 961
Greece	131 957
India	3 287 263
Indonesia	1 910 931
Lebanon	10 452
Russia	17 074 100

The surface of our planet Earth is about 510 072 000 km².

You sometimes see large numbers like this written as millions of kilometres. To convert to millions of kilometres you divide by 1 000 000.

510 072 000 ÷ 1 000 000 = 510.072
So 510 072 000 km² = 510.072 million km²
To the nearest million, this rounds down to 510 million km².

Australia covers an area of 7 692 024 km².

The surface area of the moon is 37.9 million km².
To convert these words to numbers you multiply by 1 000 000.
So 37.9 × 1 000 000 = 37 900 000 km²
To the nearest million, this rounds up to 40 000 000 km²

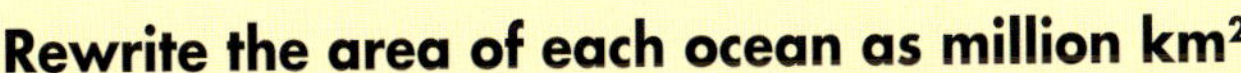

Rewrite the area of each ocean as million km²

	Name of Ocean	Surface Area in km²	Surface Area in million km²
1	Arctic	14 056 000	
2	Southern	20 327 000	
3	Indian	68 556 000	
4	Atlantic	76 762 000	
5	Pacific	155 557 000	

SQUARE METRES

Use **square metres** to measure areas less than one hectare, such as the area of a wall, floor or ceiling in a house. A square metre can be any shape. It does not have to be a square.

The symbol is m^2.

$$1\ m^2 = \frac{1}{10\,000}\ \text{hectare} = \frac{1}{10\,000\,000}\ km^2$$

$$10\,000\ cm^2 = 1\ m^2 \qquad 1\ cm^2 = \frac{1}{10\,000}\ m^2$$

Area in metres

The world's largest viewing panel in an aquarium is in the Burj Dubai. It is a rectangle measuring 32.88 m wide and 8.3 m high. What is the area?

To find the area of this rectangle, multiply the width by the height.

An efficient way to work this out is to multiply using the Italian Lattice method.

Estimate first → $30 \times 8 = 240\ m^2$

In the Italian Lattice method the place value columns are diagonal.

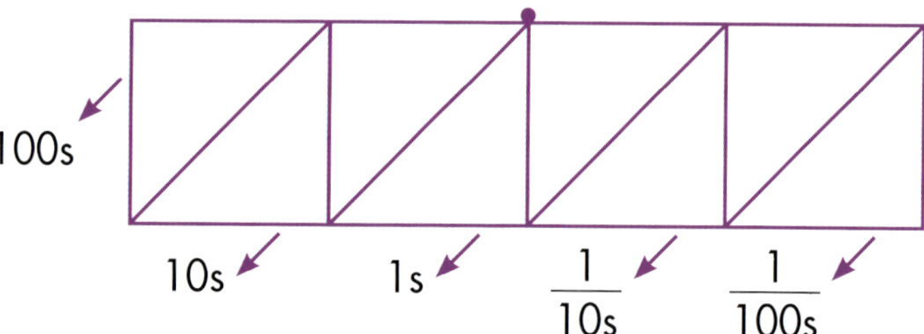

Multiply and record each pair of numbers in the small squares.

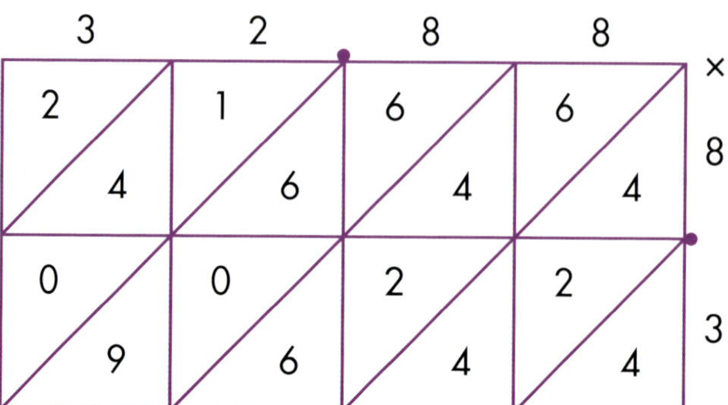

Next add within each place value column to find the total. Trade if you need to. The position of the decimal point is easy. Just draw a line until they meet and then find the nearest diagonal.

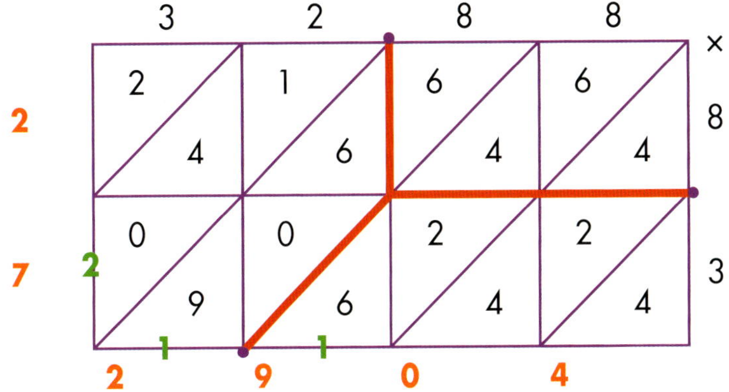

So 32.88 × 8.3 = 272.904

Rounding to the nearest square metre, the area of the viewing panel is 273 m^2.

Use the Italian Lattice method to work out the area of Japan's largest aquarium viewing panel in Okinawa. It is 22.5 m wide and 8.2 m high.

SQUARE CENTIMETRES

Use **square centimetres** to measure small areas less than one square metre. The symbol is **cm^2**.

$$1\ cm^2 = \frac{1}{10000}\ m^2$$

$$10\ cm^2 = \frac{1}{1000}\ m^2 = 0.001\ m^2$$

$$100\ cm^2 = \frac{1}{100}\ m^2 = 0.01\ m^2$$

$$1000\ cm^2 = \frac{1}{10}\ m^2 = 0.1\ m^2$$

$$10\ 000\ cm^2 = \frac{100}{100}\ m^2 = 1.0\ m^2$$

SQUARE CENTIMETRES (continued)

A square centimetre can be any shape. It does not have to be a square.

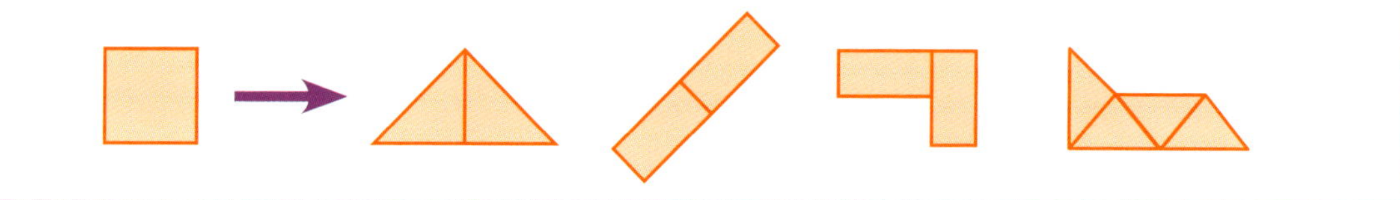

These shapes all have an area of 1 cm^2.
Use 1 cm^2 grid paper to help you calculate small areas.
Try drawing in the grid lines to help you.
Estimate when you are not sure. Try to match small gaps with overlaps.

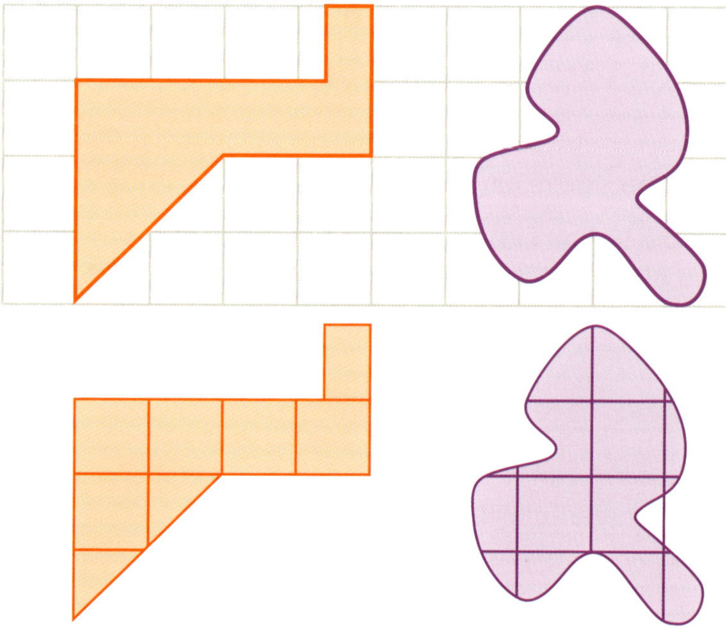

The orange shape has an area of

$$4 + 1 + \frac{1}{2} + \frac{1}{2} + \frac{1}{2} = 6\frac{1}{2} \text{ cm}^2.$$

The purple shape has an area of about 7 cm^2.

What is the area of these 2D shapes in cm^2?

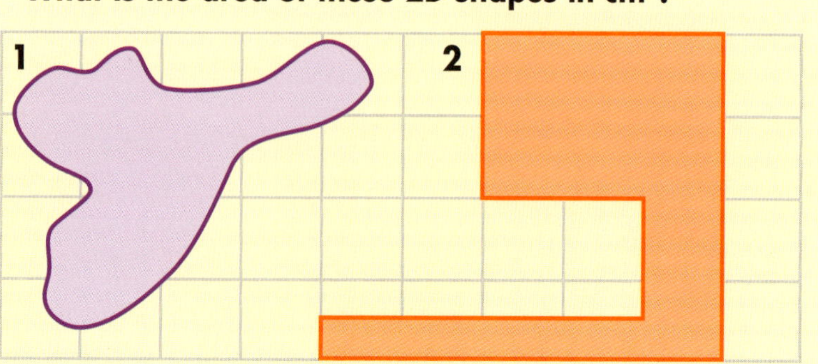

AREA OF A RECTANGLE

To find the area of a rectangle, add all the square units.

If there are no grid lines shown, measure the units using your ruler. If you can see more than one rectangle, find the area of each rectangle then add to get the total area.

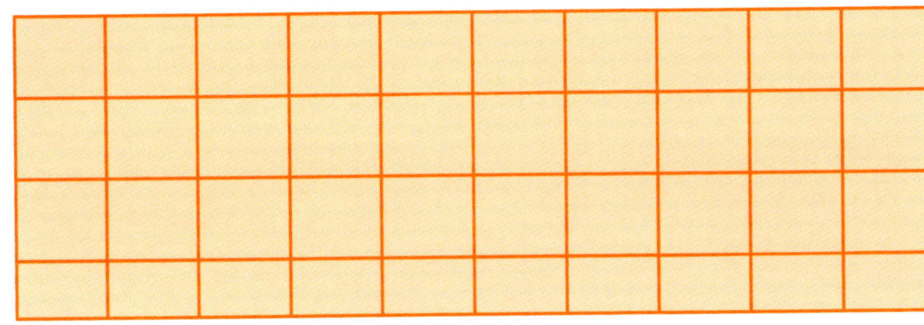

$3\frac{1}{2}$ rows high

10 cm wide

Strategies to calculate the area of a rectangle

Count how many units in one row, and then add all the rows.

$10 + 10 + 10 + (\frac{1}{2} \times 10) = 35$ cm^2

Or try counting how many units in each column, then adding all the columns.

$3\frac{1}{2} + 3\frac{1}{2} + 3\frac{1}{2} + 3\frac{1}{2} + 3\frac{1}{2} + 3\frac{1}{2} + 3\frac{1}{2} + 3\frac{1}{2} + 3\frac{1}{2}$

$+ 3\frac{1}{2} = 35$ cm^2

A fast strategy is to multiply the number in each row by the number of columns.

$10 \times 3.5 = 3.5 \times 10 = 35$ cm^2

Try this

What is the area of each of these 2D shapes in cm^2?
Which strategy works best for you?

3

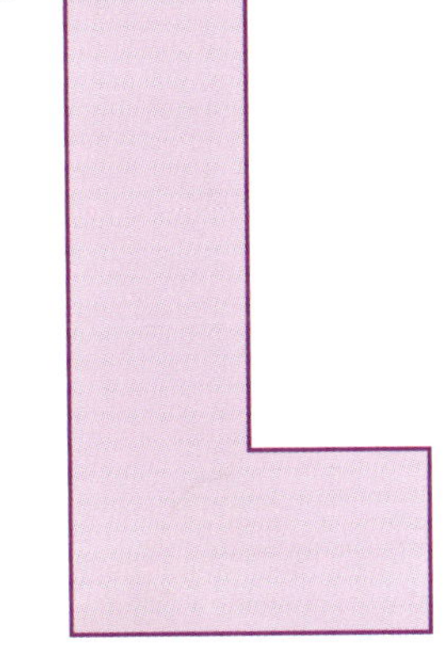

1

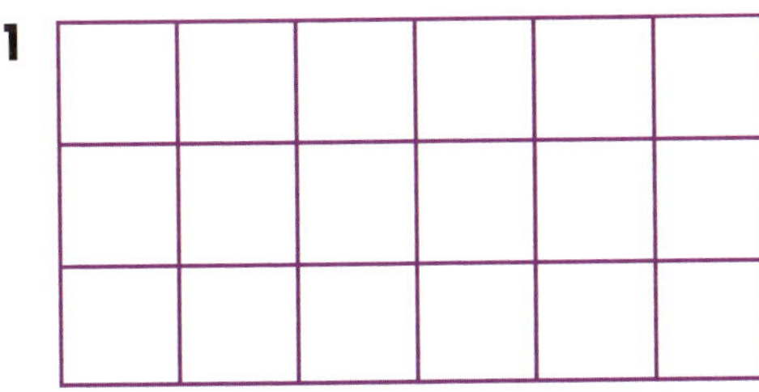

2

AREA OF A TRIANGLE

Every triangle can be surrounded by a square or an oblong.

This fact can help you work out the area of a triangle.

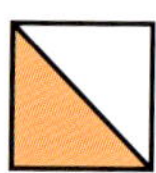

The area of this triangle is 0.5 cm^2.
It is half the area of the surrounding square.

The area of this triangle is not so easy to figure out.
The area of the surrounding square is 4 cm^2.
The area of the triangle is less than this.
What is your estimate?

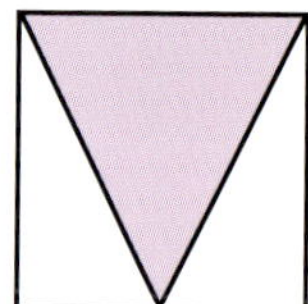

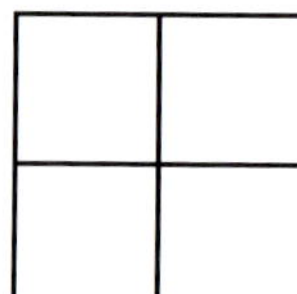

You need to subtract the orange area on the left.
The orange area is half of 2 cm^2 so that must be 1 cm^2.

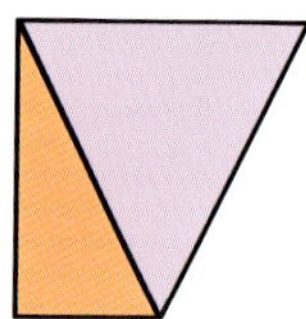

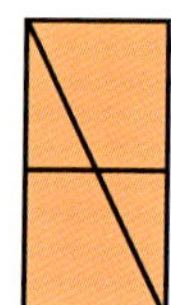

You need to subtract the orange area on the right.
The orange area is half of 2 cm^2 so that must be 1 cm^2.

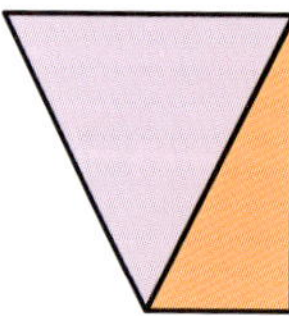

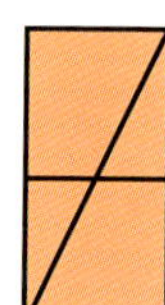

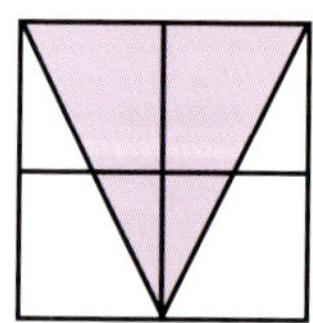

You started with an area of 4 cm^2, and then you took off 1 cm^2 and another 1 cm^2. That leaves you with 2 cm^2.
So the area of the purple triangle is 2 cm^2.

A fast strategy for working out the area of any triangle is to find half the width multiplied by the height. The purple triangle is 2 cm wide and 2 cm high.

$(\frac{1}{2} \times 2) \times 2 = 1 \times 2 = 2\ cm^2$

Draw the surrounding rectangle for each triangle on this grid.

Try this

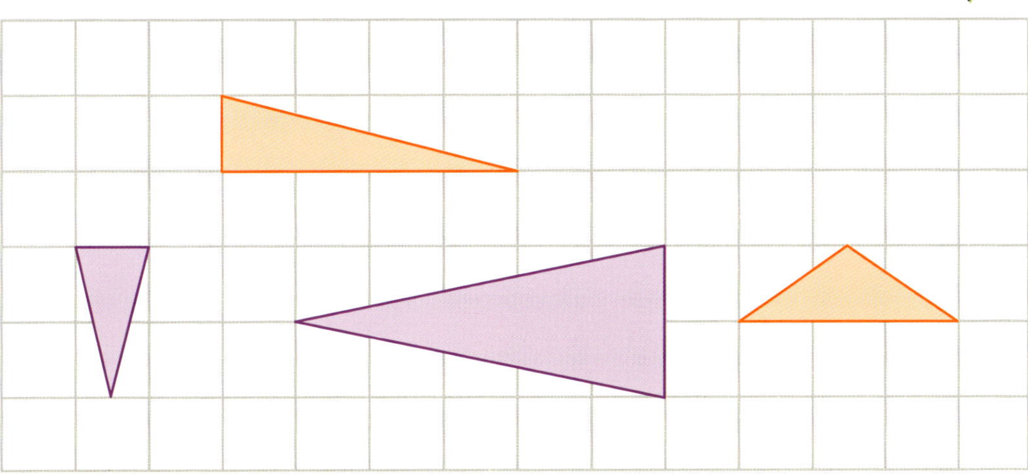

Challenge

Find the area in square centimetres for each of the above triangles.

CALCULATING AREA ON SCALE MAPS

Square metres, hectares and square kilometres are too large to draw on a sketch or a map. You can create a scale map to show these areas.

Map of Carrington Islands

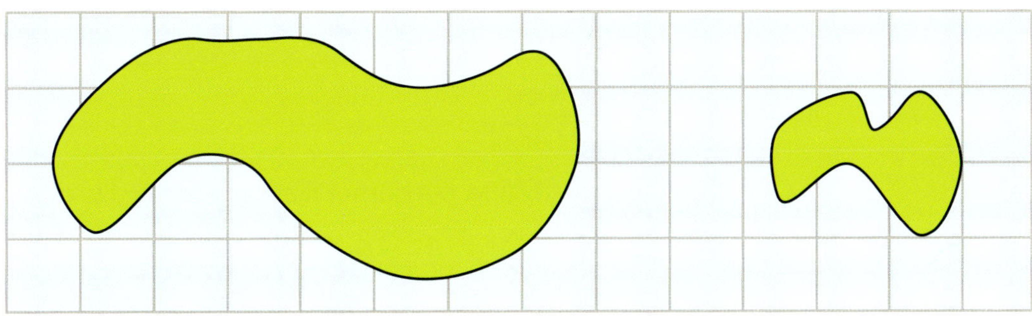

Scale 1 cm^2 = 1 ha

What is the area of the two islands?

To find the area of the islands, marked in green, draw in grid lines and estimate. My estimate is about 18 cm^2. Applying the scale means the islands cover a total area of about 18 hectares.

CALCULATING AREA ON SCALE MAPS (continued)

Map of School Library and outside paving area

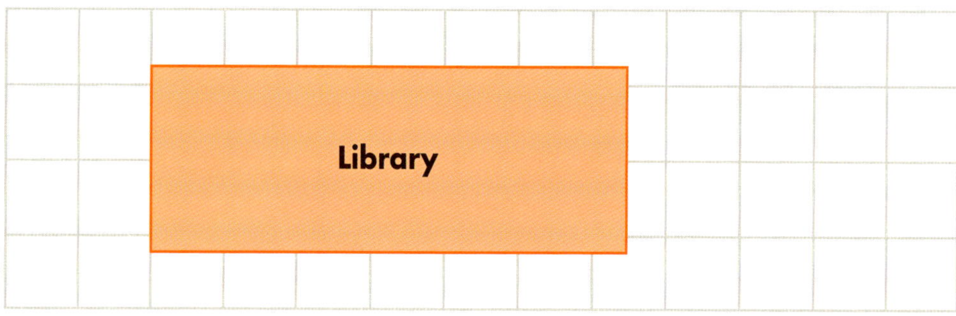

Scale 1 cm^2 = 4 m^2

How much will it cost to carpet tile the library at $75 a square metre?

To find the area of the library floor, find the area in cm^2, and then use the scale to convert your measurement to m^2.

- First find the area in cm^2

  Estimate first → 3 × 6 = 18 so it will be less than 18 cm^2

  2.5 × 6.5 = 16.25 cm^2
- Next convert this to square metres

  The scale is 1 cm^2 = 4 m^2

  4 × 16.25 = 65 m^2
- Then find the cost of the carpet tiles

  Estimate first → If I round up the $75 cost and round down the 65 square metres, then I get 80 × 60 = 4800

  65 × 75 = 4875

It will cost $4875 to put carpet tiles on the new library floor.

Challenge

Paving costs $46 a square metre. How much will it cost to pave all the area outside the library? See the map of the school library and outside area above.

MASS

Mass measures the heaviness of an object or the amount of matter in an object. It is measured in units called grams, kilograms and tonnes. The unit used depends on how heavy the object is you want to measure. A very large object may be quite light. A very small object may be quite heavy. Mass is about heaviness, not about how large an object looks.

Small cubical masses in decimal proportions have been found in Harappa, Pakistan. They are 3500 years old. The tiniest ones were probably used for measuring the mass of jewels. This shows us that humans have been using standard masses for a long time.

GRAMS

The **gram** is used for measuring the mass of objects less than a kilogram. The symbol for a gram is **g**.
1000 g = 1 kg

1000 g = 1 kg	2000 g = 2 kg
500 g = 0.5 kg	2500 g = 2.5 kg
100 g = 0.1 kg	2100 g = 2.1 kg
10 g = 0.01 kg	2010 g = 2.01 kg
1 g = 0.001 kg	2001 g = 2.001 kg

The heaviest peach ever grown had a mass of 725 g.

This cat has a mass of 3090 g.
How many kilograms is that?

If you have more than 1000 g, you have more than 1 kg.

You are asking yourself "how many groups of 1000 g can I take from 3090 grams?"

To convert **grams** to **kilograms**, divide by 1000.

$$\begin{aligned} 3090 \text{ g} &= 3090 \div 1000 \\ &= 3.090 \text{ kg} \\ &= 3.09 \text{ kg} \end{aligned}$$

The cat has a mass of 3.09 kg.

GRAMS (continued)

This kitten has a mass of 0.798 kg.
How many grams is that?

If you have less than 1 kg you have fewer than 1000 g.

You are saying to yourself "for every kilogram there are 1000 g, so I need to multiply the number of kilograms by 1000."

To convert **kilograms** to **grams**, multiply by 1000.

0.798 kg = 0.798 × 1000
= 798 g

The kitten has a mass of 798 g.

Place these mixed masses in order from lightest to heaviest.

9.2 kg   4788 g   0.999 kg   4.078 kg   920 g

KILOGRAMS

The **kilogram** is the metric standard for measuring mass. The symbol for a kilogram is **kg**. 'Kilo' means 1000, so kilogram means 1000 grams. It is the only unit still defined by an object. It is a cylinder the size of a golf-ball, made from a platinum-iridium alloy and kept in a vault in France. Scientists are trying to make a kilogram mass that never varies. One possibility is a 1 kg single silicon crystal sphere.

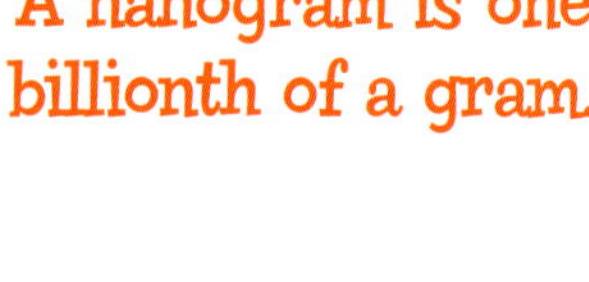

1 kg has about the same mass as 1 L of pure water
1 g has about the same mass as 1 mL of pure water

This newborn baby has a mass of 2.89 kg.

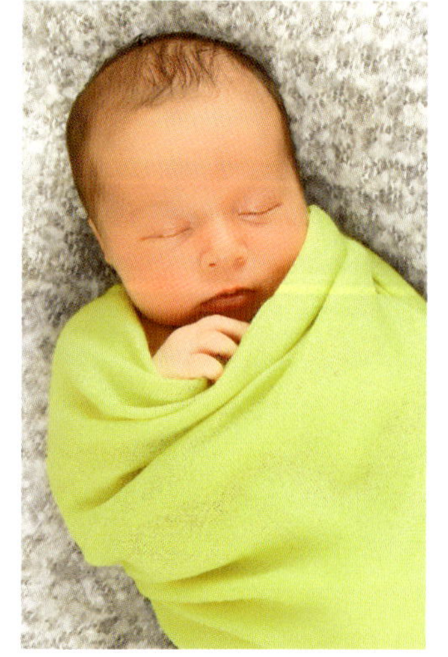

At four weeks old the baby now has a mass of 3.805 kg.

What is the difference in mass between the newborn baby and the baby at four weeks?

- Before you subtract, make the numbers the same size by writing an extra **0**.

	2		17	10	
	~~3~~	.	~~8~~	~~0~~	5
−	2	.	8	9	**0**
	0	.	9	1	5

- So the baby has increased its mass by 0.915 kg in four weeks.

Sam the Labrador puppy has a mass of 4.5 kg. Rex the Great Dane has a mass of 79.105 kg. What is the difference in mass?

When using a calibrated scale to measure mass, use proportional reasoning to work out what each mark means. This scale measures objects up to a mass of 5 kg. There are 10 spaces between each 200 g marked on the scale. The 5th mark, which is slightly longer, shows multiples of 100 g. Each of the other small marks must be $\frac{1}{5}$ of 100 or 20 g.

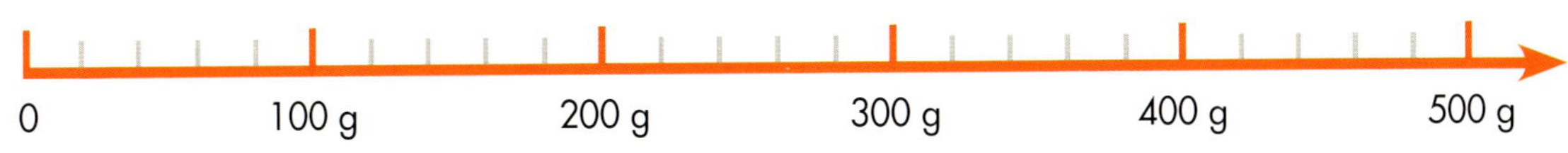

Place a cross on the number line above to show 0.25 kg, 0.07 kg and 0.19 kg.

Challenge

Create two mass problems to solve using information from this table.

Heaviest in group	Anaconda	Capybara	Gorilla	Ostrich	Echidna	Kangaroo
Group	Snake	Rodent	Primate	Bird	Monotreme	Marsupial
Mass in kg	250	78.9	224.88	156	15.5	98.8

Add more information from your own research.
For example:

- the heaviest jellyfish?
- the heaviest bat?
- the heaviest grasshopper?

TONNES

The **tonne** is used for measuring the mass of very heavy objects. The symbol for a tonne is **t**. The mass of trucks is measured in tonnes.

The counterbalance to this giant crane is made from 27 one tonne masses.

1 tonne = 1000 kg = 1 000 000 g

0.5 t = 500 kg	2.5 t = 2500 kg
0.25 t = 250 kg	3.25 t = 3250 kg
0.1 t = 100 kg	6.1 t = 6100 kg
0.01 t = 10 kg	8.01 t = 8010 kg
0.001 t = 1 kg	9.001 t = 9001 kg

A cubic metre of pure water has a mass of about 1000 kg or 1 tonne.

The estimated mass of the largest brachiosaurus was 35 t.

How many kilograms is that?

To convert **tonnes** to **kilograms**, multiply by 1000.
$35 \times 1000 = 35\,000$

So the brachiosaurus mass was about 35 000 kg.

The estimated mass of the largest T-Rex was 6800 kg. How many tonnes is that?

To convert **kilograms** to **tonnes**, divide by 1000.
$6800 \div 1000 = 6.8$
So the estimated mass of the largest T-Rex was 6.8 t.

Complete this table.

Name	Guar	Elephant	Lion	Crocodile	Hippo	Giraffe
Mass (tonnes)		7.785			3.340	1.24
Mass (kilograms)	895		225	1100		

Challenge
The largest Blue Whale has an estimated mass of 190 t. If an Indian Elephant has an estimated mass of 3910 kg, how many times heavier is the Blue Whale?

The heaviest object ever measured was a service device at Kennedy Space Centre, USA. It had a mass of 2423 tonnes.

GROSS AND NET MASS

When you measure the mass of a container, do you want to know the mass of the container itself, the mass of whatever is inside or both?

Gross mass = the mass of the container + the mass of the contents

Net mass = the total mass – the mass of the container.

This tin has a mass of 10 g.
The tuna inside has a mass of 95 g.
The gross mass = 10 + 95 = 105 g
The net mass of the tuna is 95 g.

Try this

There are 30 chocolates in a box with a net mass of 0.65 kg.

- If the box has a mass of 76 g, what is the gross mass?
- What is the approximate mass of one chocolate?

Breakfast cereal is sold by net mass. Each packet usually has a side panel packed with information in a table.

MUNCHY MUESLI Nutrition Information		
Net mass: 750 g		
Servings per box 16.7 Serving size: 45 g	Average quantity per serve	Average quantity per 100 g
Energy	895.5 kJ	1990 kJ
Protein	6.2 g	13.8 g
Fat	9.9 g	22.0 g
Sugar	3.6 g	8.0 g
Other Carbohydrate	21.6 g	48 g
Fibre	3.7 g	8.2 g
Salt	22.5 mg	50 mg

If you eat an average serve of Munchy Muesli every day, how much sugar do you get from this in one week?
7 × 3.6 = 25.2, which is about 25 g or 5 teaspoons

Try this

If you eat 1 kg of Munchy Muesli over 22 days, how much fat does this contain?

Challenge

Create three more Munchy Muesli Mass questions to answer.

VOLUME & CAPACITY

Volume measures how much 3D space an object takes up. **Capacity** measures the maximum volume inside a container or how much something can hold.

This storage box holds about 0.2 cubic metres.

Volume and capacity are both measured in cubic centimetres, cubic metres, millilitres, litres, kilolitres and megalitres.

You use about 4 L of water to wash your face in the morning.

KILOLITRES

Kilolitres are used to measure large amounts of water, such as in a drainage channel, a stream or a river.

1 kilolitre = 1000 L
The symbol for kilolitre is kL
The prefix 'kilo' comes from an old Greek word for 'a thousand'.

Your family water bill records how many kilolitres of water your family uses over three months.
This graph shows the Khoury family water usage over one year.

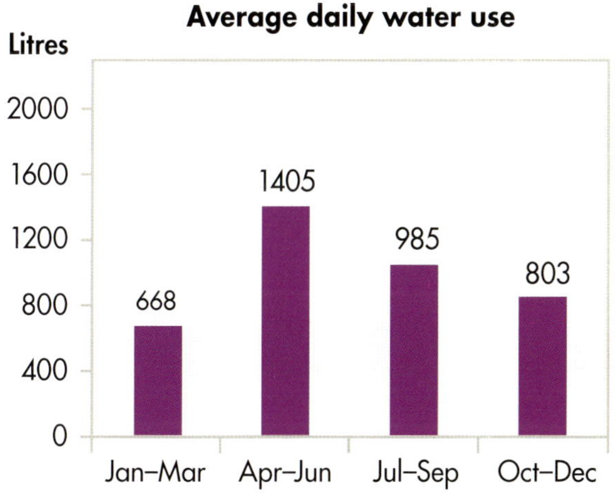

KILOLITRES (continued)

From April to June the average daily water use was 1405 L. In 91 days, the Khoury family used 91 × 1405 L. Using a calculator, this is 127 855 L. How many kilolitres is this?

To convert litres to kilolitres, divide by
1000 → L < kL, so ÷
127 855 ÷ 1000 = 127. So, they used 127 kL
in 3 months.

If the Khoury family used 350 kL in one year, how many litres is that?

To convert kilolitres to litres, divide by
1000 → kL > L, so ×
350 × 1000 = 350 000 L

How many litres of water did the Khoury family use from January to March?

MEGALITRES

Megalitres are used to measure huge volumes of water such as in a dam, a reservoir, a river or a lake.

The symbol for megalitre is ML
The prefix 'mega' comes from an old Greek word for 'great'.
It means 'one million'.

- 1 000 000 L = 1 megalitre
  1 L = $\frac{1}{1\,000\,000}$ of a ML
- 1000 kL = 1 ML
  1 kL = $\frac{1}{1000}$ of a ML
- 1000 m^3 = 1 ML
  1 m^3 = $\frac{1}{1000}$ of a ML

The world's largest aquarium, in Dubai, has a 10 000 000 L tank. How many megalitres is that?

To convert litres to megalitres divide by
1 000 000 → L < ML so ÷
10 000 000 ÷ 1 000 000 = 10
So the water in the Dubai aquarium tank has a volume of 10 ML.

That's the same amount as 10 000 kilolitres or 10 000 m^3.

Town and city water storages are measured in megalitres. These statistics are from three Melbourne Reservoirs.

Water Reservoir ML	Full Capacity ML	Current Volume ML	% Full
Thomson	1 068 000	415 575	38.9
Silvan	40 445	34 662	85.7
Maroondah	22 179	22 379	100.0
Greenvale	26 839	20 682	77.1

Information courtesy Melbourne Water, 31 May 2011

What is the difference in capacity between Maroondah and Greenvale reservoir in kilolitres?

Estimate first → 27 000 – 22 000 = 5000

$$\begin{array}{rrrrr} & & 7 & 13 & \\ 2 & 6 & \not{8} & \not{3} & 9 \\ -\ 2 & 2 & 1 & 7 & 9 \\ \hline & 4 & 6 & 6 & 0 \end{array}$$

To convert **megalitres** to **kilolitres**, multiply by 1000 → ML > kL, so ×

4660 × 1000 = 4 660 000
So the difference in capacity is 4 660 000 kL.
Rounded to the nearest million that is 5 000 000 kL.

Which is the larger volume?
3.758 ML or 2 000 579 kL

MEASUREMENT & GEOMETRY

CUBIC METRES

The **cubic metre** is the standard metric unit for measuring volume and capacity. A cubic metre can be any shape. One cubic metre takes up as much space as a 1 × 1 × 1 m cube. The symbol for a cubic metre is **m^3**.

Truckloads of soil, concrete mix and large amounts of water are measured in m^3.

1 m^3 of water = 1000 L = 1 kL
1 m^3 of water = 1 000 000 mL

Vikram ordered 1.8 cubic metres of concrete for his new garage floor. It costs \$185 for 1 m^3 plus 10% GST. How much will he pay?

Calculate the cost of the concrete: $1.8 \times 185 = 333$

Calculate 10% GST: $\frac{1}{10} \times 333 = 333 \div 10 = 33.3$

So Vikram will pay a total of \$333 + \$33.3 = \$366.30

What if Vikram ordered 2.2 cubic metres of concrete at the same price? How much will he pay now?

Fifteen people live in an apartment block. Every three people share a garden. Each garden needs 1.2 cubic metres of new soil. How much soil should they buy?

If soil costs \$45 for 1 m^3, how much will it cost each person?

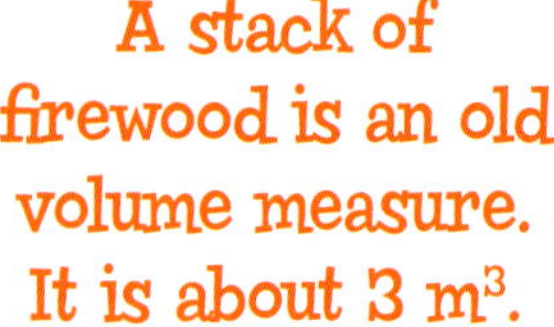

One strategy is to draw up a table of values.

No. people	3	6	9	12	15
Cubic metres	1.2	2.4	3.6	4.8	6.2

So, 15 people will need 6.2 cubic metres of soil for their new garden.

6.2 × 45 = 279, so it will cost them $279 in total.

Divided between the 15 people that is about $18.60 each.

Try this

The people in the apartments build three new gardens that need 1.2 cubic metres of soil each.

1 How much extra soil will they need?

2 What will be the extra cost for each person?

LITRES AND MILLILITRES

The **litre** is used to measure liquid volumes, like water, milk or juice. It is also used to measure the volume of a car engine. It is also used to measure gases, like air in the boot of a car or a fridge.

In 2009, the largest free-floating soap bubble had a volume of 13.67 m^3. That's about the same volume as a cube with each side 2.4 m.

A litre of pure water is the same size as a 10 cm × 10 cm × 10 cm cube. The symbol for a litre is **L**.

Th1 L = $\frac{1}{1000}$ of a cubic metre

10 L = $\frac{1}{100}$ m^3

100 L = $\frac{1}{10}$ m^3

1000 L = $\frac{1000}{1000}$ m^3 = 1 m^3

Your mum breathes in 11 000 L of air each day.

How many cubic metres is this?

To convert **litres** to **cubic metres**, divide by 1000 → L $<$ m^3 so ÷

11 000 ÷ 1000 = 11

So that's 11 m^3 of air that your mum breathes in one day.

A Boeing 747 aeroplane holds about 216 850 litres of fuel.

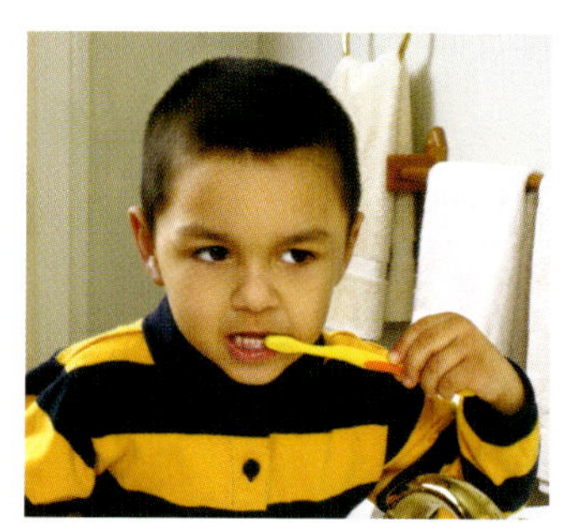

LITRES AND MILLILITRES (continued)

Brushing your teeth uses 1 L of water with the tap off and 5 L with the tap on.

This table shows some of the volumes of water used in a family home.

Average Home Water Consumption		
Shower	Old showerhead	17 L per minute
	New showerhead	8 L per minute
Bath	Full	140 L
	Half full	80 L
Toilet	Single flush	12 L
	Dual half flush	3 L
Brushing Teeth	With tap on	5 L per minute
	With tap off	1 L per minute
Washing machine	Front loader	60 L
	Top loader	150 L
Car wash	With a hose	1000 L per hour

Courtesy of Yarra Valley Water

Sonia's family does 4 washes a week using a front loader.

Jack's family does 2 washes a week using a top loader washing machine. Who uses less water?

Sonia's family: $4 \times 60 = 240$ L
Jack's family: $2 \times 150 = 300$ L
So, Sonia's family uses 60 L less water than Jack's family.

Try this

1 How much water does Sonia's family use to wash their clothes in one year?

2 At $2.01 a kilolitre, how much will this water cost them?

VOLUME OF A RECTANGULAR PRISM

To find the volume of a rectangular prism, make sure all your measurements are the same unit.

This bath is about 1.3 m long, 60 cm wide and 0.3 m deep.

How much water do you need to fill the bath?

First convert 60 cm to m → 0.6 m

You know that 0.1 × 0.1 × 0.1 m cube has the same volume as 1 L of water. So you could find out how many litres the bath holds altogether.

The bath is 13 × 0.1 = **1.3 m long**

The bath is 6 × 0.1 = **0.6 m wide**

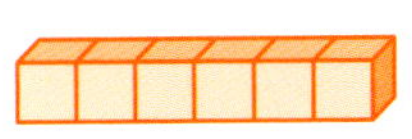

The whole bottom layer is **0.1 m high**.

This bottom layer has a volume of
1.3 × **0.6** × **0.1** = 0.078 m^3

This is the same volume as 13 × 6 × 1 = 78 L
There are 3 layers like this to the top of the bath.
3 × 0.078 = 0.234 m^3
Or 3 × 78 L = 234 L

A faster strategy is to use a calculator to multiply the length by width and then multiply this new number by the height.

1.3 × **0.6** × **0.3** = 0.234 m^3

But if you fill the bath too high, when you get into the bath you will overflow the water. Try filling it half full. So now you will have

$\frac{1}{2} \times 0.234\ m^3 = 0.117\ m^3$

So you will probably need 117 L of water for a bath.

VOLUME OF A RECTANGULAR PRISM
(continued)

Try this

Rex the Great Dane is about 0.95 m high, 1.4 m long and 0.3 m wide.

1 How big do you think his kennel should be? Why?

2 What is the volume of his kennel?

Challenge

Rex's friend is Belle the Chihuahua. Estimate her dimensions from her photograph. Then work out what you think her volume might be in m^3.

CUBIC CENTIMETRES

The **cubic centimetre** is used for measuring small volumes. It is also used to make scale models of larger objects. The symbol for a cubic centimetre is **cm^3**.

1 cm^3 displaces 1 mL of water
1000 cm^3 displaces 1 L of water

This cube is made from three layers of small cm^3 units. There are 27 units altogether. The volume is 27 cm^3.

This square pyramid is made from 5 layers of blocks. Each block has a volume of 1 cm^3.

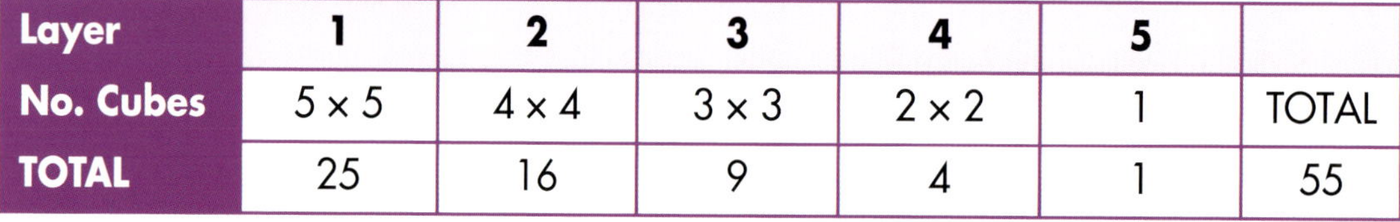

Layer	1	2	3	4	5	
No. Cubes	5 × 5	4 × 4	3 × 3	2 × 2	1	TOTAL
TOTAL	25	16	9	4	1	55

There are 55 cm^3 altogether. The volume is 55 cm^3.

When you calculate the volume of an object made from cubic centimetres, sometimes not all the blocks are shown. Sometimes blocks are hidden. Sometimes no blocks are shown. Use proportional reasoning to work out how many units are in each layer.

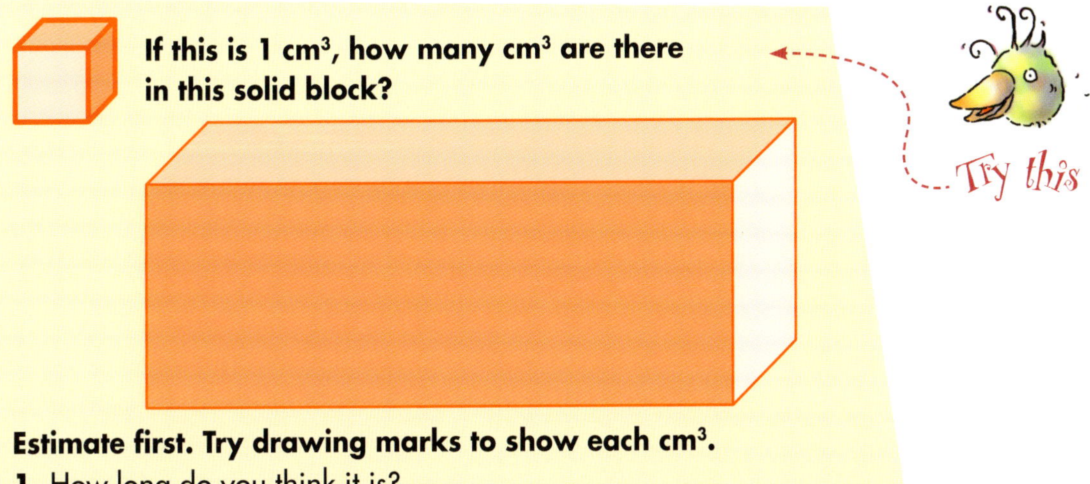

If this is 1 cm^3, how many cm^3 are there in this solid block?

Try this

Estimate first. Try drawing marks to show each cm^3.

1 How long do you think it is?
2 How deep do you think it is?
3 How high do you think it is?
4 What do you think the total volume is in cm^3?

How close was your estimate?
This block above is:

3 cm^3 deep 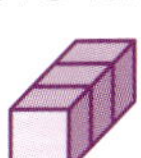 3 cm^3 high 

8 cm^3 long 

The volume of the bottom layer is:
3 × 8 blocks = 24 blocks.
The whole block is 3 layers high.
That's 24 + 24 + 24 = 3 × 24 = 72.
So the solid block has a volume of 72 cm^3.

This is what the model looks like when it is only partially built. How many blocks are missing?

Try this

MILLILITRES

The **millilitre** is the unit for measuring small volumes of liquids, such as shampoo, detergent or medicine. The symbol for a millilitre is **mL**.

1000 mL = 1 L

500 mL = 0.5 L

250 mL = 0.25 L

200 mL = 0.2 L

100 mL = 0.1 L

10 mL = 0.01 L

1 mL = 0.001 L

Shampoo and conditioner are on special this week. You get 25% more for the same price. Each bottle used to be 330 mL. The sale price is 2 for $10.50. About how much is that now for each 100 mL of shampoo and conditioner?

How many millilitres normally?	2 × 330 mL	= 660 mL
For 25% more	25% × 660	$= \frac{1}{4} \times 660$
		= 660 ÷ 4
		= 165 mL
Normal size plus 25%	660 + 165	= 825 mL
Price per mL	10.50 ÷ 825	= 1.27 cents
Price for 100 mL	100 × 1.27	= 127 cents

So the new price is about $1.30 for 100 mL.

You want to make triple quantities of Mango Punch for your birthday party.

One punnet of strawberries and one mango together have a volume of 600 mL.

1 How large a container will you need?

2 If one lemon makes 50 mL of juice, how many lemons will you need to buy?

3 If a glass holds 250 mL, how many glasses of punch can you serve?

Mango Punch

500 mL mango juice
250 mL orange juice
125 mL lemon juice
750 mL mineral water
1 punnet strawberries (sliced)
1 mango (peeled and chopped)
Fresh mint leaves

Mix all ingredients well. Pour into a large punch bowl. Sprinkle with mint leaves.

Challenge

Everyone at your party had three glasses of Punch each and between them drank it all. How many people were at your party?

Try this

CONVERTING MILLILITRES AND LITRES

You need 1000 mL before you get the same capacity as 1 L.
If you have fewer than 1000 mL you have a volume less than 1 L.

$495 \text{ mL} < 1 \text{ L}$

$\frac{495}{1000} \text{ L} < 1 \text{ L}$

$0.495 \text{ L} < 1 \text{ L}$

If you have more than 1000 mL you have a volume more than 1 L.

$4723 \text{ mL} > 1 \text{ L}$

$4 \text{ litres and } \frac{723}{1000} \text{ L} > 1 \text{ L}$

$4.723 \text{ L} > 1 \text{ L}$

Notice that there are different ways to record the same volume.
Always put the unit name after each number.

CONVERTING MILLILITRES AND LITRES (continued)

You have a 2.5 L jug to fill with fresh orange juice. One orange makes about 60 mL of juice. How many oranges will you need?

To convert **litres** to **millilitres**, multiply × 1000.

How many millilitres in 2.5 L?
This is more than 1 L, so there will be more than 1000 mL.
2.5 L = 2.5 × 1000 mL = 2500 mL
So, 2.5 L is the same volume as 2500 mL.

How many 60 mL in 2500 mL?
2500 ÷ 60 = 41.6
You will need 42 oranges to fill a 2.5 L jug with juice.

You buy a 250 mL sample pot of paint. If you can paint about 15 square metres with 1 L, how much area can you cover with 250 mL?

To convert **millilitres** to **litres**, divide by ÷ 1000.

How many litres in 250 mL?
This is less than 1000 mL, so there will be less than 1 L.

250 ÷ 1000 = 0.250 L = 0.25 L = $\frac{1}{4}$ of a litre
15 ÷ 4 = 3.75

You will be able to paint about 3.75 square metres with 250 mL of paint.

Circle the larger amount in each pair:
1 0.06 L or 50 mL
2 3.49 L or 2980 mL
3 1.5 L or 1459 mL

TIME

24-HOUR AND 12-HOUR TIME

One **24-hour time** period is called a day, even though it includes day and night. In the past, people broke this day into two parts with sunrise and sunset. Or they measured time in 12-hour units based on midnight and midday. We still use this 12-hour time system in Australia as well as 24-hour time.

A 24-hour time cycle starts at midnight with 00:00 and finishes just before the next midnight at 23:59, 23 hours and 59 minutes. The numbers in the 24-hour time system tell you what part of the day is being measured.

1 day = 24 hours = 24 h
= 1440 minutes = 1440 min
= 86 400 seconds = 86 400 s

This 24-hour clock reads 12:00 so it must be midday.

The first 12-hour time cycle starts at midnight and finishes at midday. The first group of 12 is the morning or am hours.
am is short for 'ante meridiem' or before midday

The second 12-hour cycle starts at midday and finishes at midnight. The second group of 12 is the afternoon and evening or pm hours. The am and pm can also be written without the dots.
pm is short for 'post meridiem' or after midday.

This 12-hour analogue clock reads 10:08 or 8 minutes past 10.
You cannot tell whether it is am or pm just by looking at the clock.
If you read it in the morning it is 10:08 am. If you read it in the evening it is 10:08 pm.

24-hour clock	12-hour clock
00:00	12:00 midnight
01:00	1:00 am
02:00	2:00 am
03:00	3:00 am
04:00	4:00 am
05:00	5:00 am
06:00	6:00 am
07:00	7:00 am
08:00	8:00 am
09:00	9:00 am
10:00	10:00 am
11:00	11:00 am
12:00	12:00 midday
13:00	1:00 pm
14:00	2:00 pm
15:00	3:00 pm
16:00	4:00 pm
17:00	5:00 pm
18:00	6:00 pm
19:00	7:00 pm
20:00	8:00 pm
21:00	9:00 pm
22:00	10:00 pm
23:00	11:00 pm

24-HOUR AND 12-HOUR TIME (continued)

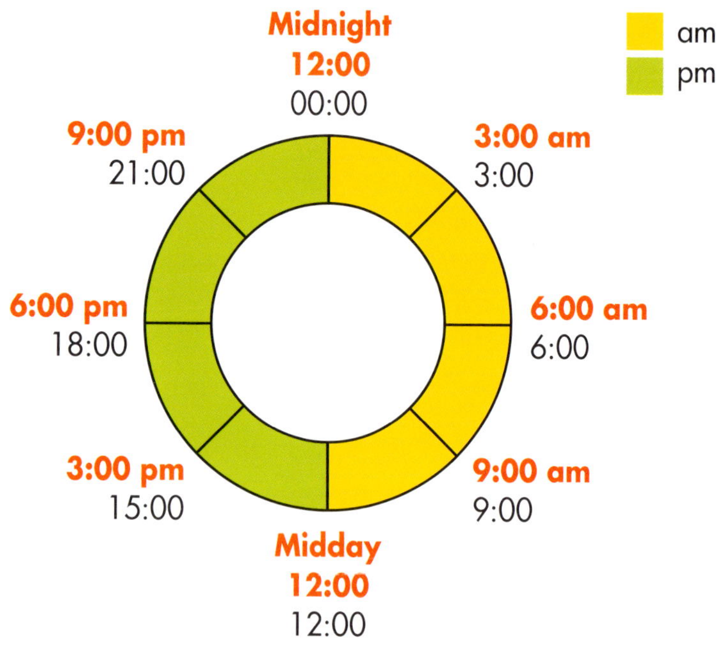

CONVERTING 24-HOUR TIME TO 12-HOUR TIME

A 24-hour time system is a more efficient way to communicate.

It is used all over the world in:

- airline flights
- military manoeuvres
- sporting timetables
- computers.

The funny thing is, in 24-hour time there is no 24:00. Once your 24-hour clock gets to 1 minute and 59 seconds before midnight, the next number is the start of a new cycle so it will show 00:00. Some timetables for convenience will show 24:00 for the end of a journey and 00:00 for the start of a journey. Or they show 23:59 or 00:01.

For times from 00:01 to 00:59, convert 24-hour time to 12-hour time by **adding 12 hours** and recording **am**.

This 24-hour clock reads 00:46.

That's 46 minutes past midnight.

In 12-hour time, this is 00:46 + 12 = 12:46 **am**.

For times from 1:00 until 11:59, convert 24-hour time to 12-hour time by just recording **am**.

For times from 12:00 **midday** until just before 12:59, convert 24-hour time to 12-hour time by just recording **pm**.

For times from 13:00 until just before 23:59, convert 24-hour time to 12-hour time by **subtracting 12 hours** and recording **pm**.

This 24-hour clock reads fifteen fifty-six.

You know it is after midday because it is more than 12.

This time is 15:56 – 12 = 3:56.

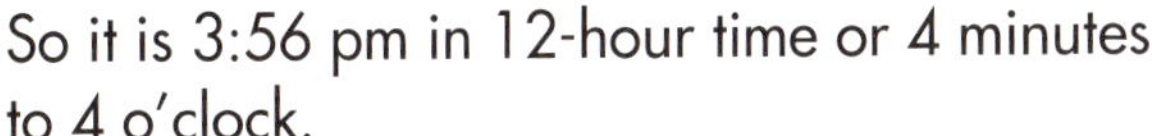

So it is 3:56 pm in 12-hour time or 4 minutes to 4 o'clock.

Record these times in both 24-hour and 12-hour time.

1

2

3

CONVERTING 12-HOUR TIME TO 24-HOUR TIME

The time shown on this watch is 8:24 or 24 minutes past 8. There is nothing to tell you whether it is am or pm.

If you arrange to meet your friends at 8:30, you will be far too early if you arrive at 8:30 am and they meant 8:30 pm. You will be far too late if you arrive at 8:30 pm and they meant 8:30 am.

Convert 12-hour time to 24-hour time to communicate with your friends more effectively.

For times from 12 midnight to 59 minutes later, convert 12-hour time to 24-hour time by **subtracting 12 hours**.

This 12-hour clock reads 12:45.

If it is night time, you can record this as 12:45 am.
In 24-hour time, this is 12:45 – 12 = 00:45
So it is 00:45 in 24-hour time.

From 1:00 am until just before 1:59 pm, 12-hour time and 24-hour time is identical. Just **remove the pm** symbol.

From 1:00 pm until just before midnight, convert 12-hour time to 24-hour time by **adding 12 hours** to all times.

This clock reads 8 minutes past 10.
If it is daytime, you can record this as 10:08 am.
So it is 10:08 in 24-hour time.
If it is night time, this time is 10:08 pm.
10:08 + 12 = 22:08
So it is 22:08 in 24-hour time.

Record the times on these clocks in both 12-hour and 24-hour time.

1

2

3

Try this

TIME ZONES

The Earth rotates on its axis in a 360° circle. It takes 24 hours to complete one rotation.

$360° \div 24 = 15°$

This means that every hour the Earth spins 15 degrees or $\frac{1}{24}$th of a circle. The whole world is divided into a system of 24 time zones, based on these 15° units. All places in the same time zone have the same time, except for some daylight saving differences.

The starting point traditionally is Greenwich in England. It is called Greenwich Mean Time or GMT. When this zone is 00:00, it is 8:00 am in Perth. Today clocks around the world are based on Universal Coordinated Time (UTC). UTC is the standard time for most internet and World Wide Web devices. But in everyday use, people still refer to GMT.

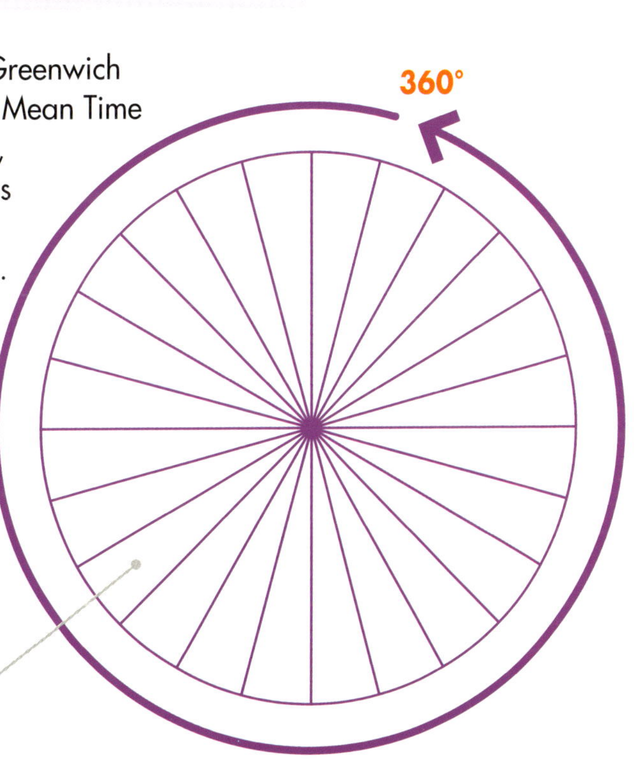

TIME ZONES (continued)

Australia lies within 3 time zones.

Australian Western Standard (AWST)

Australian Central Standard (ACST)

Australian Eastern Standard (AEST)

AEST = GMT + 10

ACST = GMT + $9\frac{1}{2}$

AWST = GMT + 8

This means it is 8:00 am all over Western Australia when it is 10:00 am in the Eastern Standard zone.

Daylight Saving Time

During Daylight Saving Time, it is 1 hour later to take advantage of the warmer weather, the early sunrise and later sunset. You turn your clock 1 hour ahead. It begins at 2:00 am on the first Sunday in October and usually ends at 2:00 am on the first Sunday in April. Western Australia, Queensland and the Northern Territory do not use Daylight Saving Time.

Converting between time zones

At 10:45 am on Saturday 12th December, you phone from Melbourne, Vic, to your Great Gran who lives in Fremantle, WA. What time is it for her?

Is it Daylight Saving Time? Yes.
Which zone are you in? Melbourne, Vic, is in the AEST zone.
Daylight Saving Time is AEST + 1.
Which zone is Great Gran in? Fremantle, WA, is in the AWST zone.
The time for Great Gran will be 10:45 – 3 hours.
That's 7:45 am. Will she be up then?

Complete this table using 24-hour time:

GMT	AWST	ACST	AEST
7:00			
	23:15		
		14:25	
			00:16

WRITING THE DATE

There are at least three different ways to record the date.

Christmas Day 2012 is on:

- Tuesday 25th December
- 25 December 2012
- 25.12.12.

In USA, they write the short date in a different order. They put the month first, then the day, then the year. So Christmas Day will be 12.25.12 in the USA.

July 2011 was an unusual month. There were 5 Fridays, 5 Saturdays and 5 Sundays. In Chinese culture this makes it a very lucky month.

Use the December 2012 calendar to answer these questions:

1. What is the 3rd Monday in December?
2. If it is Friday 7th, how many days until Tuesday 25th?
3. What day will it be on 4th January 2013?
4. If it is Monday 17th December, what was the date 3 Mondays ago?

December 2012						
Su	**M**	**T**	**W**	**Th**	**F**	**S**
30	31					1
2	3	4	5	6	7	8
9	10	11	12	13	14	15
16	17	18	19	20	21	22
23	24	25	26	27	28	29

Number of days in a month		
28/29 days	30 days	31 days
February	April	January
	June	March
	September	May
	November	July
		August
		October
		December

TIMETABLES

A transport timetable is a list of times or a table showing the departure and arrival time for buses, trains, ferries or planes.

City to Tarbar Train Timetable								
City	4:15 pm	4:30 pm	4:45 pm	5:00 pm	5:15 pm	5:30 pm	5:45 pm	6:00 pm
Burbank	4:29 pm	4:44 pm	4:59 pm	5:14 pm	5:29 pm	5:42 pm	5:59 pm	6:14 pm
Arion	4:47 pm	5:02 pm	5:17 pm	5:32 pm	5:47 pm	6:02 pm	6:17 pm	6:32 pm
Tarbar	5:03 pm	5:18 pm	5:33 pm	5:48 pm	6:03 pm	6:18 pm	6:33 pm	6:58 pm

Use a timetable to help you plan a travel itinerary.

You need to work out what time to leave home and what time you would like to arrive at your destination.

When do you need to leave home if it takes 13 minutes to walk to Burbank station and you want to catch the 5:29 train to Arion?

- You probably need to leave a 5-minute gap between arrival at the station and the train's departure.
- 13 + 5 = 18, so you need to leave 18 minutes before 5:29.
- 5:29 – 18 = 5:11, so you need to leave home no later than 5:11.

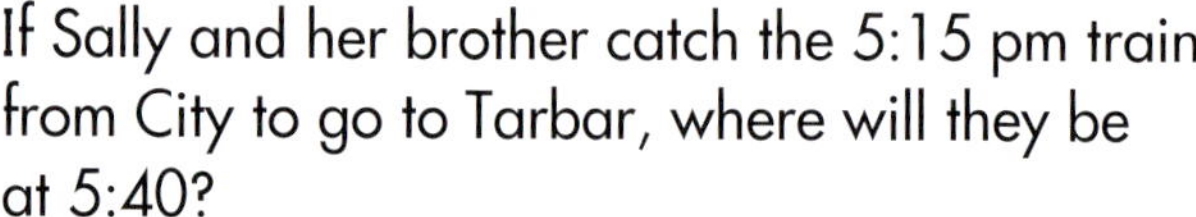

If Sally and her brother catch the 5:15 pm train from City to go to Tarbar, where will they be at 5:40?

Sally and her brother will be on the train between Burbank and Arion stations.

If Khi misses the 4:30 train from City, does he still have enough time to get to Tarbar by train before 5:30 pm?

The next train departs for Tarbar at 4:45 pm. It does not arrive in Tarbar until 5:33 pm. So Khi will be 3 minutes late.

Try this

Use this timetable about opening hours at the Blue Hardware store to write T (True) or F (False) to the statements below.

Blue Hardware EASTER Trading Hours	
THURSDAY 6 April	GOOD FRIDAY
9 am – 9 pm	Closed
SATURDAY 8 April	EASTER SUNDAY
8 am – 5 pm	10 am – 4 pm

1 The store is open between 15:00 and 16:00 on Sunday.

2 The store is closed between 13:00 and 17:00 on Saturday.

3 You cannot buy anything there between 7 and 9 am on Thursday.

Challenge

Write and solve three more problems using the City to Tarbar train timetable.

TIMELINES

A timeline is often a number line showing historical events in order.

Collect all the dates and events you want to show on your timeline in a list sorted from the earliest to the latest times.

History of hot air balloon flight from 1783 to 2012

1783 1st flight

1960 1st on board heat source

1991 Longest distance flight (7672 km)

Largest balloon flight (74 000 m^3)

2002 Shortest round-the-world flight (320 h 33 min)

2005 Highest flight (21 027 m)

TIMELINES (continued)

To work out an appropriate scale to use

- Find the difference between the 1st and the last dates.
  2005 – 1783 = 222
  This means you need a scale to represent 222 years.
- Decide the length of your time line in cm, for example about 12 cm
- Divide the number of years by this number.
  222 ÷ 12 =18.5
  This can be rounded to the nearest 10 years.
  This means that 1 cm represents about 20 years.

To use this scale with your facts:

- Start the timeline with the earliest event. 1783 = 0
- 1960 – 1783 = 177 and 177 ÷ 20 = 8.85, so 1960 will be at the 8.85 cm mark.
- 1991 – 1783 = 208 and 208 ÷ 20 = 10.4, so 1991 will be at the 10.4 cm mark.
- Continue calculating like this until your time line is complete.

History of Balloon Flight

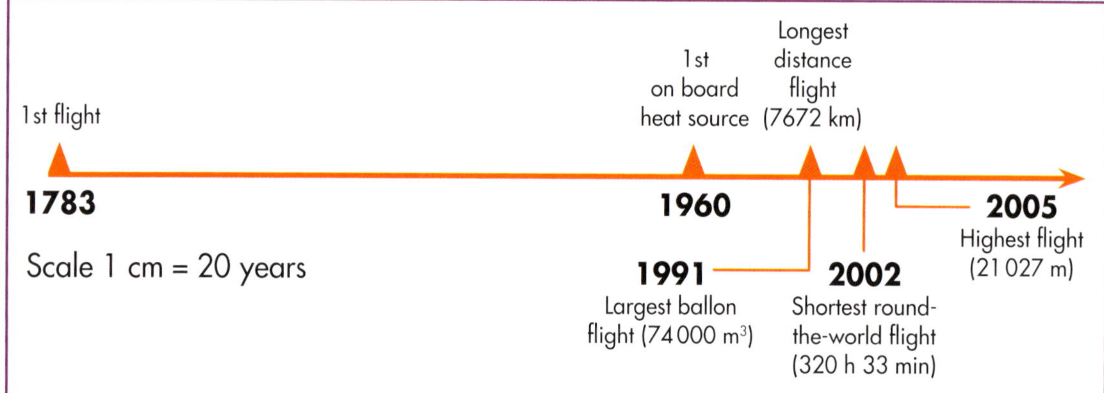

Challenge

Create your own 'History of the Mobile Phone' timeline to show these events:

1876 1st long distance phone call
1880 1st wireless telephone call
1927 1st video phone call
1935 1st round-the-world phone call
1961 1st public touch phone
1973 1st hand-held mobile phone call (Motorola)
2007 1st iPhone

3D PRISMS & PYRAMIDS

Prisms are 3D **solids** with flat faces, or planes. Prisms have one pair of parallel bases joined by rectangles. Prisms are named by the shape of their bases.

Pyramids are 3D solids with flat faces, or planes. You describe pyramids by their base, just like prisms. But pyramids have only one base. Pyramids have triangular faces. These triangular faces always meet at one point, one **apex** or **vertex**.

A **skeleton model** shows the **edges** and vertices of a prism or a pyramid. The faces are invisible. Construct a skeleton model of a prism or a pyramid using sticks, straws or toothpicks for the edges. Join the corners together using blu tac or small spheres such as soaked dried peas.

These nine sticks and six small spheres can be rearranged to construct a skeleton model of a triangular prism.

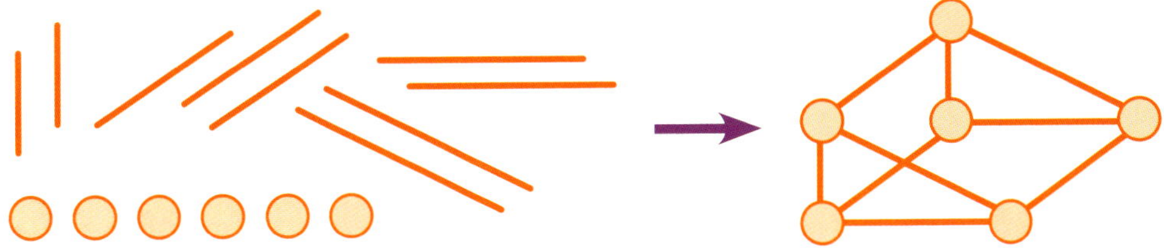

A **net** shows only the **faces** of a prism or a pyramid. It is a 2D representation that can be drawn on card or paper, cut out and folded up to construct a 3D model.

These faces can be rearranged to create the net of this 3D object.

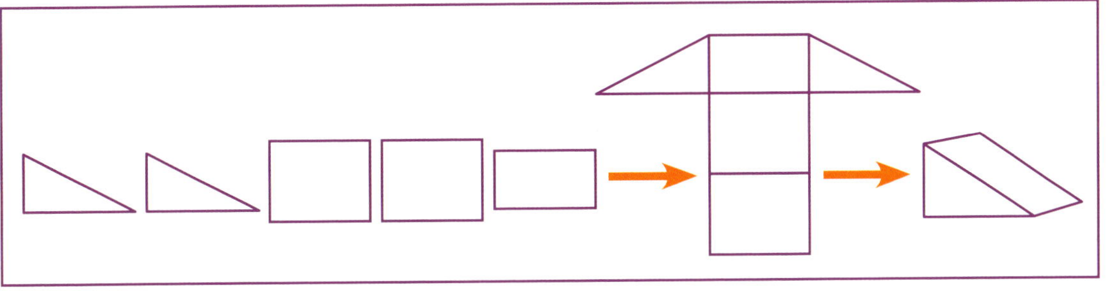

TRIANGULAR PRISMS AND TRIANGULAR PYRAMIDS

	Triangular Prism	Triangular Pyramid
Real life example		
Shape of base	triangle	triangle
Number of faces	5	4
Number of vertices	6	4
Number of edges	9	6
Number of curved surfaces	0	0
Skeleton model		
Example of a 2D net		
Sketch from different angles	at an angle front bottom	at an angle top front

The base triangle can be a scalene, isosceles, right-angle, obtuse or equilateral triangle.

Name these 3D objects. Draw one of them from at least three different viewpoints.

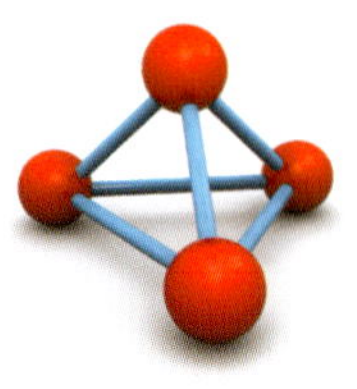

RECTANGULAR PRISMS AND RECTANGULAR PYRAMIDS

	Rectangular Prism	Rectangular Pyramid
Real life example		
Shape of base	rectangle	rectangle
Number of faces	6	5
Number of vertices	8	5
Number of edges	12	8
Number of curved surfaces	0	0
Skeleton model		
Example of a 2D net		
Sketch from different angles	at an angle; front; top	at an angle; top; front

A prism with a square base can also be called a square prism. A cube is a square prism that has every face a square. It is the only regular prism. If a pyramid has a square base it is called a square pyramid.

Try this

Name these 3D objects. Draw one of them from at least three different viewpoints.

OTHER COMMON 3D PRISMS AND PYRAMIDS

Shape	Faces	Vertices	Edges
Pentagonal prism	7 faces (2 pentagons, 5 rectangles)	10 vertices	15 edges
Pentagonal pyramid	6 faces (1 pentagon, 5 triangles)	6 vertices	10 edges
Hexagonal prism	8 faces (2 hexagons, 6 rectangles)	12 vertices	18 edges
Hexagonal pyramid	7 faces (1 hexagon, 6 triangles)	7 vertices	12 edges
Octagonal prism	10 faces (2 octagons, 8 rectangles)	16 vertices	24 edges
Octagonal pyramid	9 faces (1 octagon, 8 triangles)	9 vertices	16 edges

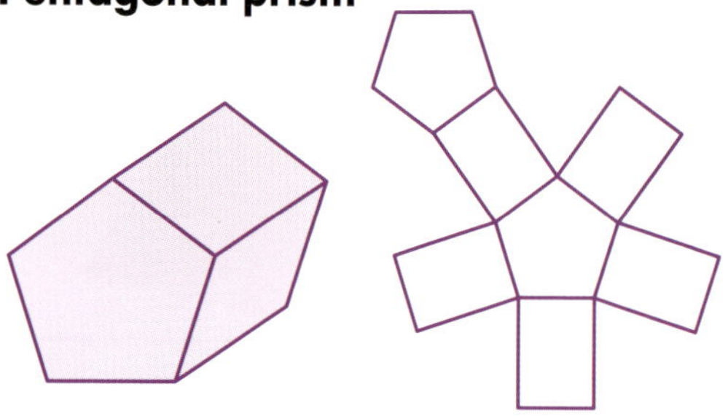

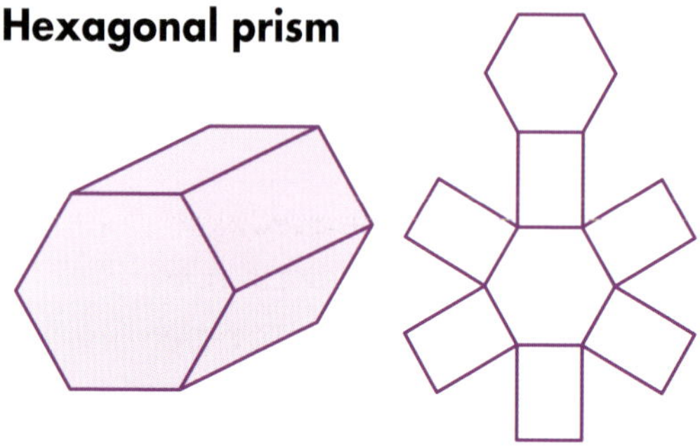

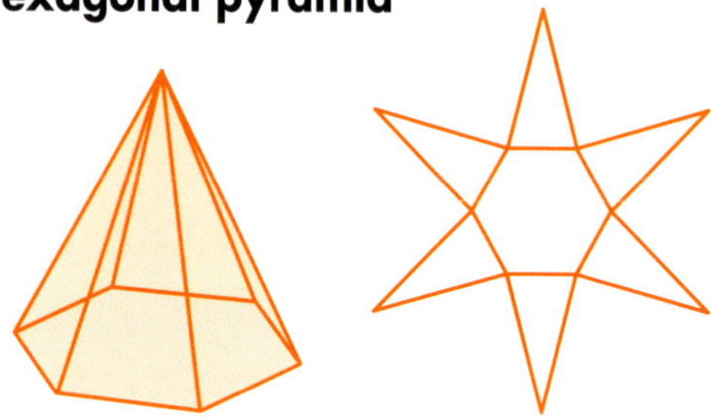

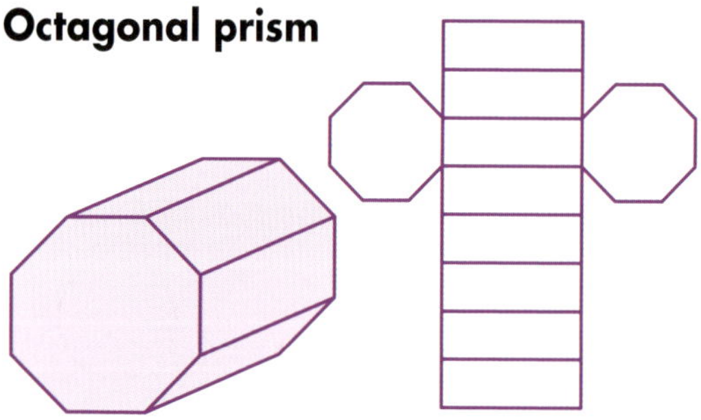

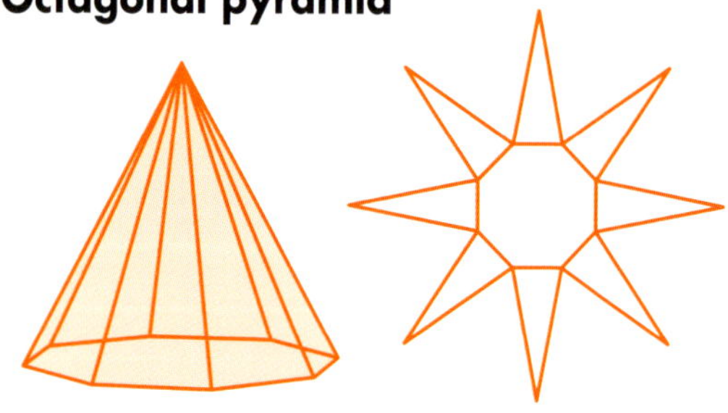

The world's tallest pentagonal prism building is the Baltimore World Trade centre designed by IM Pei

Construct one of these 3D objects, from the table above, using small spheres and sticks. Try small pieces of plasticine and toothpicks.

CYLINDERS AND CONES

	Cylinder	Cone
Real life example		
Shape of base	circle	circle
Number of faces	2	1
Number of vertices	0	1
Number of edges	2	1
Number of curved surfaces	1	1
Skeleton model	It is too difficult to make a skeleton model of a cylinder because it has a circular base.	It is too difficult to make a skeleton model of a cone because it has a circular base.
Example of a 2D net		
Sketch from different angles	at an angle, side, bottom	front, bottom

Try this

Name these 3D objects. Draw one of them from at least three different viewpoints.

PLATONIC SOLIDS

These solids are named after Plato, who was a famous Greek mathematician 2400 years ago.

These are the only five **regular 3D solids** in the whole universe. These amazing solids each have identical faces and vertices.

No matter which way you turn them, they look the same shape and size.

tetrahedron

hexahedron

octahedron

dodecahedron

icosahedron

Complete this Platonic Solids fact table.

Name of Platonic Solid	Tetrahedron (triangular pyramid)	Hexahedron (cube)	Octahedron	Dodecahedron	Icosahedron
Shape of all faces					Equilateral triangle
Number of faces (F)					20
Number of vertices (V)				20	12
Number of edges (E)				30	30

Challenge

Look at the octahedron. Imagine it unfolding and lying flat as a 2D net. Draw what you think the net of an octahedron looks like.

EULER'S RULE

Euler was a famous Swiss mathematician who discovered a pattern rule linking the number of faces, vertices and edges in any 3D solid with flat faces.

Look at the number of faces and vertices in the Platonic Solids fact table. Then look at the number of edges. Can you discover a pattern?

Euler discovered a pattern rule that works for all **polyhedra**:

F (faces) + **V** (vertices) = **E** (edges) + 2

Another way of saying this is the number of edges is always 2 less than the number of faces and vertices combined.

An icosahedron has 20 faces and 12 vertices. You can use Euler's pattern rule to work out how many edges there must be.

$\mathbf{20} + \mathbf{12} = \square + 2.$

$32 = \square + 2$

So $\square = 30$

An icosahedron has 30 edges.

So if you know how many faces and vertices there are, you can calculate the number of edges without actually counting them.

Try this

1 A rectangular prism has 6 faces and 8 vertices. Without looking at a model, use Euler's pattern rule to work out how many edges there must be.
2 A 9-sided nonagonal pyramid has 10 faces and 10 vertices. How many edges does it have?

Challenge

Investigate the table for 'Other common 3D prisms and pyramids'. Does Euler's pattern rule still work for these 3D objects?

MEASURING ANGLES

Over 4000 years ago, the ancient Mesopotamians thought that the Sun took 360 days to complete a full revolution of the sky. Today you still say that a complete turn, or one **revolution**, is 360°.

Angles measure the amount of turn between two straight lines (arms or rays), joined at a vertex or a point. Angles are measured in **degrees**. You draw a curved line near the vertex to highlight the angle.

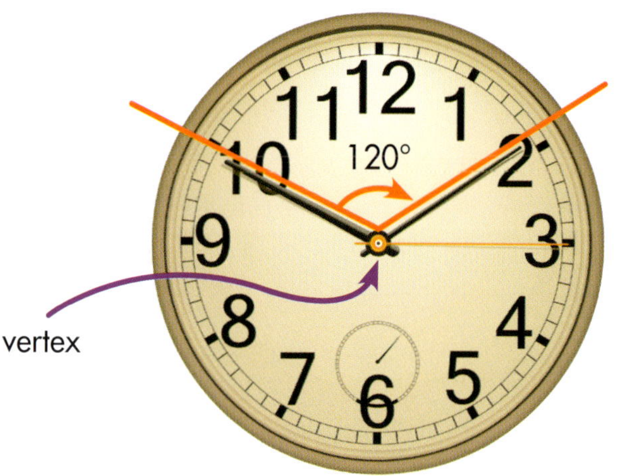

When the two arms are together at the start, there is no angle.

When one arm makes a full turn, the angle is 360°.

USING A 180° PROTRACTOR

A **protractor** is a device to help you accurately measure and draw angles. A 180° protractor is a semi-circular shape with two scales that divide the shape into degrees from 0° to 180°.

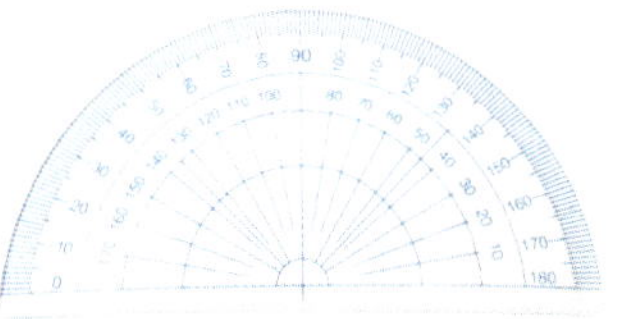

The centre is halfway between the 0° and 180° marks. Line up the 0° and 180° straight angle on your protractor along one arm of the angle that you are measuring.

One scale starts at 0° on the left and finishes at 180° on the right. Use this to measure angles with a vertex on the right. The other scale starts at 0° on the right and finishes at 180° on the left. Use this to measure angles with a vertex on the left.

All measurements start by placing the centre mark along the bottom edge of the protractor over the vertex of an angle to be measured.

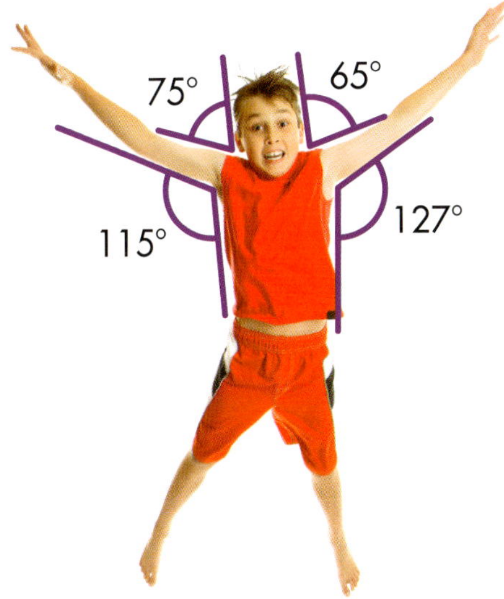

USING A 360° PROTRACTOR

A 360° protractor is a circular shape with two scales that divide the shape into degrees from 0° to 360°.

This is a useful device for measuring angles larger than 180°. The centre is halfway between the 0° and 180° marks. It has two scales. One scale starts at 0° and goes clockwise to 360°. The other scale starts at 0° and goes anti-clockwise to 360°.

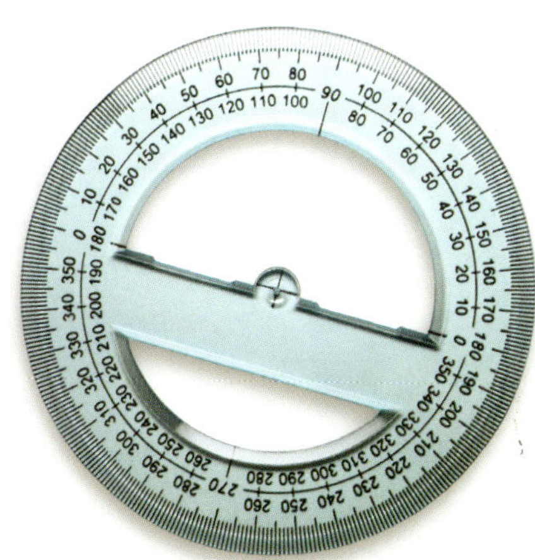

USING A 360° PROTRACTOR (continued)

To measure an angle, place the centre of the protractor over the vertex of the angle you want to measure. Line up the 0° and 180° straight angle on your protractor along one arm of the angle.

Check whether you need to use the clockwise or the anticlockwise scale.

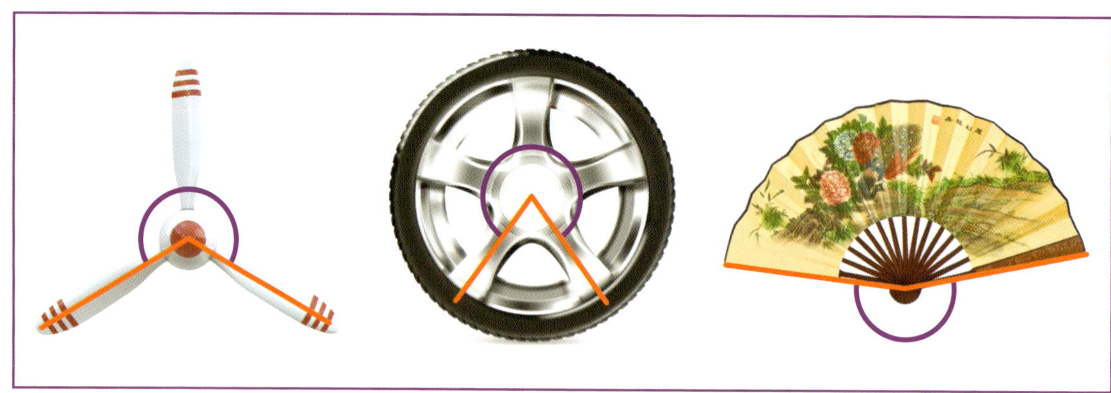

Try this

Use a 180° or 360° protractor to measure the angles marked.

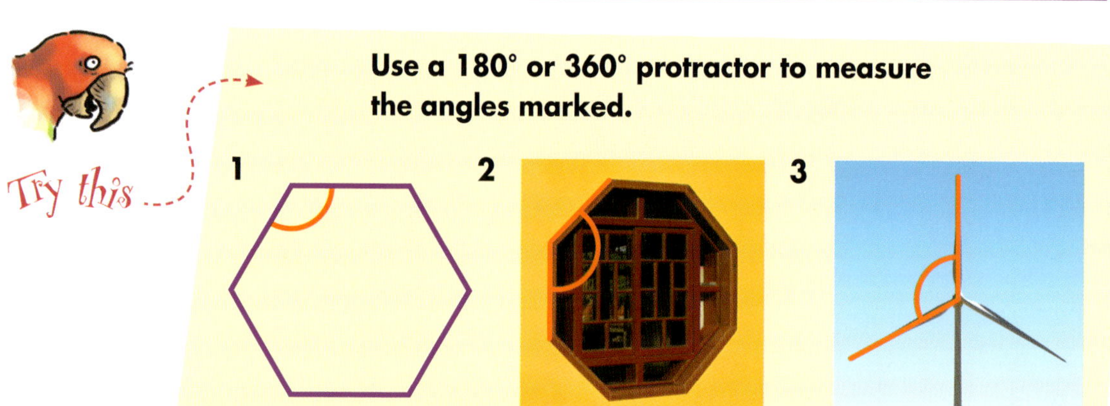

Challenge

Look at this circle of 3 leaf clover cards. An invisible arm joins the ace and the dot. If you rotate this arm clockwise, which card is at 25°? Which card is at 135°? Which card is at 305°?

CONSTRUCTING AN ANGLE

Use a 180° or a 360° protractor, a ruler and a pencil to draw an angle up to 180°.

For example, to draw an angle of 60°, first draw your fixed **ray**. A ray can be any length and in any direction you want.

1. Place a mark where you want the vertex to be.
2. Place the centre mark of your protractor exactly over the vertex mark, lining up the 0° and 180° line along the ray.
3. Read the scale that starts at 0° on the right and finishes at 180° on the left.
4. Find 60° and make a pencil mark at that spot.
5. Draw a straight line from the vertex through the marked point. This line can be any length.
6. Record the size of the angle and draw in the curved angle marker.

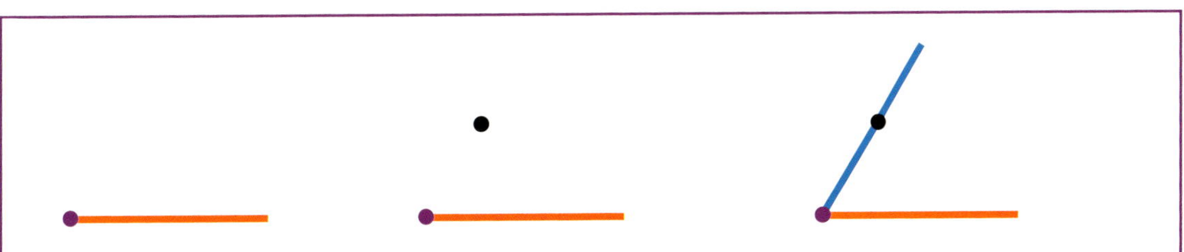

Use a 360° protractor to draw a reflex angle, for example 290°. If you do not have a 360° protractor, then subtract 290° from 360° to get 70°. Use a 180° protractor to draw this acute angle of 70°. Once you do this, you have automatically drawn the matching reflex angle of 290°.

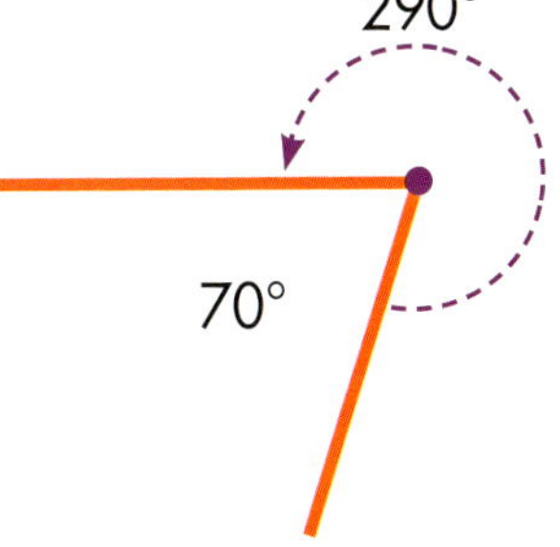

Try this

Draw the following angles.

1 85° **2** 135° **3** 285°

TYPES OF ANGLES

Name of angle	Description	Example*	Real-life example
Acute (less than a quarter turn)	More than 0°, less than 90°	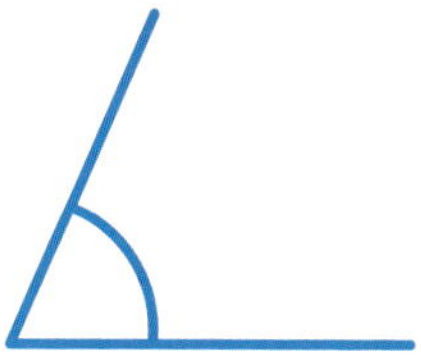	
Right (quarter turn)	Exactly 90° (draw a small square at the vertex to show it is exactly 90°)	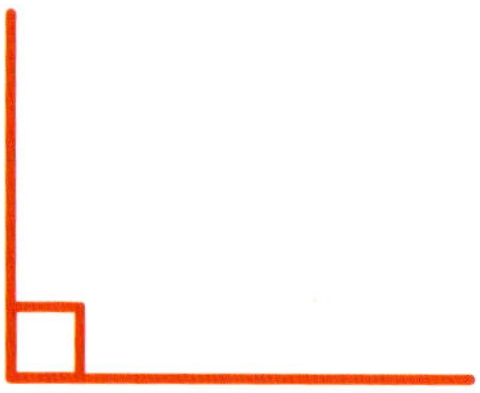	
Obtuse (more than a quarter turn)	More than 90°, less than 180°	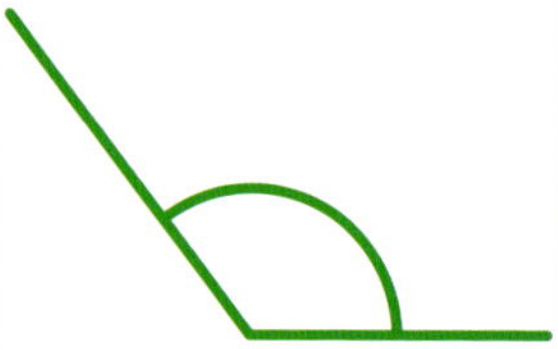	
Straight (half turn)	Exactly 180°		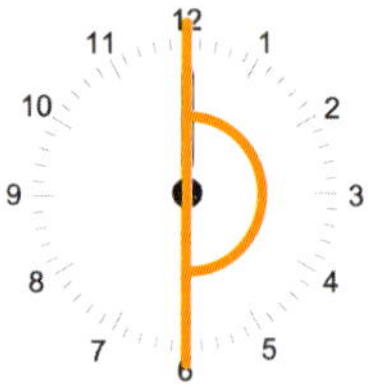
Reflex (more than a half turn)	More than 180°, less than 360°		
Revolution (full turn)	Exactly 360°	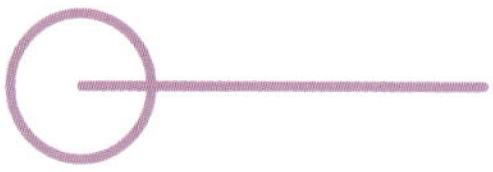	

* Each angle has a small curved line near the vertex to highlight the angle

Try this

Estimate in degrees first, then use a protractor to measure the angles shown in these photographs.

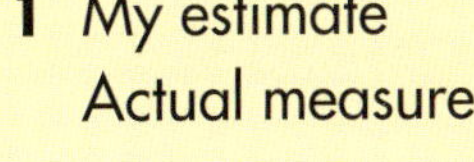

1 My estimate
Actual measure

2 My estimate
Actual measure

3 My estimate
Actual measure

4 My estimate
Actual measure

ANGLES ON A STRAIGHT LINE

A **straight angle** is half a full turn, or 180°. So if another line intersects a straight line to create two angles, these two angles will always add to exactly 180°.

You can use this fact to solve problems. If you know the size of one angle, you can easily work out the size of the other angle without measuring. Just subtract the known angle from 180°.

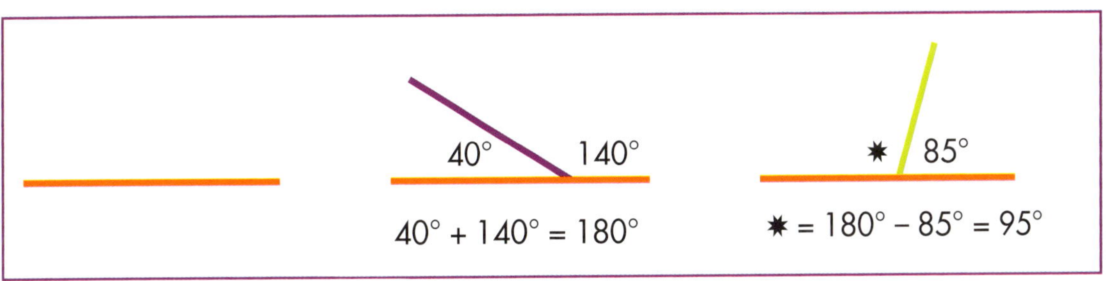

ANGLES ON A STRAIGHT LINE (continued)

Try this

Work out the size of each missing angle without using your protractor.

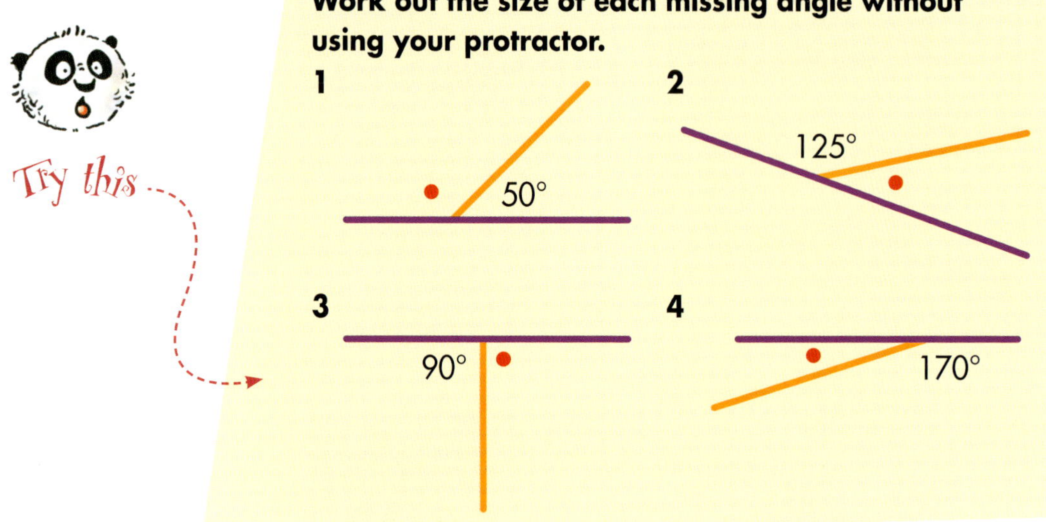

Challenge

What angle will you tell the carpenter to make each of these window panes if they are all the same size?

COMPLEMENTARY ANGLES

Complementary angles add to 90°. They are any two angles that make a right-angle. They do not have to be side by side.

63°
27°

63° + 27° = 90°

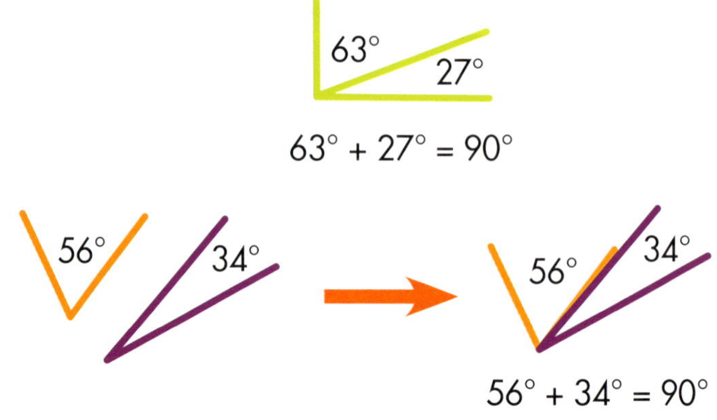

SUPPLEMENTARY ANGLES

Supplementary angles add to 180°. They are any two angles that make a straight angle. They do not have to be side by side.

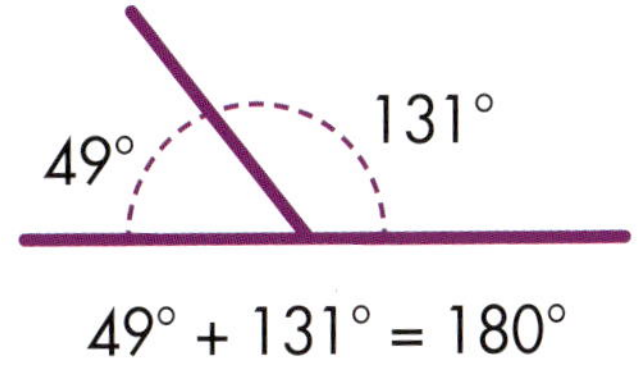

$49° + 131° = 180°$

Use your understanding of complementary and supplementary angles to work out and record the missing angles.

1

115° ●

2

89° ●

3

● 42°

CO-INTERIOR ANGLES

Co-interior angles are formed when two straight lines are crossed by a third straight line. Interior means inside. Co-interior means inside together.

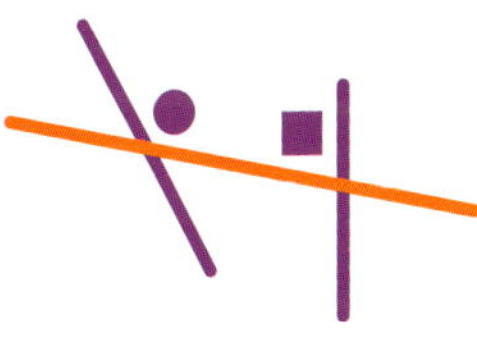

Angles ● and ■ are co-interior angles. They are above the orange line but inside the two purple lines.

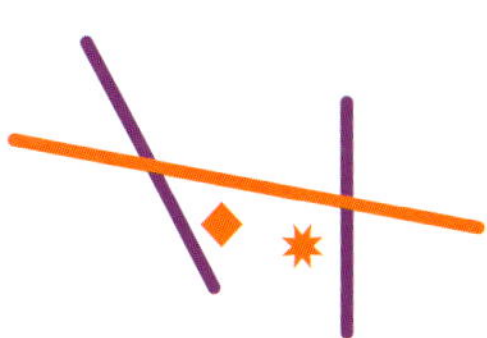

Angles ◆ and ✸ are also co-interior angles. They are below the orange line but inside the two purple lines.

CORRESPONDING ANGLES

Corresponding angles are also formed when two straight lines are crossed by a third straight line. They are in a similar position either above or below the intersecting line.

Angles ● and ■ are corresponding angles. They are both above the orange line. They are both to the right of the other two lines.

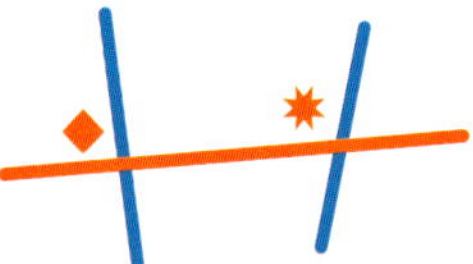

Angles ◆ and ✷ are corresponding angles. They are both above the orange line. They are both to the left of the other two lines.

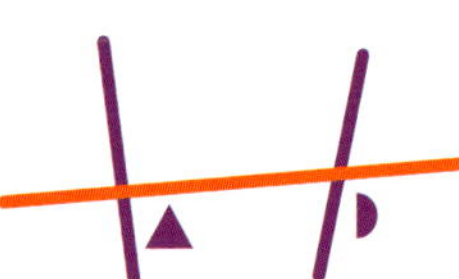

Angles ▲ and ◗ are corresponding angles. They are both below the orange line. They are both to the right of the other two lines.

Angles ★ and ❖ are corresponding angles. They are both below the orange line. They are both to the left of the other two lines.

Here is a section from this town plan showing intersecting roads. Mark two pairs of co-interior angles. Mark two pairs of corresponding angles.

ANGLES AT A POINT

A revolution is a full turn, or 360°. If you have two straight lines meeting at a point, the sum of both angles will always be 360°.

If you know the size of one angle, you can easily work out the size of the other angle without measuring. Just subtract the known angle from 360°.

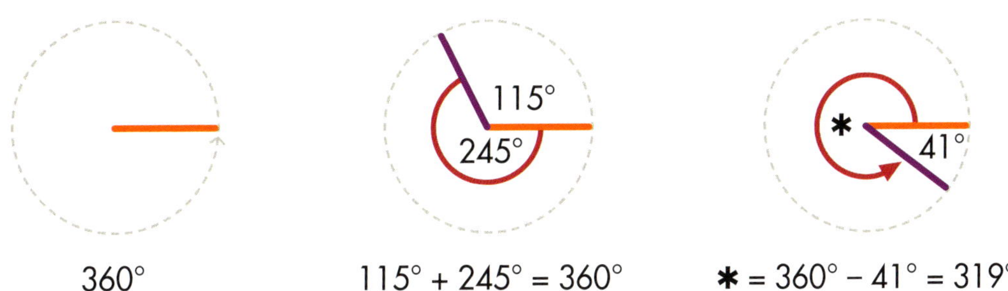

360°

115° + 245° = 360°

* = 360° – 41° = 319°

If you have more than two straight lines meeting at a point, the sum of all the angles will still be 360°. To find your missing angle, just add up all the other known angles and subtract the total from 360°.

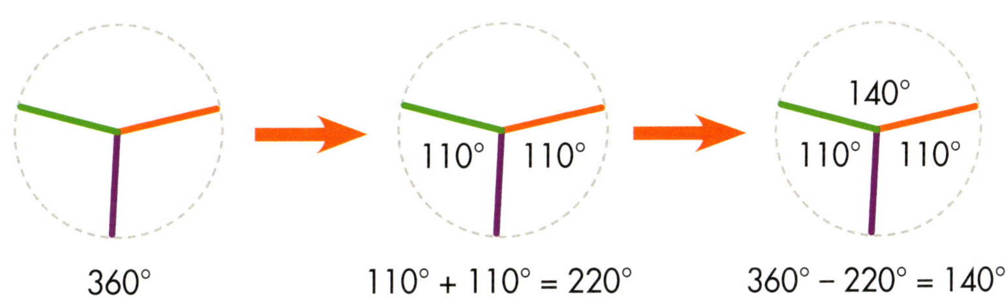

360°

110° + 110° = 220°

360° – 220° = 140°

Use your protractor to work out the size of each missing angle.

1

2

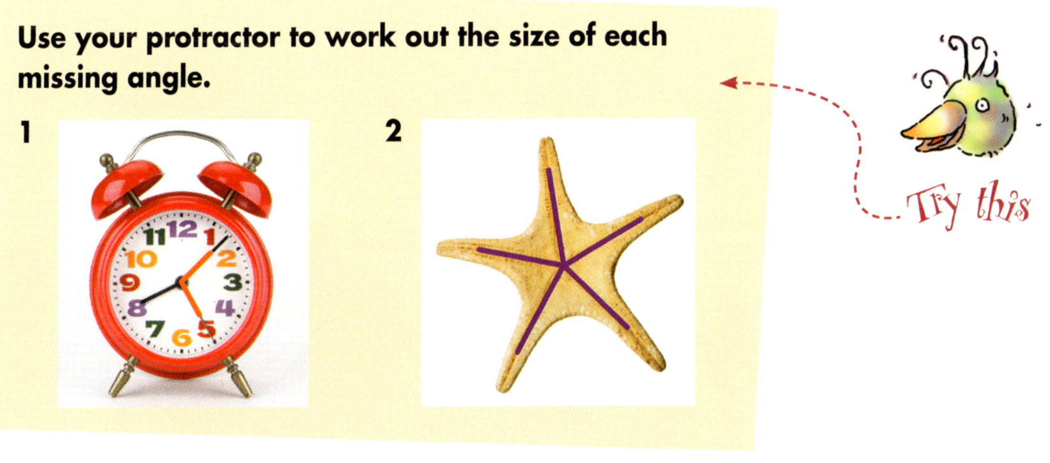

VERTICALLY OPPOSITE ANGLES

When any two straight lines intersect, or cross over, four angles are created. You can label these with alphabet letters **a**, **b**, **c** and **d**. The amazing thing is that the opposite pairs of angles are the same size.

- Angles **a** and **c** match
- Angles **b** and **d** match

These matching pairs are called **vertically opposite angles**.

Angles **a** and **c** are both 50°.
Angles **b** and **d** are both 130°.

You can use this fact to solve problems. If there is one missing angle, you can easily work out the size without measuring. To find your missing angle, just look for any vertically opposite angles.

Angle **a** must be 32°.
Angle **b** must be 148°.

Remember that all four angles will always add to 360°. When two straight lines intersect, you can use this fact to work out the size of all four angles if you are given just one angle. You can label these four angles with shapes ●, ■, ◆ and ✷.

If ● = 85° then ◆ must also equal 85° as it is a vertically opposite angle. The angles at a point always add to 360°, so the vertically opposite angles ■ and ✷ must equal 360° – (2 × 85°) or 360° – 170° = 190°
Together ■ and ✷ = 190°
So each angle must be half that or 95°

Use your understanding of angles at a point and vertically opposite angles to work out and record the size of each angle.

1

2

TRANSFORMING 2D SHAPES

Two-dimensional shapes can be repeated, divided and rearranged to make new shapes, designs or patterns.

A **design** is where random shapes, colours and sizes are put together however you want. You can't predict where each piece will go.

A **pattern** is where shapes, colours and sizes are put together in a way that can be predicted. It is not random. You repeat a design at least once.

A **tessellation** is where all of an area is covered with one or more shapes that fit together with no gaps and no overlaps.

A **transformation** is where 2D shapes are repeated using flips, slides and turns. When you transform a shape, it stays the same shape and size but may change direction.

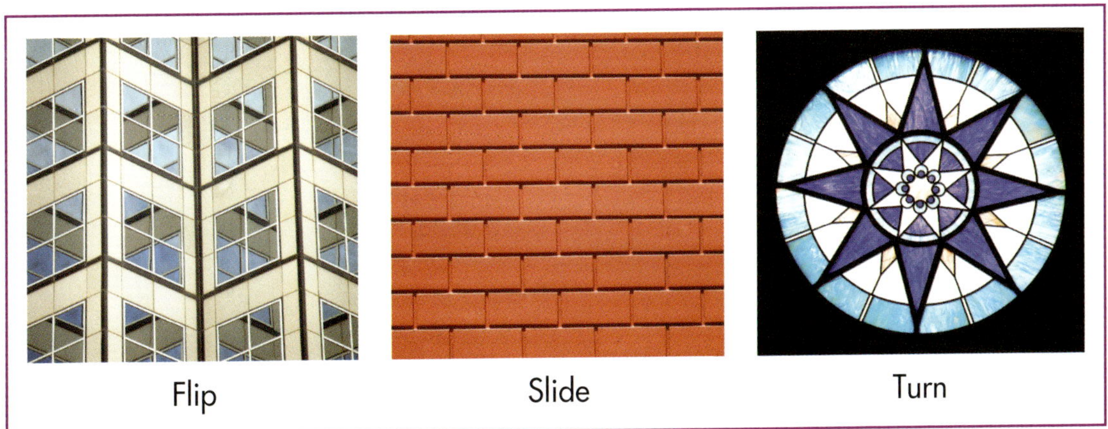

TRANSFORMING 2D SHAPES (continued)

You can also transform 2D shapes by enlarging or reducing them. When you do this the shape still stays the same but the size gets larger or smaller.

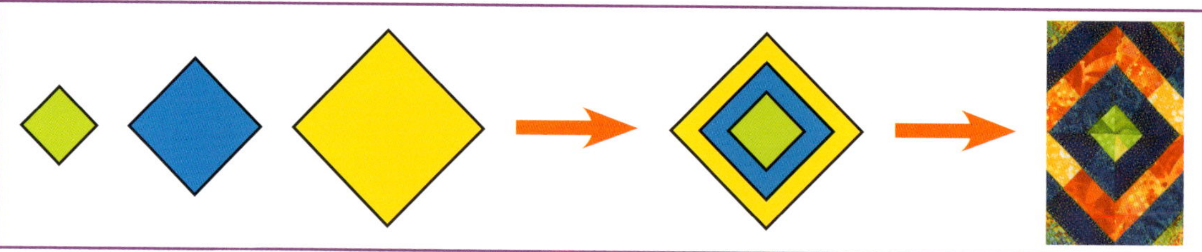

REFLECTIONS OR FLIPS

To make a **flip** pattern, take an exact copy of your first shape or design and reflect it across an **axis of symmetry**.

A flip creates a mirror image or **reflection** of the original shape or design. A flip can be in any direction.

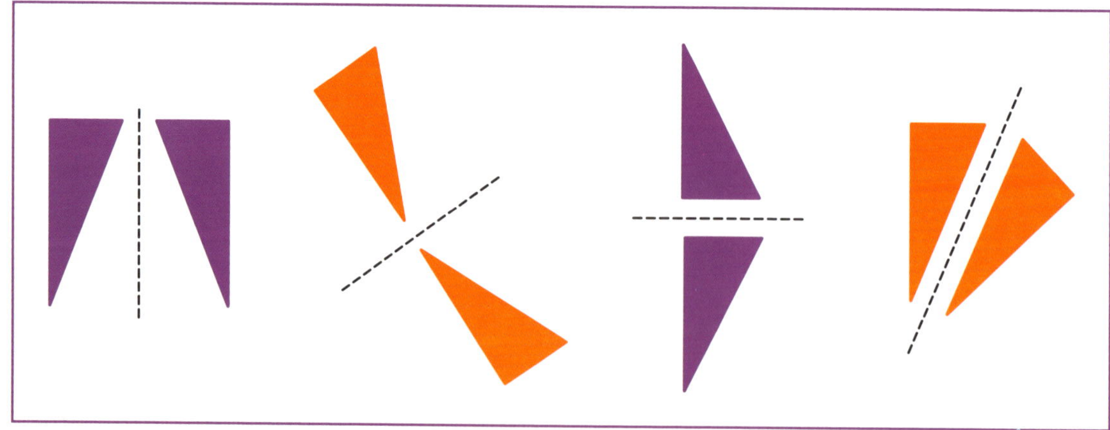

The second shape is now facing in the opposite direction to the first shape. You have created a new shape or part of a pattern. Your pattern is now **symmetrical**.

Look closely at different parts of each flipped shape to notice what happens to each side or each corner. As you get better at flipping shapes, try to predict what the reflection will look like in your mind before reflecting the shape.

You can flip your shapes more than once. You can trace around them on paper to make a permanent pattern.

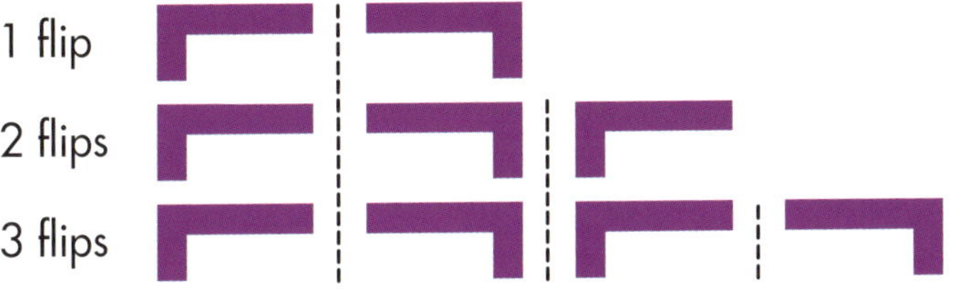

Some shapes look the same when they have been reflected across an axis of symmetry.

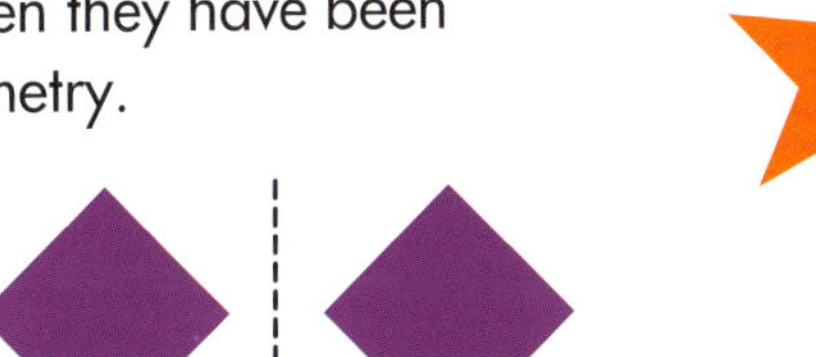

Try this

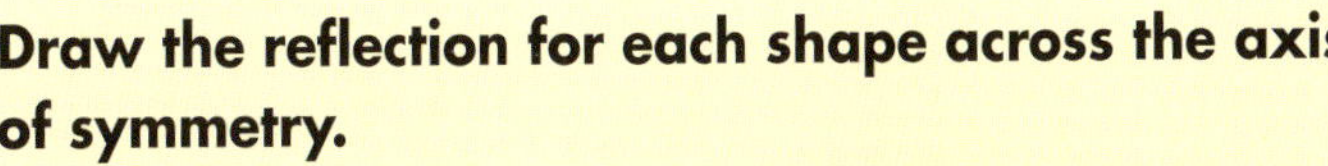

Draw the reflection for each shape across the axis of symmetry.

TRANSLATIONS OR SLIDES

To make a **slide** pattern, keep taking an exact copy of your first shape or design and slide it without flipping it or turning it.

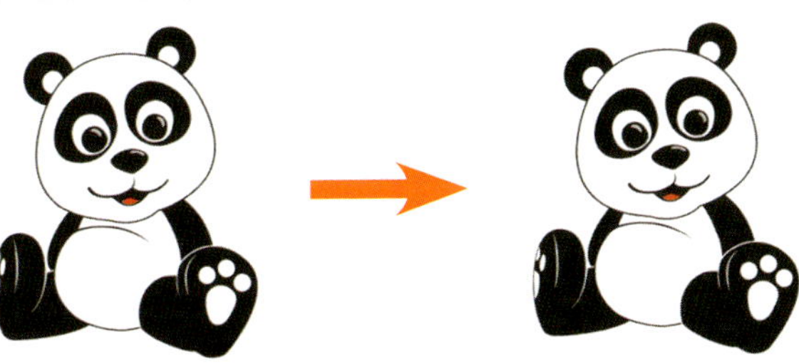

TRANSLATIONS OR SLIDES (continued)

This is called a **translation**. You have created a new shape or part of a pattern.

In a translation, you can overlap shapes as you slide.

Each new shape is still facing the same direction as the first shape.

If you rotate or flip your shape, then it is no longer a slide.

More examples of translation patterns:

Draw a slide pattern by repeating this shape without flipping or turning.

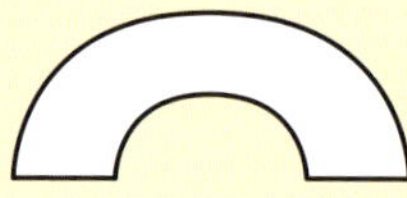

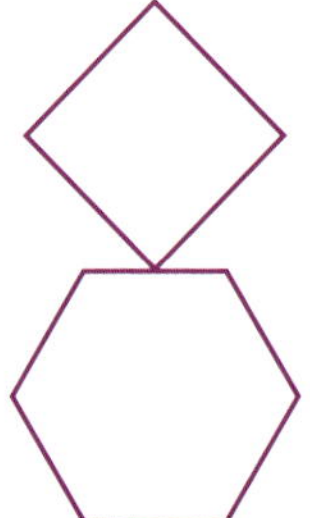

Challenge

Draw a slide pattern by repeating this shape without flipping or turning.

ROTATIONS OR TURNS

To make a **rotation** pattern, turn shapes or designs around a point and copy them in the new position.

To rotate **clockwise** means to turn a shape or design in the same direction as the hands of a clock.

To rotate **anti-clockwise**, or counter-clockwise, means to turn a shape or design in the opposite direction as the hands of a clock.

To make a rotation pattern:

1 Decide where your turning point will be.
2 Decide the rotation angle. This can be between 1° and 180°. A common rotation angle is a quarter turn or 90°.
3 Copy your first shape, and then turn your shape clockwise or anti-clockwise around the turning point.
4 Trace each new position.

More examples of rotation patterns:

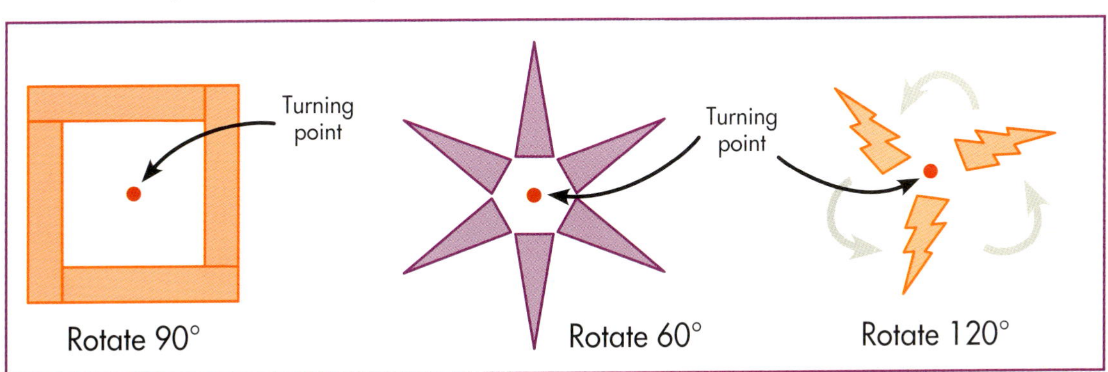

ROTATIONS OR TURNS (continued)

Other examples of real-life rotation patterns:

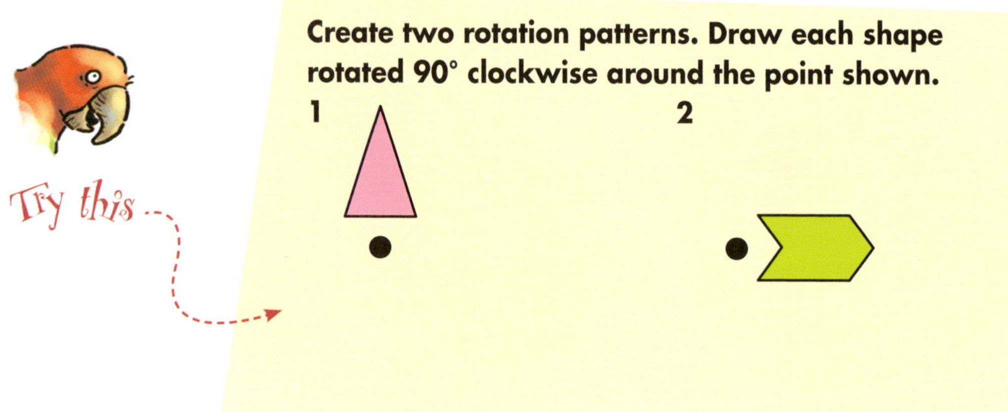

LINE SYMMETRY

A shape, drawing or photo has **line symmetry** if one half is a reflection of the other half. The line cuts the shape into two equal halves or mirror images. The line of symmetry is also called a **mirror line**.

If you can fold the shape along this mirror line each part of one side will match the other side exactly. The line of symmetry can go in any direction.

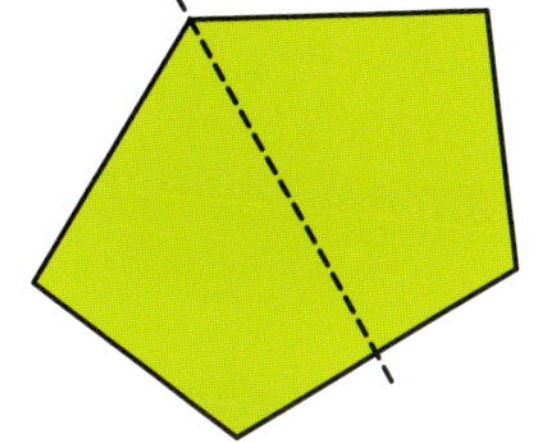

Some shapes, drawings or photos have no line of symmetry. There are no matching halves.

Some shapes and patterns have more than 1 line of symmetry.

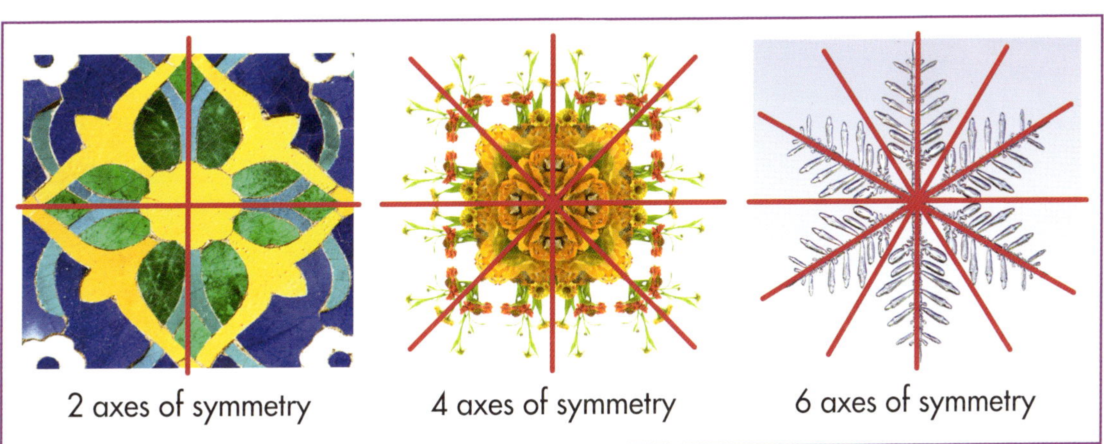

2 axes of symmetry | 4 axes of symmetry | 6 axes of symmetry

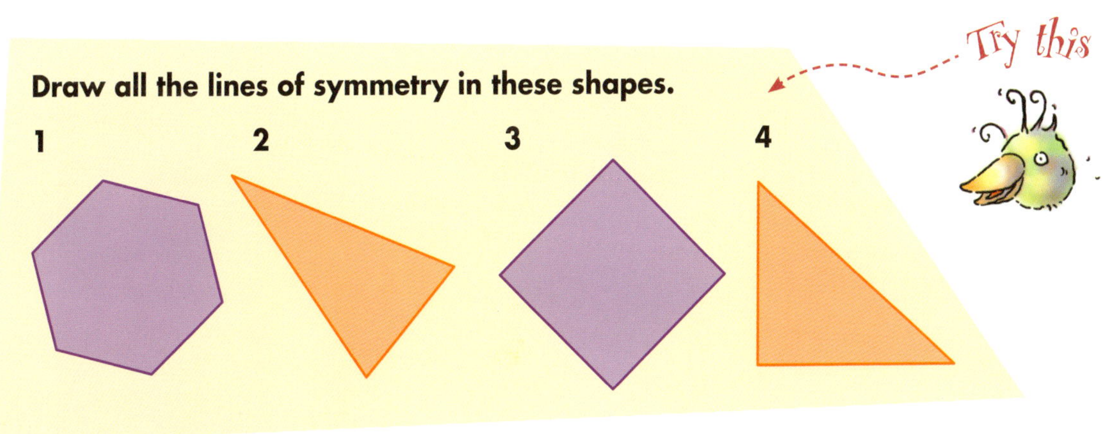

Draw all the lines of symmetry in these shapes.

1 **2** **3** **4**

ROTATIONAL SYMMETRY

If a shape is rotated about its centre and it matches itself at least once within this turn, you say the shape has **rotational symmetry**.

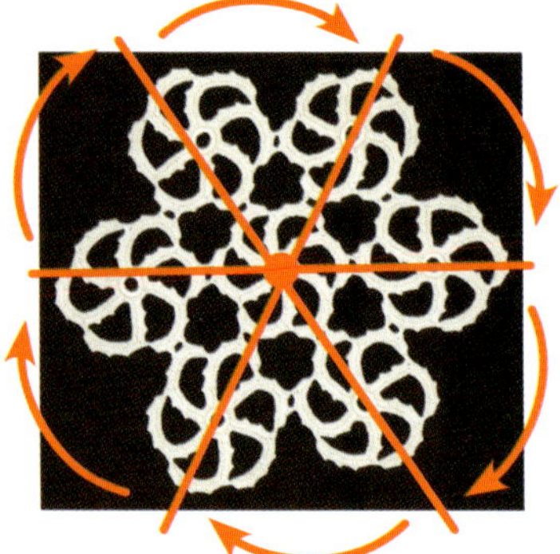

The **order of rotation** is how many times the shape or design matches itself exactly at a point within a full turn of 360°. Start at the top then visualise rotating the shape. Count how many times you would see the shape matching itself.

3 matches in 360°

5 matches in 360°

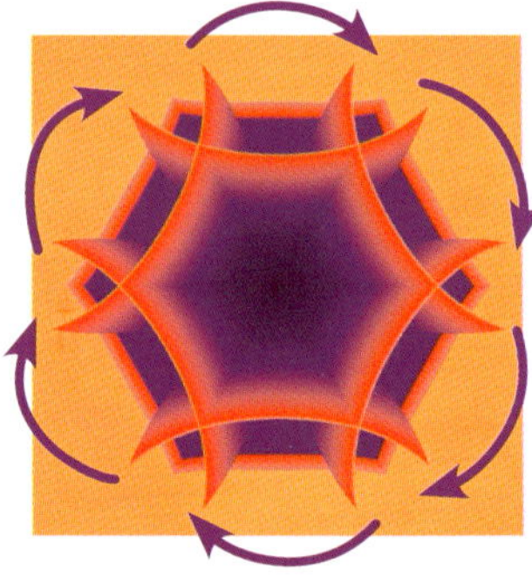

6 matches in 360°

If the shape only matches when it returns to its original position it has no points of rotational symmetry. These shapes have no rotational symmetry.

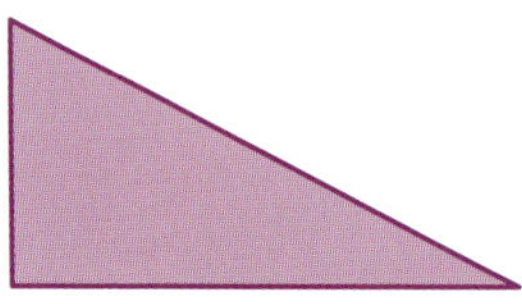

Rotational symmetry is not the same as line symmetry. A shape can have no line symmetry but still have rotational symmetry. This parallelogram has no line symmetry, but matches itself twice when it is rotated around its centre. It has two points of rotational symmetry.

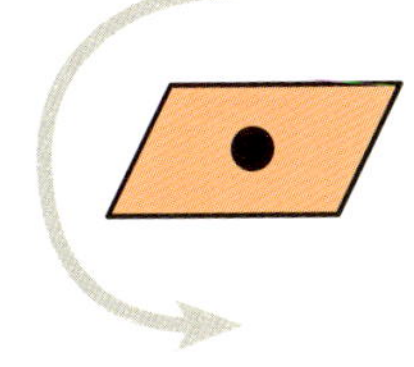

Mark the points of rotational symmetry where each of these shapes, would match if rotated.

1

2

3

Challenge

Mark the points of rotational symmetry where each of these photos would match if rotated.

1

2

ENLARGING AND REDUCING 2D SHAPES

Use a grid system to help you enlarge a 2D shape or drawing. Use a scale to suit the size of your enlargement.

For example, the second grid is 4 times the size of the first grid. Use proportional reasoning to work out where each part of the shape goes on the enlarged grid. Match each point in the same position.

Notice that the new enlarged shape is the same but the size is 4 times larger.

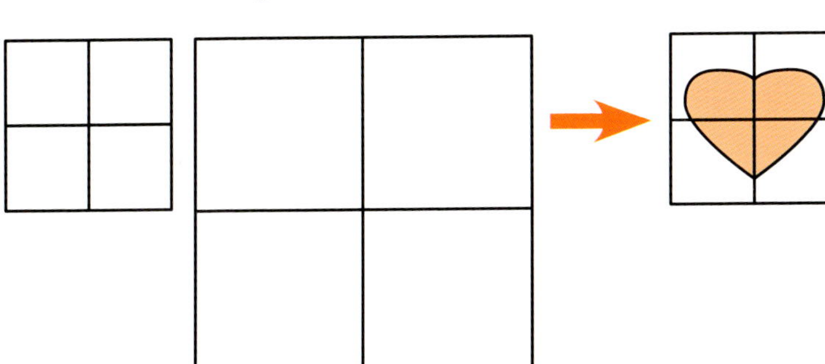

MEASUREMENT & GEOMETRY

ENLARGING AND REDUCING 2D SHAPES
(continued)

To reduce a shape or design, draw a smaller grid, and then match each part of the original shape in the new position. The new shape should be the same but the size is now decreased.

Enlarge each shape using the grid.

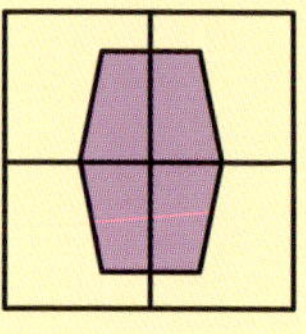
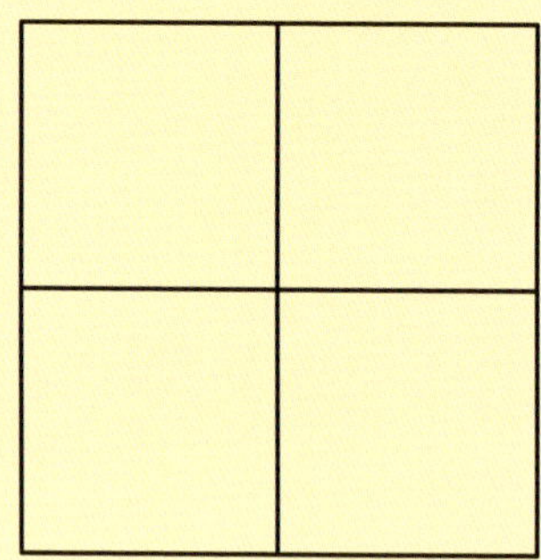

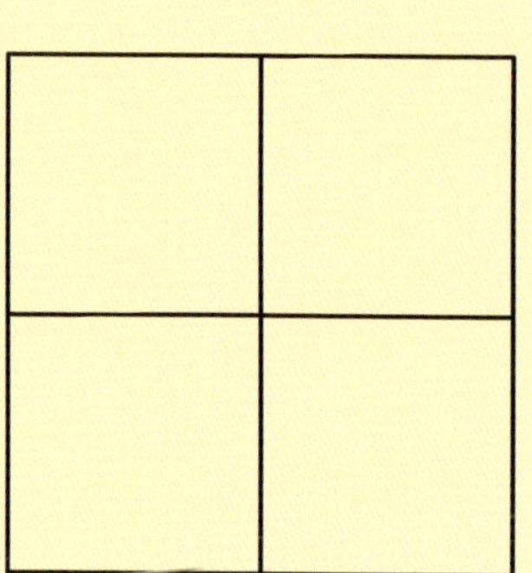

Challenge

Reduce each drawing using the grid.

1

2

LOCATING POSITION

LOCATING POSITION USING A STREET DIRECTORY

A **street directory** is a book of street maps that shows the names of all the streets in a whole area such as a city. It shows important features such as rivers, schools and hospitals, sporting venues and shops. These features help you to locate a specific street or plan a route from one place to another.

North is usually at the top of each map.

The map **legend** at the front of each directory tells you what each symbol on a street map means, for example:

	Motorway	P	Car park		Airport		Service station
	Highway		Hospital	$	Shops		Post office
	Local road	S	School		Library		Telephone

Each page has a **map number** at the top and a grid that divides the page into columns and rows to help you find your location:

- The **horizontal axis** at the bottom and top of each page labels the columns with alphabet letters.
- The **vertical axis** at the side of each page labels the rows with numbers.
- The **co-ordinate reference** is the intersection of a row and a column such as D3.

To locate a street, look up the name and suburb in alphabetical order in the index at the front of the directory. This tells you which map number to use and the co-ordinate reference for that position.

Aerial map of Hawksville
Scale: 1 cm = 25 m

Legend: Grass / Houses / Roads / Water

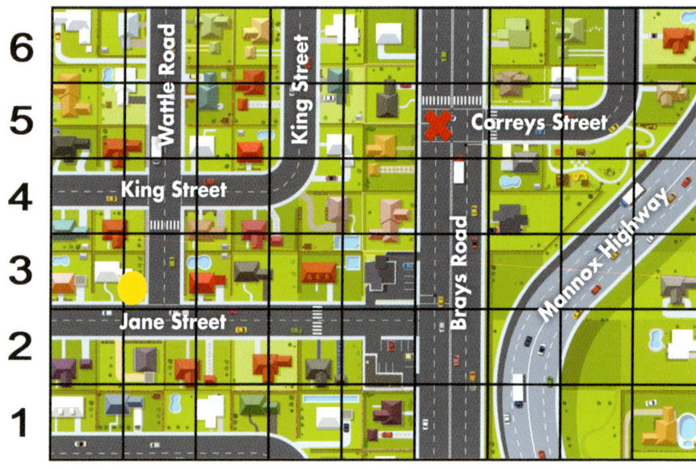

Use this aerial map of Hawksville to complete the following:

1 At the cross at F5, what are the co-ordinates for two different swimming pools you can see?

2 What are the names of the two intersecting streets at F5?

3 If you travel 50 m north from the yellow circle at B3, turn right and travel another 50 m, what is your new co-ordinate position?

4 What is your new co-ordinate position if you travel 100 m east of the yellow circle position, turn left then travel another 50 m?

Challenge

Start at the position marked with a yellow circle at B3. Write directions using co-ordinates and position words to describe one way to travel to the position of the cross at F5.

LOCATING POSITION USING EIGHT COMPASS POINTS

Many people now use a Global Positioning System or **GPS navigation device** in their car, on their computer or on their mobile phone. These devices use satellites to accurately pinpoint a specific place.

If you do not have access to a GPS device, you can still work out where you are using compass points.

Captain James Cook sailed from England to Australia over 200 years ago, using a compass, the stars and maps to navigate.

A compass is based on four cardinal points:

North
South
East
West

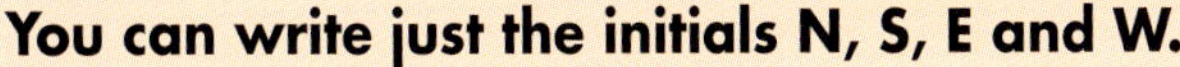

You can write just the initials N, S, E and W.

In the southern hemisphere, east is where the sun appears to rise each day. North will be at a quarter turn anti-clockwise, or 90° from this position. South is directly opposite north. West is directly opposite east.

The four directions in between each of the cardinal points make up the eight points of a compass. You always say and write the north or south name first. The other four points of the compass are:

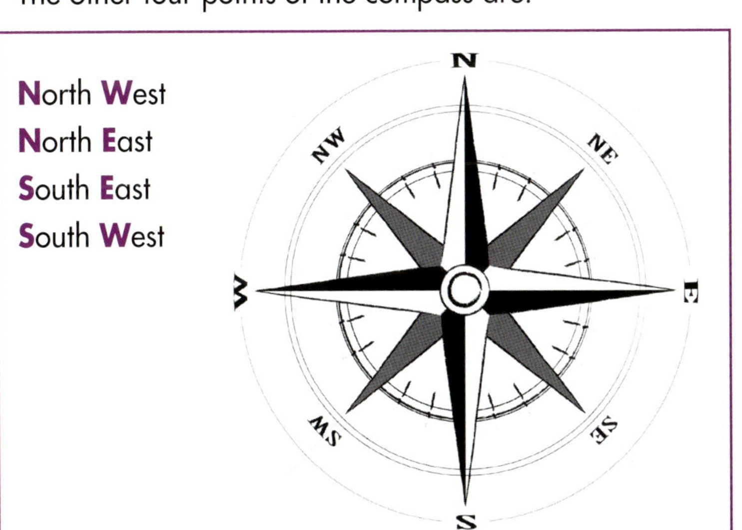

LOCATING POSITION USING EIGHT COMPASS POINTS (continued)

Road maps are 2D aerial views of our 3D world. They help us orient ourselves in space. Look at this road map showing some of the main beaches on the Gold Coast.

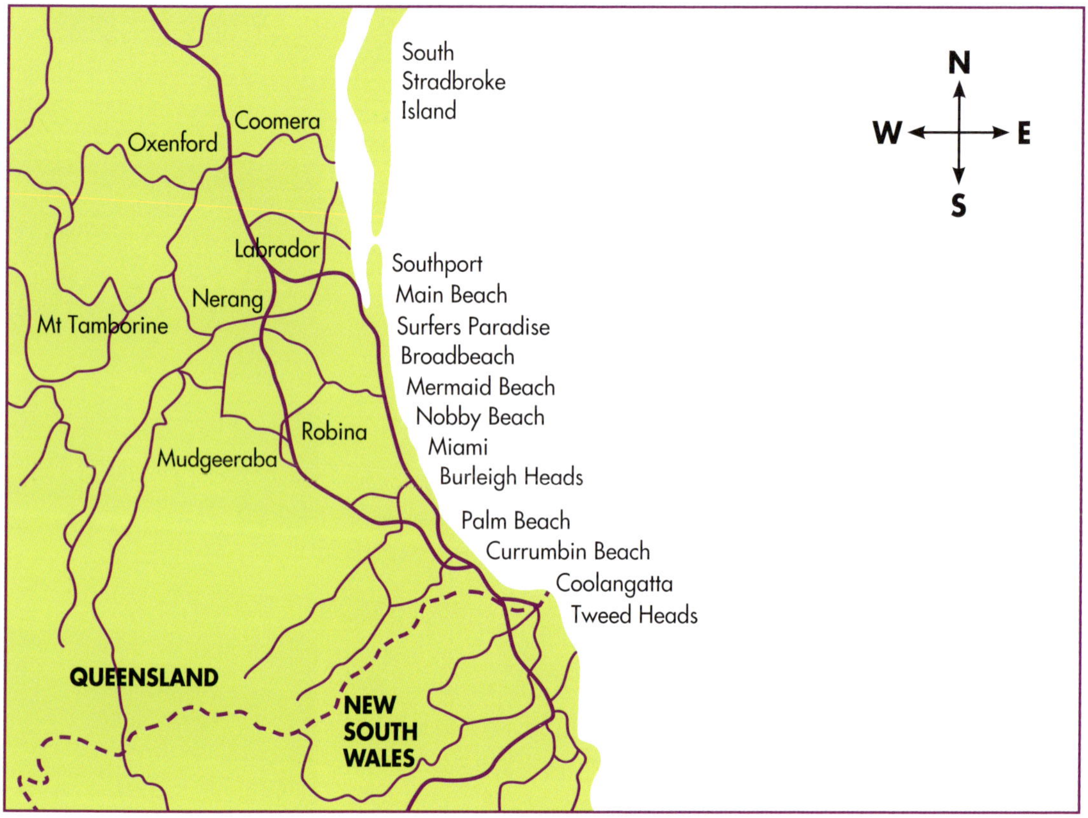

South
Stradbroke
Island
N
W
E
S
Oxenford
Coomera
Labrador
Nerang
Mt Tamborine
Southport
Main Beach
Surfers Paradise
Broadbeach
Mermaid Beach
Nobby Beach
Miami
Burleigh Heads
Robina
Mudgeeraba
Palm Beach
Currumbin Beach
Coolangatta
Tweed Heads
QUEENSLAND
NEW SOUTH WALES

You can locate specific places on this map using compass directions.

Labrador is directly NW of Surfers Paradise.

Coolangatta is SE of Burleigh Heads.

Palm Beach is SE, not south, of Mt Tambourine.

To find a specific street in one of these towns you need to use a street directory. The road map just gives you the overall directions.

Use the map of SE Queensland to answer these questions:

1 Where is Coomera?

2 Is Main Beach north or south of Miami?

3 Mermaid Beach is to the NE of Robina. True or False

Challenge

Use the map shown to create your own adventure map.

1 Add at least three extra features of your own to this map.
2 Create an appropriate scale.
3 Use the 8 compass points to record a route showing how to get from the ship to the village.
4 Ask a friend to follow your directions to check how accurately you planned your route.

LOCATING POSITION USING CARTESIAN CO-ORDINATES

Usually a number line lies horizontally from left to right.

Numbers after 0 are all **positive numbers** such as 3, 94 or 217.8.

Numbers before 0 are all **negative numbers** such as –2, –29 or –356.5.

negative numbers 0 positive numbers

LOCATING POSITION USING CARTESIAN CO-ORDINATES (continued)

About 350 years ago, a French mathematician called Descartes invented a system to locate the position of any object using **co-ordinates**. Some say he was trying to describe the exact position of a fly on his bedroom ceiling.

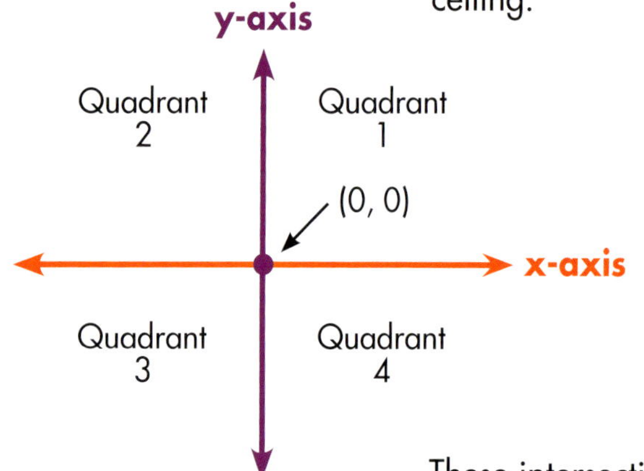

Descartes called the horizontal number line the **x-axis**. He then added a second number line, but turned it 90° anti-clockwise so that the two number lines intersect. This new number line goes up and down vertically. It is called the **y-axis**.

These intersecting number lines create four quarters or quadrants. All four quadrants together are called the **Cartesian number plane**.

Every point on the number plane can be labelled using co-ordinates. Imagine the number plane is Descartes' ceiling and the dot is Descartes' fly. Where is the fly?

The intersection is the centre of the ceiling, the point of origin or (0, 0). All locations are measured from here.

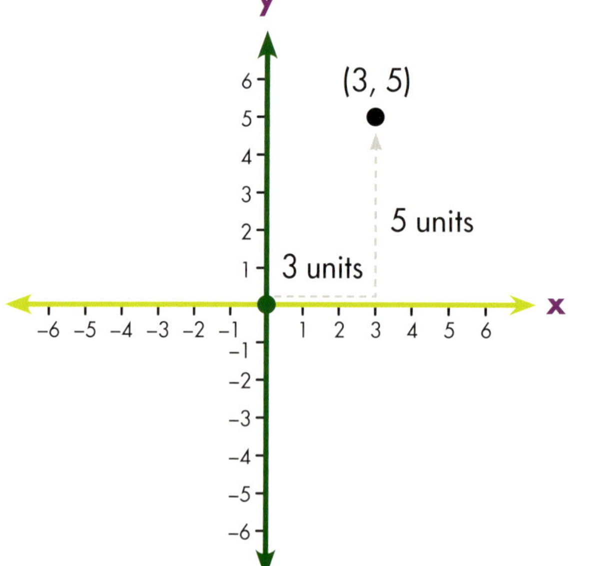

To describe the position of the fly

- Start with the x-axis and count the number of units along.
- Next count the number of units up the y-axis.
- Write the co-ordinates inside parentheses with a comma in between. The fly is at (3, 5).
- It is 3 units along the x-axis and 5 units up the y-axis.

This is called plotting a point.

LABELLING CO-ORDINATE POINTS IN ANY QUADRANT

To plot a point on a number plane, always start with the number of units along the x-axis. The second number is always the number of units along the y-axis.

The centre of each shape below can be described or plotted using co-ordinates.

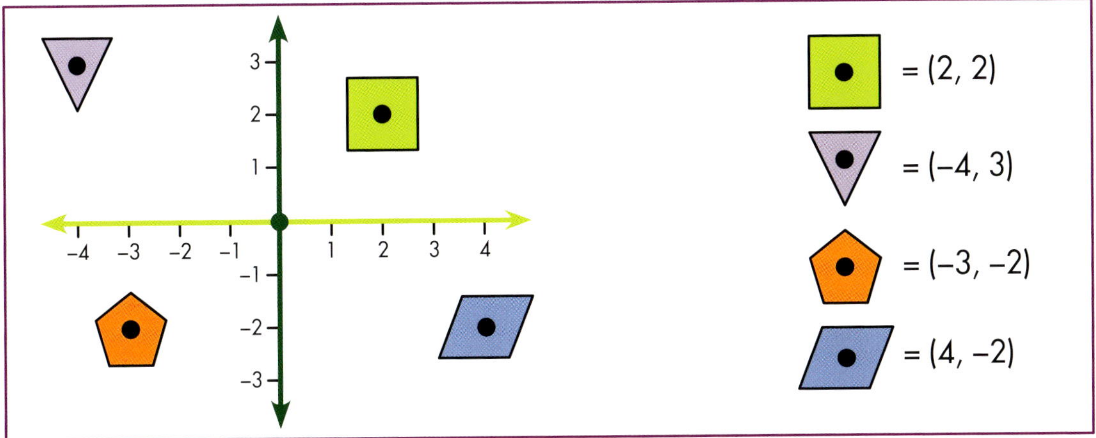

Play 'Where's my nose?'
Plot the co-ordinates that show the exact position of each dog's nose.

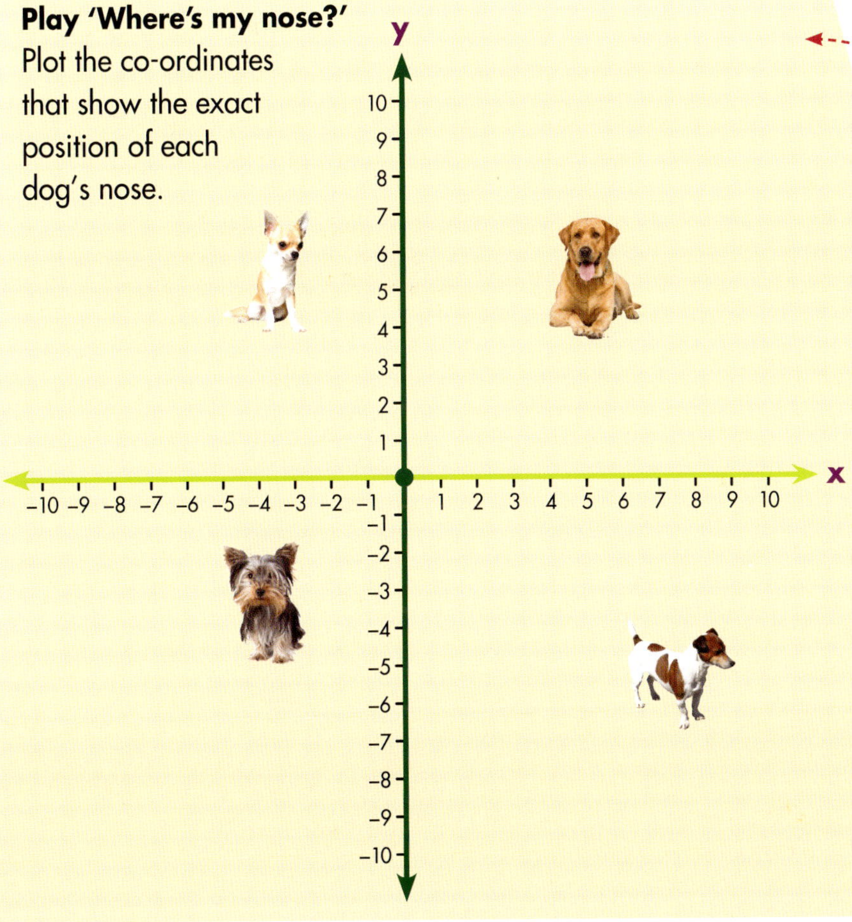

Try this

1 =

2 =

3 =

4 =

DRAWING SHAPES USING CARTESIAN CO-ORDINATES

Use co-ordinates to draw simple shapes on a number plane by joining up points with a ruler and a pencil.

These co-ordinates are marked on this number plane:
(3, 6) (–3, 6) (–3, –6) (3, –6)

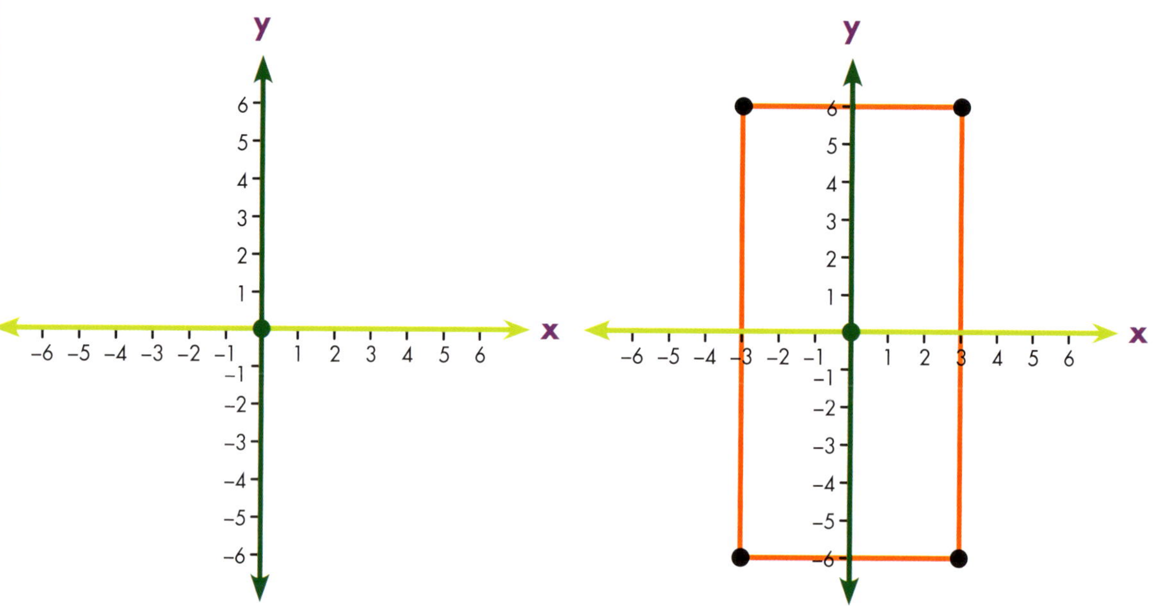

When you join the dots with straight lines, you create a rectangle.

Try this

Look at these co-ordinates.
(4, 0) (2, 2) (0, 4) (–2, 2) (–4, 0) (–2, –2) (0, –4) (2, –2)
Visualise what shape you think they make before plotting them on the number plane. Join them up with straight lines to reveal the shape.

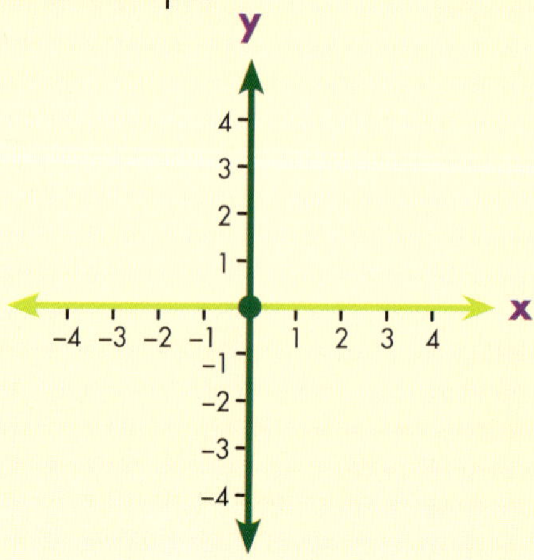

CHANCE

MEASURING CHANCE EVENTS

You can measure chance events in order of certainty and give them a value from 0 to 1. This is called a **probability scale**.

Chance is about whether something will or won't happen. If something is impossible, it scores 0. It is not a chance event. If the result is certain, it scores 1. It is also not a chance event.

Even though chimps can do many things you can do, it is impossible for a chimp to read this Maths Guide.

No-one else has identical fingerprints to you. It is 100% certain that fingerprints are unique.

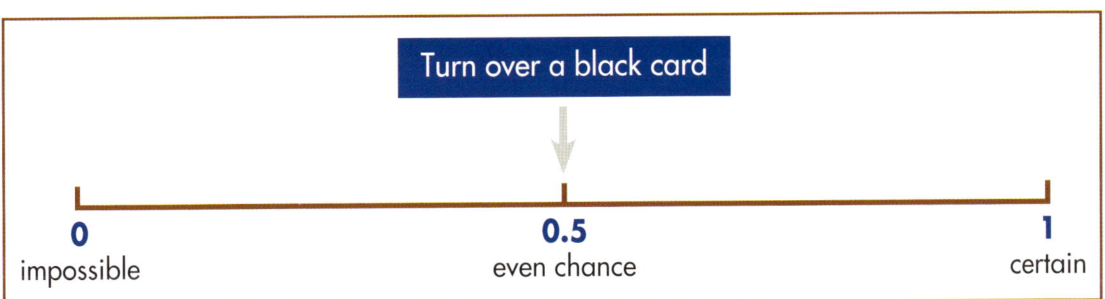

Chance is about all the random events that score more than 0 but less than 1 on the probability scale. Shuffle a pack of playing cards, place them face down and turn over the top card. You have a 1 in 2 chance of turning over a black card, as there is an equal number of red and black cards in any pack. That's the same as $\frac{1}{2}$, 50% or 0.5. You have an even chance.

MEASURING CHANCE EVENTS (continued)

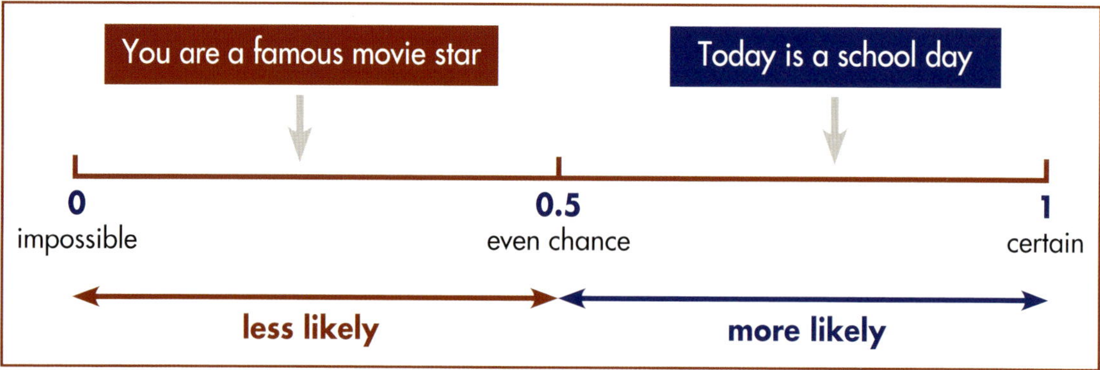

It is less likely that you are a famous movie star. You have less than an even chance of being one.

It is more likely that today is a school day as there are at least 5 out of 7 days when you go to school. Today has more than an even chance of being a school day.

Look at each photo. Work out the chance of each event happening. Draw an arrow to where you would place them on a probability scale.

Your cat goes shopping

The sun will rise in the morning

You win $500 in a lottery

Your dog is pleased to see you

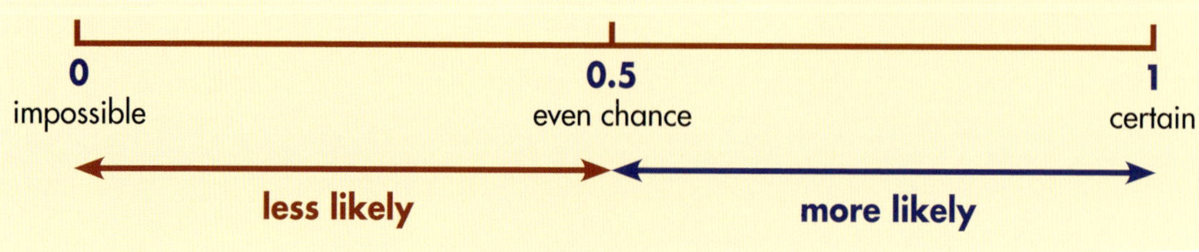

You have a 1 in 10 456 chance of being struck by lightning in your lifetime.

TOSSING COINS

When you toss a coin, it can land on heads **H** or tails **T**.

There are only two possibilities. You have a 1 in 2 chance of tossing **H**. You have a 1 in 2 chance of tossing **T**. Both have an even chance of happening.

Remember these are just the probable outcomes. You need to check your real results after tossing a coin 10 times and recording the results.

Heads	Tails
H	**T**

When you toss two coins, you can list four possible outcomes:

H H **H T** **T T** **T H**

Although each coin can land on either heads **H** or tails **T** you now have a 1 in 4 chance of tossing two heads **H H**. It is no longer an even chance.

Tossing **H H** would score $\frac{1}{4}$, 0.25 or 25% on the probability scale.

Tossing **T T** would score $\frac{1}{4}$, 0.25 or 25% on the probability scale.

What chance do you have of tossing at least one **H**? You have a 3 out of 4 chance, as 3 out of 4 possible outcomes include a **H**.

Toss two coins 10 times and record the results.

1. How close are your tosses of the coins to the predicted results?
2. Are the results any closer if you toss 20 times?
3. Are the results any closer if you toss 50 times?
4. Are the results any closer if you toss 100 times?

Try this

Challenge

List all the possible outcomes if you toss 3 coins.
What chance do you have of tossing **H H H**?

OTHER CHANCE EVENTS

Macaroons

You have a bag with five different coloured macaroons in it. You put your hand in and select one at random. What is the chance of selecting an orange macaroon?

You have a 1 in 5 chance of selecting the orange one. This is the same as $\frac{1}{5}$, or 0.2 or 20%. It is not very likely. You have less than an even chance of selecting an orange one.
If you have 10 of each colour, you will have 50 macaroons. But you still have a 10 out of 50 chance, or 1 in 5, of selecting an orange macaroon.
If you have 100 of each colour, you will have 500 macaroons. But you still have a 100 out of 500 chance, or 1 in 5, of selecting an orange macaroon.

Balls in a bag

You have 12 balls in a bag, 3 red balls and 9 blue balls.

If you put your hand in and take out one ball at random, you have 9 out of 12 chances of getting a blue ball. That's $\frac{9}{12}$ or $\frac{3}{4}$. That's a 0.75 or 75% chance of selecting blue.

On the probability scale, it's more likely that you will select a blue ball.

1 What is the chance of selecting a blue ball?
2 In which bag do you have the best chance of selecting blue?

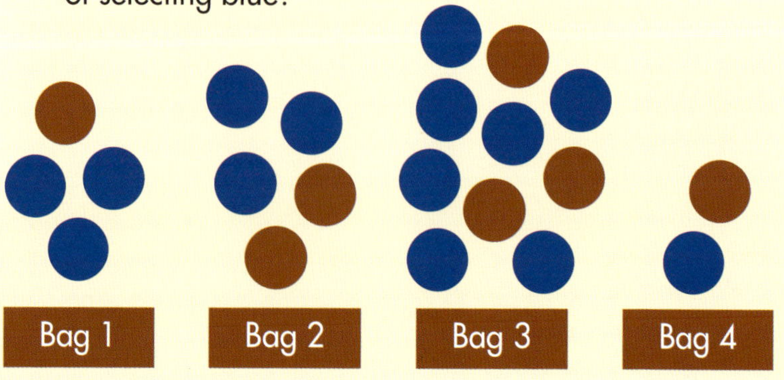

DATA DISPLAYS

Data is the information you collect to answer a question. It helps you analyse, discuss and explain your results. **Statistics** is a way to put this information into numbers to help you make predictions.

DESIGNING A SURVEY

Once you have a question you would like to ask, you need to design a **survey** to collect your facts. Decide whether you are conducting a sample or a census. A **sample** is where you collect data from only some members of a group. A **census** is where you collect data from every single person in the group.

As part of a study on animals, Ava found out which of seven creatures her friends found the scariest. She printed a colour photo of each creature, and asked her friends to label a survey form in order from 1, the least scary, to 7, the most scary. She did a **pre-test** first with just two friends to check that her survey made sense to them. She then asked a sample of 28 more friends to participate. Altogether she collected results from 30 friends.

The scariest creatures

What would you do next with all this information? As each creature had received a score from 1–7, Ava added all the scores for each creature. Spiders had the highest score, so her friends thought they were the scariest.

These are the results from Ava's survey, shown in a table:

The scariest creatures						
Poison dart Frogs	Spiders	Mosquitoes	Sharks	Snakes	Crocodiles	Bats
53	191	91	155	149	60	141

DESIGNING A SURVEY (continued)

Mosquitoes are one of the most deadly creatures on earth.

Ava could be more certain of her survey results if she sampled 100 or more people. Some surveys are conducted by telephone, by mail or on a computer. If you could survey a sample of 1500 people, that would give you very precise results.

Look at the results from Ava's survey. Put the results in order from the most scary to the least scary creature. Write three more statistical statements about Ava's results.

DIFFERENT WAYS TO DISPLAY DATA

Tables are just one way to display the data you collect. Most people find it easier to read and analyse data when it is presented in a **graph**. Your graph might be a dot plot, a column graph, a line graph or a pie graph. A graph makes comparing numbers easier.

Dot plots

A **dot plot** is a simple data display. You plot the dots over a number line. It is useful when there are not huge quantities of data to display. It is also useful for comparing two sets of data. Even though it is called a dot plot, you can use any symbol to display your data. You do not have to use dots. Make sure you keep everything in line as a messy dot plot is not worth creating.

Ryan wanted to see how long it took his friends to run 100 m. He plotted this information at the school Athletics Carnival.

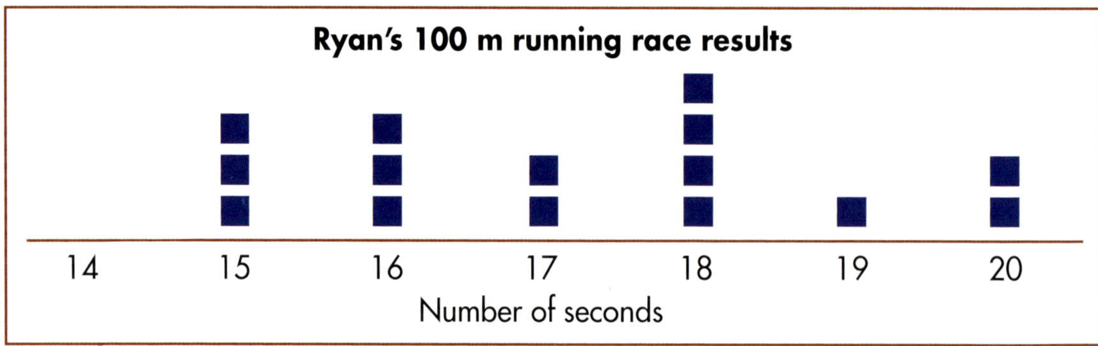

How many friends were in his survey?
The total number of dots is 15, so Ryan had 15 friends involved.

You can now use Ryan's information to make statistical statements. For example:

- The most common time was 18 seconds.
- Slightly more than half took between 15 and 17 seconds.
- The difference between the fastest and the slowest runner was only 5 seconds.

What else could you say?

Other questions you could investigate:

- Do taller people run 100 m faster?
- Do people with longer feet run 100 m faster?
- Do younger people run 100 m faster?

The Jamaican runner Usain Bolt holds the 2009 world record for running 100 m in 9.58 seconds.

Ryan also recorded how long it took the same friends to swim 100 m freestyle. He plotted this information at the school Swimming Carnival. As the results were so spread out he recorded the results in groups of 5 seconds.

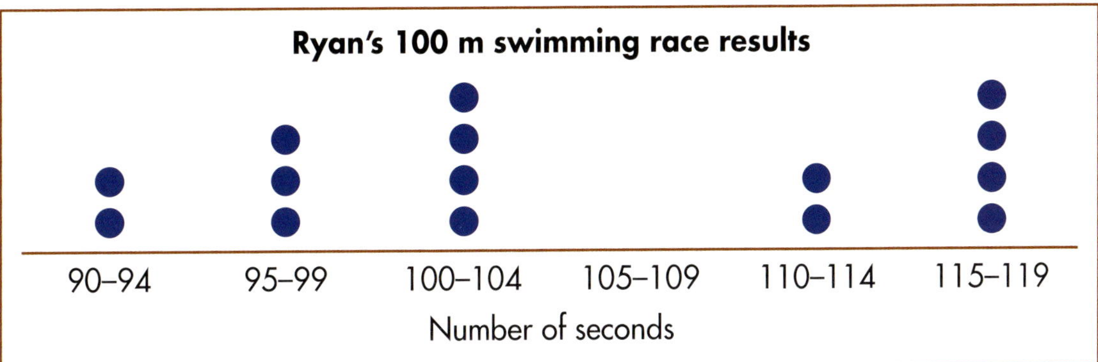

The German swimmer Britta Steffen holds the 2009 women's world record for swimming 100 m in 52.07 seconds.

Use the information on Ryan's dot plot to answer the following questions.

1. What is the difference between the fastest and the slowest swimmers?
2. How many friends swam between 105 and 109 seconds?
3. What was the most common time?

Try this

DIFFERENT WAYS TO DISPLAY DATA (continued)

Two-way tables

A **two-way table** helps you collect more specific data. Instead of just recording how many students can or cannot swim 100 m, the swimming coach can divide the responses into Year groups.

	Can swim 100 m	Cannot swim 100 m
Year 5	19	11
Year 6	24	8

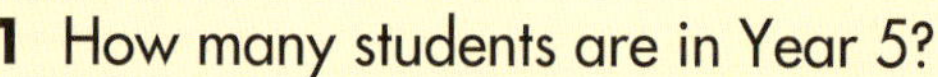

1 How many students are in Year 5?
2 How many students are there altogether?
3 How many students cannot swim 100 m?
4 What fraction is this?

To create your own two-way table:

- Think of a question you want answered. E.g. How many students received a certificate for swimming 100 m freestyle?
- Think of how to break swim certificates into more specific parts. E.g. How many students received a gold, a silver or a bronze certificate?
- Think of how to break students into more specific parts. E.g. Boys and girls
- Design your survey form. E.g.

	Gold	Silver	Bronze
Girls			
Boys			

- Collect your data. E.g.

	Gold	Silver	Bronze
Girls	37	15	14
Boys	42	4	8

- Analyse your results and make statistical statements about what you discovered.
  E.g. Altogether 120 students received a certificate. More boys received a gold certificate. About 20% of girls received a bronze certificate. $\frac{8}{54}$ boys received a bronze certificate.

Challenge

Design your own survey to collect data for a two-way table.

Side-by-side column graphs

If you collect data from a survey that involves a two-way table, you can construct **side-by-side column graphs** to show your data. This makes it very easy to see comparisons.

Sam collected this data about favourite dance styles and recorded it as a 2-way table.

	Jazz	Tap	Ballet	Hip Hop	Jive	Other
Girls	8	5	9	4	3	3
Boys	3	2	3	10	4	4

You can use a computer program to make each of the following graphs.

This is what the data looks like in a vertical side-by-side column graph.

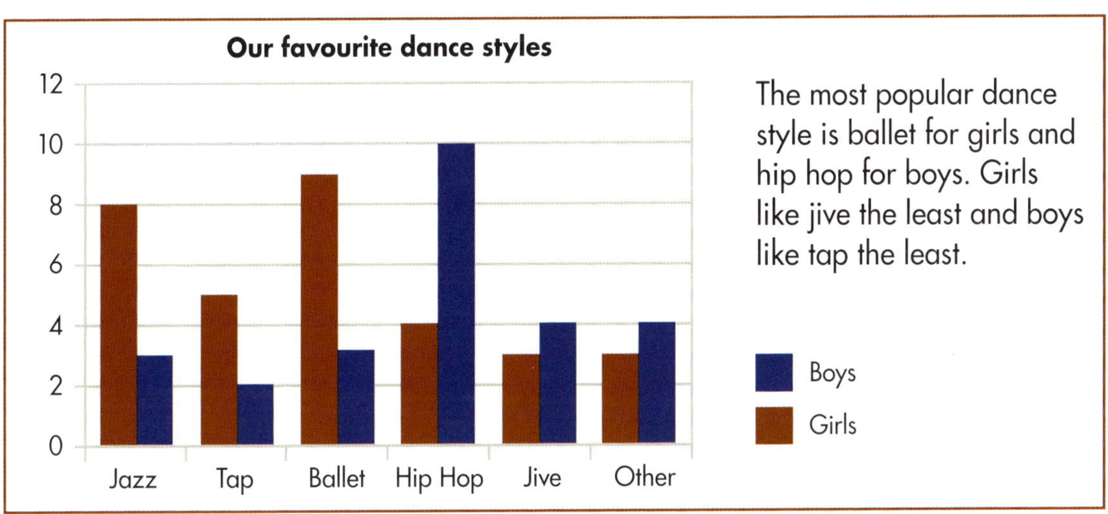

The most popular dance style is ballet for girls and hip hop for boys. Girls like jive the least and boys like tap the least.

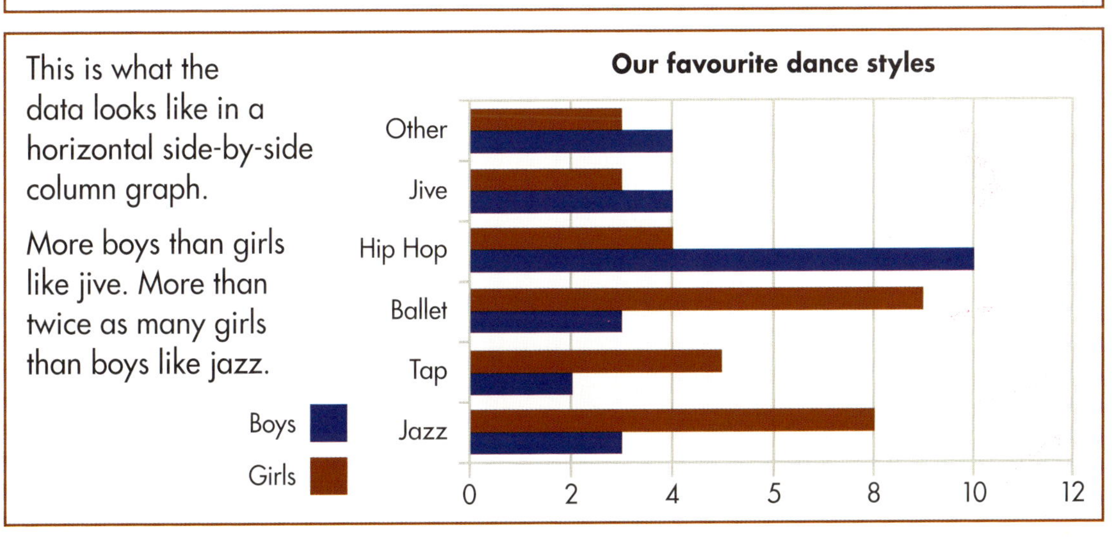

This is what the data looks like in a horizontal side-by-side column graph.

More boys than girls like jive. More than twice as many girls than boys like jazz.

DIFFERENT WAYS TO DISPLAY DATA (continued)

This is what it looks like if you put them both together on top of each other.

The most popular dance style overall is hip hop. More students like ballet than jazz.

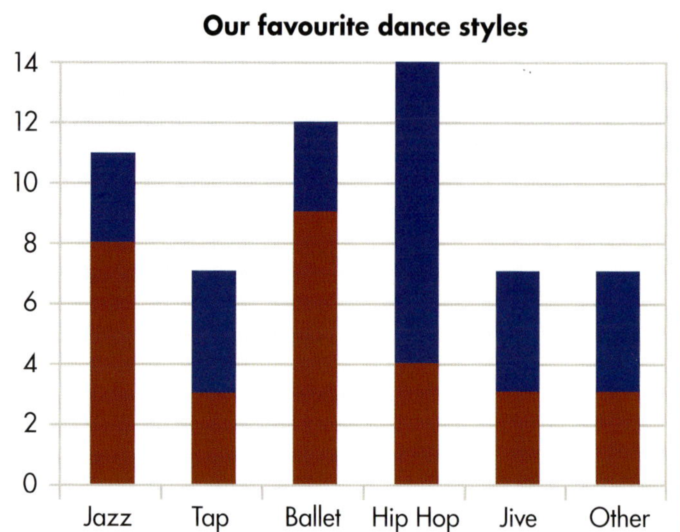

1 Which graph do you find easier to read? Why?
2 What are three new statistical statements you can now make?

Line graphs

A **line graph** can be used to show data over a period of time. A major advantage is that you know every point along the line has meaning, based on the information you collect in a table.

One disadvantage is that only things that change over time can be represented in a line graph. E.g. temperatures, money raised for a charity, your height plotted each year as you grow.

This table shows the increase in mass of two babies over six months. You can use two different colours to plot their growth on the same graph.

Growth in Mass over 6 months							
Month	**0**	**1**	**2**	**3**	**4**	**5**	**6**
Emily	3.2 kg	4.1 kg	5.0 kg	5.7 kg	6.3 kg	6.6 kg	7.2 kg
Jacob	3.3 kg	4.5 kg	5.4 kg	6.2 kg	6.8 kg	7.3 kg	7.8 kg

Label the x-axis with the months. Label the y-axis with the mass in kg.
Remember to give the whole graph a title too.
Plot marks on your graph then join the marks to create a continuous line.

GROWTH IN MASS OF 2 BABIES OVER 6 MONTHS

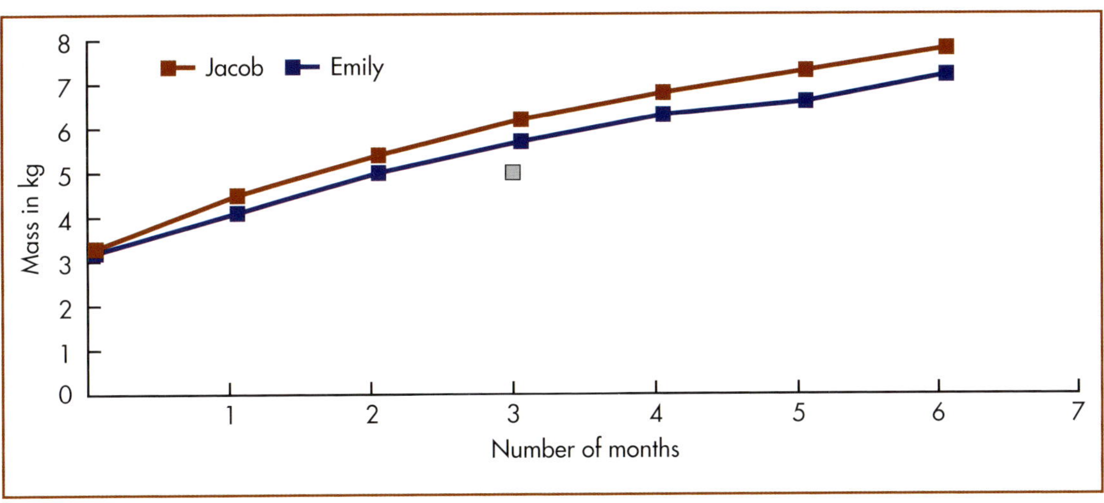

You can see that both babies increase in mass over time. Emily never catches up to Jacob. She is always lighter than Jacob.

The heaviest baby ever born had a mass more than 10.5 kg.

This table shows the number of people who caught the Pelican Point ferry to the city on Monday.

6.00 am	8.00 am	10.00 am	12.00 noon	2.00 pm	4.00 pm	6.00 pm
5	56	21	18	30	10	28

1 Draw and label your own line graph based on this data.

2 Write three statistical statements based on your line graph.

Try this

Pie graphs

A **pie graph**, also called a pie chart, represents data as **sectors**, or fractions of a circle. The size of each sector shows the quantity for each group of data. The larger the sector, the larger the amount of data it represents. The size of each sector is usually shown with a percentage label, showing the proportion of the total circle area.

It is not easy to construct a pie graph as it can involve very complex fractions. Most computers include a program which will create one for you.

DIFFERENT WAYS TO DISPLAY DATA (continued)

Animals sold at Mo's Pet Shop this weekend:

Guinea pigs	Dogs	Cats	Rabbits	Birds	Fish
4	9	5	2	9	20

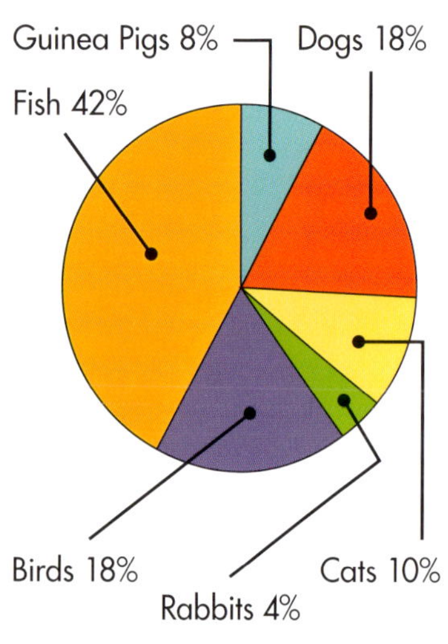

One **advantage** is that a pie graph quickly shows the data as proportions. You can easily see that Mo sold more fish than any other creature. Rabbits were the least popular.

One **disadvantage** is that a pie graph is difficult to analyse if the sectors look too similar in size. You can see that birds and dogs look the same size. But you need to check the percentage label to see they both sold 18%.

A pie graph can be **misleading**. Here fish obviously sold the most. Yet fish are so small and people tend to buy more than one at a time if they have an aquarium. If the owners are concerned about making money, they probably should focus more on how many of the larger pets were sold. You may need more information before you make useful statistical statements.

MISLEADING DATA DISPLAYS

Advertisers sometimes use graphs to represent data in a way that is misleading. Each graph gives a specific message to its audience.

Look at the heights of these 5 friends:

Sam	Jack	Kia	Mike	Ella
153 cm	149 cm	147 cm	148 cm	147 cm

If you want to show that the friends are all very similar in height, you can make the scale on your graph cover a large range. On this scale, each mark represents 5 cm, but it starts at 100 cm and finishes at 154 cm.

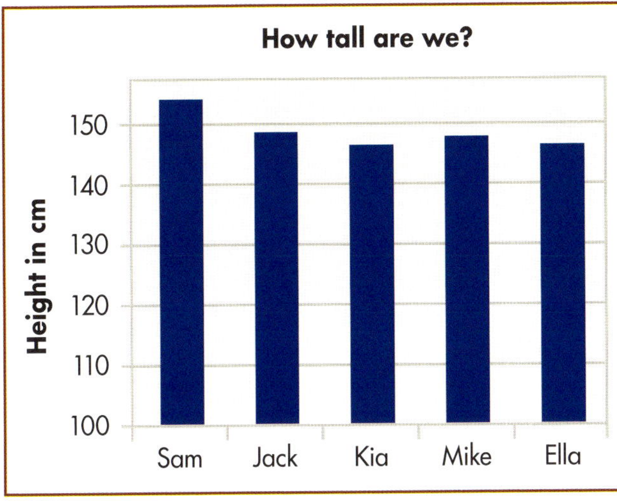

By making the scale cover so many cm, you make the differences in height appear quite small.

If you want to show that the friends are very different in height, you can make the scale on your graph cover a small range. On this scale, each mark represents 1 cm, but it starts at 146 cm and finishes at 154 cm.

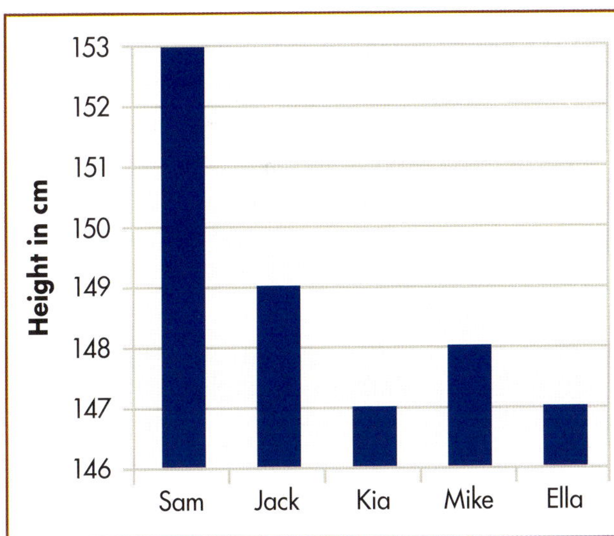

By making the scale cover only a few cm, you make the differences in height appear quite larger.

The sample you select can also be very misleading. Perhaps the survey omitted friends who were smaller than 147 cm or taller than 153 cm. It all depends on what message you want to send to your audience.

Challenge

Find two different graphs in a newspaper, magazine or on the internet. Think about what message each graph conveys to you. What are some possibly misleading points you may need more information about?

GLOSSARY

apex	The pointy end of a shape or object where two or more straight lines or faces meet to create a corner
ascending	When you sort mixed numbers into place value order from the smallest to the largest number
axis of symmetry	A straight line that cuts a 2D shape into two matching halves
bill	A list of items you have purchased that shows what each item costs and the total amount you have to pay, also called an invoice
budget	A list of items showing how much you can afford to spend on each item and what you can afford to spend altogether
capacity	A measure of how much a container can hold, measured in litres, millilitres and kilolitres
cardinal points	The four main directions of the compass – North (N), East (E), South (S) and West (W)
Cartesian number plane	The four quadrants, or sections, created by the intersection of a horizontal and a vertical line, where every point on the number plane can be given a co-ordinate label
cash	The notes and coins that make up a country's money system such as in Australia, where we have dollars and cents.
chunking	Looking for large enough amounts to subtract easily in a division problem
co-ordinates	The name given to the intersection of one row and one column on a Cartesian number plane
debt	When you owe someone more than what you have paid them and is often an amount of money that you have borrowed and will later pay back
decimal	Another name for a number which has been divided into $\frac{1}{10}$s, $\frac{1}{100}$s, $\frac{1}{1000}$s and so on
degrees	A measure of the amount of turn between two straight lines (arms or rays) joined at a vertex or point
denominator	The bottom number in a fraction or the total number of equal parts into which something has been divided
descending	When you sort mixed numbers into place value order from the largest to the smallest number

digit	The ten symbols from 0–9 used to record any number in the base 10 number system
edges	The line where two faces meet
estimate	A rough idea of an answer to a calculation, based on mentally finding an easy way to work out the problem but it is not the correct answer
face	Any flat two-dimensional surface on a three-dimensional object
flip	The action of repeating a 2D shape by flipping it onto the opposite side of a line of symmetry; also called reflecting
gram	A small metric unit for measuring the mass or heaviness of an object
graph	A representation of data you have collected and sorted to demonstrate visually what you have discovered
hundred thousand	A six-digit number, including all numbers from 100 000 to 999 999
invoice	A type of bill that you don't always have to pay immediately and it lists the items you have bought and the total amount you owe
legend	A diagram or table showing the meaning for each symbol used on a map or in a street directory
line graph	A graph that shows a line connecting the different points, where every part of the line has meaning; often used to show changes over time
line symmetry	A way to describe a shape, drawing or photograph where one half is an exact mirror image of the other half
litre	A metric unit for measuring liquid volumes and capacities less than 1 cubic metre
kilolitre	A metric unit for measuring large volumes and capacities where 1 kilolitre is the same amount as 1000 litres
long division	An algorism used when you have a two-digit (or larger) divisor and a two-digit (or larger) dividend that you can't divide mentally
lowest common multiple	This is the smallest multiple that two factors have in common
map number	The reference number that tells you which map you want to use in a street directory
megalitre	A metric unit for measuring extremely large volumes of water or other liquids, such as in dams or rivers
million	A seven-digit number including any number from 1 000 000 to 9 999 999

negative number	Any number less than 0, written using a – (minus) sign
net	A flat 2D shape that can be cut out and folded to make a 3D solid
number pattern	A sequence of numbers where you can see a relationship between the numbers and predict what the next number will be
numerator	The top number in a fraction, the selected number of equal parts
order of operations	A rule for working out what calculations to do first in a complicated number sentence
pie graph	A way to show the data you have collected as fractions or sectors of a circle
place value	This is the base 10 value a digit represents in specific positions in a number
polyhedron	A three-dimensional solid with four or more flat faces
positive number	Any number more than 0, sometimes written with a + (plus) sign
pre-test	A small data survey before you start a larger survey to check that you are asking the relevant questions
probability scale	The numbers between 0 and 1 showing the chance or probability of an event
ray	Any two straight lines that meet at a point to create an angle
regular 3D solid	A 3D solid with identical shaped faces and equal length edges such as tetrahedron, cube, octahedron, dodecahedron, icosahedron
regular polygon	Any straight-sided 2D shape where every side is exactly the same length and every angle is the same size
revolution	An angle that turns a complete rotation measuring 360°
rotation	The action of repeating a 2D shape by turning it any amount in a clockwise or anti-clockwise direction; also called a turn
running total	Where you are adding lots of different numbers but you record the total, or sub-totals, after each separate addition
side-by-side column graphs	A way to record information from a two-way table as a graph in columns representing each piece of information
skeleton model	A three-dimensional model showing only the edges and vertices; the faces are invisible
slide	The action of repeating a 2D shape by moving it across, up and down in any direction without turning or flipping; also called a translation

solid	Another name for a three-dimensional object
speed	A measure of how fast something is travelling, which is a measure of both time and distance
survey	A collection of smaller questions you would like a group of people to answer to help you investigate a problem or larger question
symmetrical	A way to describe any shape that has at least one line of symmetry or one mirror line, where one half of the shape is perfectly reflected in the other half
terms	The parts or separate numbers in a number pattern
transformation	The action of flipping, sliding or turning a shape to change its direction or enlarging or reducing the size of the shape
two-way table	Information collected from more than one source and recorded in a table or grid
unit fraction	A fraction where the numerator, the top number, is 1 and the denominator can be any number
volume	A measure of how much 3D space an object takes up, measured in cm^3, m^3, L and mL
x-axis	A horizontal line of a co-ordinate reference grid, usually marked with letters or numbers to represent the columns in the grid
y-axis	A vertical line of a co-ordinate reference grid, usually marked with letters or numbers to represent the rows in the grid

SYMBOLS & ABBREVIATIONS

Number

$=$	equal
$+$	plus
$-$	minus
$\times$	multiply
$\div$	divide
$<$	less than
$>$	more than
%	percentage

Length

mm	millimetre
cm	centimetre
m	metre
km	kilometre

Speed

km/h	kilometres per hour

Area

ha	hectare
km^2	square kilometre
m^2	square metre
cm^2	square centimetre
mm^2	square millimetre

Volume and capacity

m^3	cubic metre
cm^3	cubic centimetre
kL	kilolitre
ML	megalitre
L	litre
mL	millilitre

Mass

g	gram
kg	kilogram
t	tonne

Time

h	hour
min	minute
s	second
am	before midday (ante meridiem)
pm	after midday (post meridiem)

Space

2D	Two dimensional
3D	Three dimensional

Temperature

°C	degrees Celsius

Angles

$\angle$	angle
∟	right angle

ANSWERS

NUMBER & ALGEBRA

Page 1 **Roman numerals**
1 8 **2** 44 **3** 2770
4 1 600 255

Page 4 **Place value to 1 000 000**
7 553 100 **Challenge:** 7 553 010

Page 8 **Ordering large numbers**
Mercury, Mars, Venus, Earth, Jupiter
Challenge: Earth, Mars, Jupiter, Saturn, Uranus

Page 11 **Facts to 20**
1 Answers starting at 0:
7 11 14 13 10 16 9 15 8 12
2 Answers starting at –2:
6 3 17 9 2 5 15 8 4 0
3 Answers starting at –1:
8 13 19 6 0 17 2 9 4 14

Page 12 **Magic squares**

1

2	7	6
9	5	1
4	3	8

2

4	9	2
3	5	7
8	1	6

Challenge:
Adds to 30

12	2	16
14	10	16
4	18	8

Adds to 45

18	3	24
21	15	9
6	27	12

Page 14 **'Counting up to' strategy**
1 744 **2** 519 **3** 195

Page 18 **Other subtraction algorisms**
52 543

Page 20 **Factors and multiples**
1 1, 2, 3, 4, 6, 8, 12 and 24: any 4.
2 8, 16, 24, 32, 48, 56, 64, 72, 80, 88

Page 22 **Prime and composite numbers**
4, 6, 8, 9, 10, 12, 14, 15, 16, 18

Page 24 **Essential table facts to 10 × 10**
1 Starting at 6: 42 28 7 63 0 21 35 56 14 49
2 Starting at 27: 3 0 8 4 9 2 10 5 7 6
3 Starting at × 8: 64 4 48 1 56 8 40 2 72 80

Page 31 **Division estimates**
1 200 ÷ 4 = 50 **2** 540 ÷ 6 = 90

Page 33 **Divide mentally by 10 and 100**
1 2.3 **2** 7.9 **3** 39.8
4 5.02 **5** 144 **6** 856.9

Page 34 **Division using chunking**
The binoculars cost $794

Page 36 **Division using long division**
Challenge: 49 km

Page 42 **Ordering fractions with same denominator**
$\frac{6}{6}, \frac{5}{6}, \frac{4}{6}, \frac{3}{6}, \frac{2}{6}, \frac{1}{6}$

Page 43 **Equivalent fractions**
1 Examples are $\frac{2}{4}, \frac{3}{6}, \frac{4}{8}, \frac{5}{10}, \frac{6}{12}$
2 Examples are $\frac{2}{2}, \frac{3}{3}, \frac{4}{4}, \frac{5}{5}, \frac{6}{6}$

Page 51 **Ordering decimals**
20.855, 17.999, 12.0, 3.92, 1.3, 0.1

Page 52 **Rounding decimals**
1 67 **2** 14 **3** 1
4 2 **5** 1 **6** 16

Page 54 **Subtracting decimals**
1 0.633 tonnes **2** 5.847

Page 56 **Multiplying decimals by 10, 100 or 1000**
1 0.8, 8, 80
2 171.05, 1710.5, 17 105
3 913.72, 9137.2, 91 372

Page 57 **Dividing decimals by 10, 100 or 1000**
1 0.2, 0.02, 0.002
2 3.14, 0.314, 0.0314
3 10.35, 1.035, 0.1035

Page 60 **Calculating with percentages**
1 6 **2** 220
Challenge:
1 69
2 A discount of 70% is better. You only pay $30 for a $100 pair of shoes. 60% off $80 means the other pair will cost $32.

Page 61 **Savings plan**
Just over 21 weeks

Page 63 **Discounts**
5 haircuts normally 3 × $20 and
2 × $35 = $130
30% discount the haircuts will only cost $91,
10% of $130 = $13, 30% is 3 × $13 = $39,
$130 – $39 = $91

Page 64 **Comparing discounts**
10% off $70 = $7, 40% off = $28,
$70 – $28 = $42
10% off $80 = $8, 50% off = $40,
$80 – $40 = $40
So 50% off $80 is a slightly better deal.

Page 68 **Converting money overseas**
1 211 250 **2** $100

Page 70 **Number patterns based on shapes**
600

Page 71 **Table of values**
Top row: 30, 45, 75
Bottom row: 32, 40
1 75 km, 5 L **2** 600 km, 40 L
Challenge:

No. Boxes	1	2	3	4	5
Chicken	3	6	9	12	15
Beef	5	10	15	20	25
Veg	4	8	12	16	20
TOTAL	12	24	36	48	60

There are 15 chicken pies in 5 boxes.

Page 72 **Number patterns with whole numbers**
Pattern A rule: Multiply by 2
8, 64, 128, 256
Pattern B rule: Add 13
54, 67, 93, 106
Pattern C rule: Divide by 10
350, 3.5, 0.0035, 0.00035
Pattern D rule: Subtract 7
64, 36, 22, 15

Page 73 **Number patterns with fractions and decimals**
Pattern A rule: Subtract $\frac{5}{12}$
$1\frac{5}{12}$, $\frac{-3}{12}$
Pattern B rule: Add 0.05
3.12, 3.32, 3.37
Challenge:
Pattern rule: Multiply by 3
29.25, 789.75, 2369.25

Page 74 **Number sentences**
1 5 **2** 0.5 **3** 5

Page 76 **Order of operations**
1 B: 5 × (65 – 6) **2** $295

MEASUREMENT & GEOMETRY

Page 77 **Kilometres**
96 500 m

Page 78 **Kilometres**
The shorter route is Clareville, Wanda, Mudbar, Clinton at 57 km. The other route is 62 km.

Page 80 **Metres, centimetres and millimetres**
1 2.5 km **2** 4.01 m **3** 6.7 cm

Page 82 **Calculating perimeters of rectangles**
1 6.2 cm **2** 8.8 cm **3** 12.8 cm

Page 82 **Calculating perimeters of other polygons**
1 11.9 cm **2** 8.1 cm **3** 11 cm

Page 83 **Calculating perimeters of other polygons**
18 + (2 × 30) + (2 × 11) + (2 × 15) + 40
= 170 mm or 17 cm

Page 84 **Interpreting speed**
(2 × 80) + (3 × 100) = 460 km

Page 86 **Hectares**
659 600 square metres
6.75 hectares

Page 87 **Square kilometres**
Russia, China, Australia, India, Indonesia, Greece, Lebanon
1 14.056 **2** 20.327 **3** 68.556
4 76.762 **5** 155.557

Page 89 **Square metres**
184.5 m^2

Page 90 **Square metres**
1 about 6 cm^2 **2** 10 cm^2

Page 91 **Area of a rectangle**
1 18 cm^2 **2** 15 cm^2 **3** 10.5 cm^2

Page 93 **Area of a triangle**

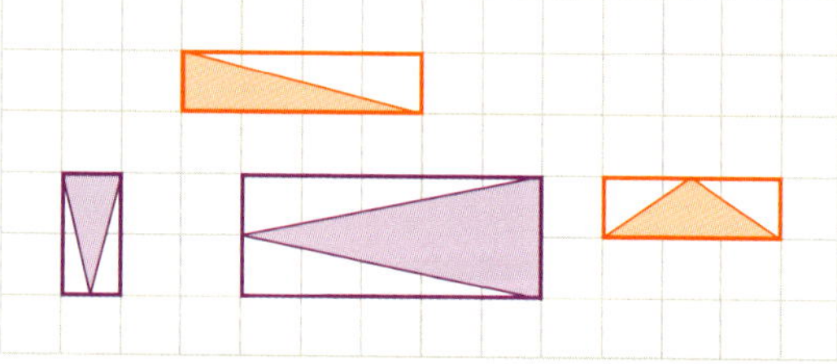

Challenge: Orange1 = 2 cm^2
Orange2 = 1.5 cm^2
Purple1 = 1 cm^2 Purple2 = 2 cm^2

Page 93 **Calculating area of scale maps**
Challenge: Area of whole area is 13 × 4 = 52 m^2. Area of Library is 2.5 × 6.5 = 16.25 m^2. The area to pave is 52 – 16.25 = 35.75 m^2. This will cost 35.75 × $46 = $1644.50.

Page 96 **Grams**
950 g, 0.999 kg, 4.078 kg, 4788 g, 9.2 kg

Page 97 **Kilograms**
74.605 kg

Page 99 **Tonnes**
Top row: 0.895, 0.225, 1.1
Bottom row: 7785, 3340, 1240
Challenge: Indian Elephant is 3.91 tonnes. 190 ÷ 3.91 = 48.59 so the Blue Whale is about 49 times heavier than the Indian Elephant.

Page 100 **Gross and net mass**
Gross mass is 650 g + 76 g = 726 g or 0.726 kg. Mass of 1 chocolate is 650 g ÷ 30 = 21.67 g so about 22 g
22 g of fat in 100 g, so 10 × 22 g = 220 g of fat in 1000 g

Page 102 **Kilolitres**
668 kilolitres

Page 103 **Megalitres**
2 000 576 kL ÷ 1000 = 2000.576 ML, which is larger than 3.758 ML

Page 104 **Cubic metres**
$185 × 2.2 = $407

Page 105 **Cubic metres**
1 3 × 1.2 m^3 = 3.6 m^3
2 $15.50 × 3.6 = $55.80. 15 people sharing cost, $55.80 ÷ 15 = $3.72

Page 106 **Litres and millilitres**
1 52 × 240 L = 12 480 L or 12.48 kL
2 12.48 kL × $2.01 = $25.08

Page 108 **Volume of a rectangular prism**
1 One example: 1.2 m high, 1.7 m long and 0.7 m wide
2 Volume is 1.2 × 1.7 × 0.7 = 1.43 m^3
Challenge: One example – 0.3 high, 0.3 long and 0.1 wide. Volume is 0.3 × 0.3 × 0.1 = 0.009 m^3

Page 109 **Cubic centimetres**
1 8 blocks
2 3 blocks
3 3 blocks
4 8 cm × 3 cm × 3 cm = 72 cm^3
There are 20 blocks missing

Page 111 **Millilitres**
1 3 × 2225 = 6675 mL so a container that holds about 7 L
2 3 × 125 = 375 mL, 375 ÷ 50 = 7.5 so you will need 8 lemons
3 6675 ÷ 250 = 26.7 so about 27 glasses
Challenge: 27 ÷ 3 = 9

Page 112 **Converting mL and L**
1 0.06 L **2** 3.49 L **3** 1.5 L

Page 115 **Converting 24-hour time to 12-hour time**
1 00:35 or 12:35 am
2 22:30 or 10:30 pm
3 14:27 or 2:27 pm

Page 117 **Converting 12-hour time to 24-hour time**
1 13 minutes to 2, 0147 or 1347
2 5 past 4, 04:05 or 16:05
3 22 minutes to 7, 06:38 or 18:38

Page 119 **Time zones**

GMT	AWST	ACST	AEST
7:00	15:00	16:30	17:00
15:15	23:15	12:45	01:15
04:55	12:55	14:25	14:55
14:16	22:16	23:46	00:16

Page 119 **Writing the date**
1 Monday 17 December
2 18 days
3 The 4th January 2013 is a Friday
4 It was Monday 26th November

Page 121 **Timetables**
True, False, True

Page 124 **Triangular prisms and pyramids**
Triangular prism, triangular pyramid, triangular prism, triangular prism

Page 125 **Rectangular prisms and pyramids**
Rectangular prism, rectangular prism, rectangular pyramid, rectangular prism

Page 127 **Cylinders and cones**
cylinders, cone, cylinder, cone

Equilateral triangle	Square	Equilateral triangle	Regular pentagon	Equilateral triangle
4	6	8	12	20
4	8	6	20	12
6	12	12	30	30

Challenge:

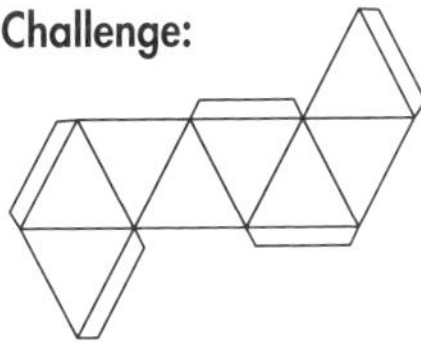

Page 129 **Euler's rule**
1 6 + 8 = 14 so there must be 12 edges
2 10 + 10 = 20 so there must be 18 edges

Page 132 **Using a 360° protractor**
1 120° **2** 140° **3** 120°
Challenge: 2, 6, king

Page 135 **Types of angles**
1 90° **2** 25° **3** 112° **4** 360°

Page 136 Angles on a straight line
1 130° **2** 55° **3** 90° **4** 10°
Challenge: 180° ÷ 10 = 18°

Page 137 Supplementary angles
1 65° **2** 91° **3** 48°

Page 139 Angles at a point
1 105°, 95°, 160° **2** 72° each

Page 140 Vertically opposite angles
1 90° **2** 60°, 120°

Page 143 Reflections or flips
1 **2** **3** **4**

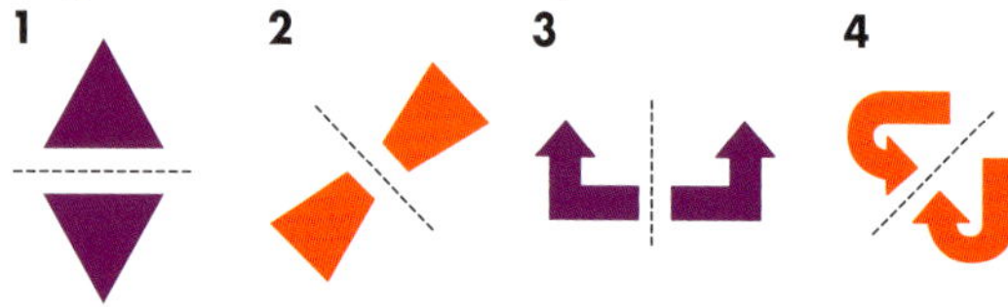

Page 146 Rotations or turns
1 **2**

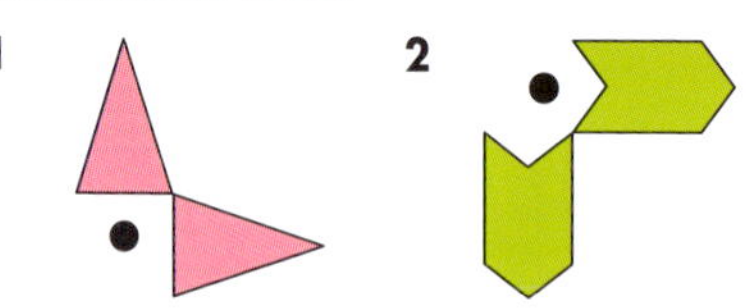

Page 147 Line symmetry

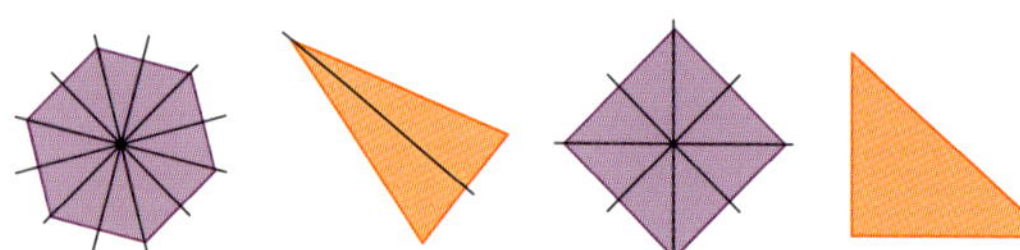

Page 149 Rotational symmetry
1 **2** **3**

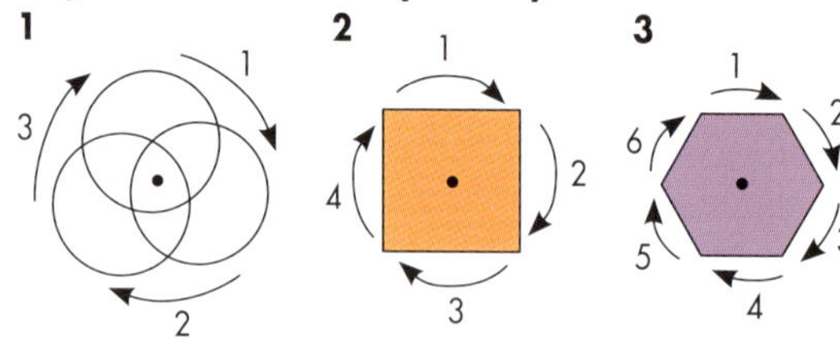

1 **2**

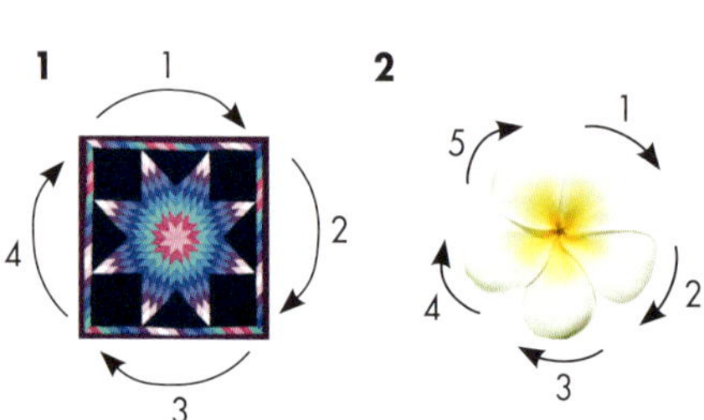

Page 150 Enlarging and reducing 2D shapes

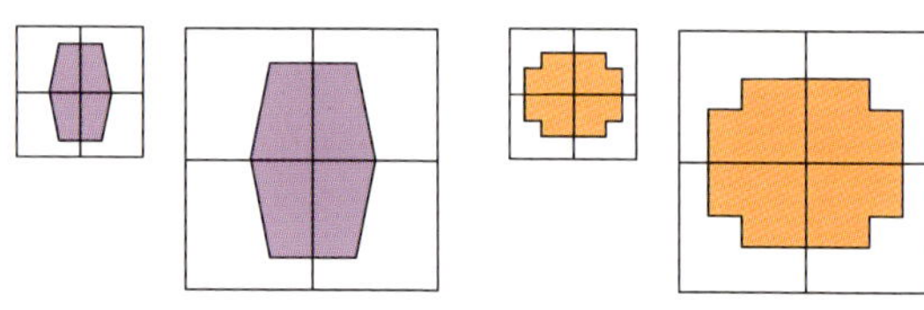

Page 152 Locating position
1 Examples: I1, E3 and G4
2 Brays Road and Correys Street
3 D5
4 F5

Page 154 Locating position using eight compass points
1 Coomera is north of Labrador, east of Oxenford, west of South Stradbroke Island
2 Main Beach is north of Miami
3 True

Page 157 Labelling co-ordinate points in any quadrant
1 (5, 6) **2** (–3, 6)
3 (–4, –3) **4** (9, –5)

STATISTICS & PROBABILITY

Page 160 Measuring chance events
Your cat goes shopping: impossible
The sun will rise in the morning: certain
You win $500 in the lottery: less likely
Your dog is pleased to see you: more likely

Page 161 Tossing coins
Challenge: HHH, HHT, HTH, HTT, TTT, TTH, THT, TTH. You have a 1 in 8 chance of getting HHH or $\frac{1}{8}$ or 0.125 or 12.5%.

Page 162 Other chance events
1 Bag 1: 3 out of 4 or 75%, Bag 2: 3 out of 5 or 60%, Bag 3: 7 out of 10 or 70%, Bag 4: 1 out of 2 or 50%.
2 Bag 1 has the best chance of selecting a blue ball.

Page 164 Designing a survey
Spider, sharks, snakes, bats, mosquitoes, crocodiles, poison dart frogs

Page 165 Dot plots
1 25–29 s **2** none **3** 100–104 s and 115–119 s

Page 166 Two-way tables
1 30 **2** 62 **3** 19 **4** $\frac{19}{62}$

INDEX